# LOVE AND DANGER

*A Beach Reads Billionaire Bodyguard Contemporary Romance*

~ *Book IIII* ~
*The Summer Sisters Tame the Billionaires*
*Book Club Edition*

*Jean Oram*

*Oram Productions Alberta, Canada*

This is a work of fiction and all characters, organizations, places, events, and incidents appearing in this novel are products of the author's active imagination or are used in a fictitious manner—unless stated in the book's front matter. Any resemblance to actual people, alive or dead, as well as any resemblance to events or locales is coincidental (unless noted) and, truly, a little bit cool.

Love and Danger: A Beach Reads Billionaire Bodyguard Contemporary Romance
Copyright © 2015 by Jean Oram

All rights reserved, including the right to reproduce this book or portions thereof in any form whatsoever, unless written permission has been granted by the author, with the exception of brief quotations for use in a review of this work. For more information contact Jean Oram at JeanOramBooks@gmail.com. www.JeanOram.com

Printed in the United States of America unless otherwise stated on the last page of this book. Published by Oram Productions Alberta, Canada.

LIBRARY OF CONGRESS CATALOGING-IN-PUBLICATION DATA

Oram, Jean.
    Love and Danger: A Beach Reads Billionaire Bodyguard Contemporary Romance / Jean Oram.—$1^{st}$. ed.
    p. cm.
    ISBN 978-1-928198-04-8 (paperback)
    Ebook 978-1-928198-05-5 ISBN
1. Romance fiction. 2. Sisters—Fiction. 3. Bodyguards—Fiction. 4. Romance fiction—Small towns. 5. Love stories, Canadian. 6. Small towns—Fiction. 7. Muskoka (Ont.)—Fiction. 8. Interpersonal relations—Fiction. 9. Hippies—Fiction. 10. Single parents—Fiction. 11. Mothers and daughters—Fiction. I. Title.

Summary: Single mother Daphne Summer wants nothing more than a father for her five-year-old daughter, Tigger. The father, Mistral Johnson, is more concerned with creating a development across from the Summer's family cottage than being a father. When things escalate between the two, a former military man and bodyguard, Evander de la Fosse, is hired to protect Daphne and Tigger. Will the two opposites attract? Or will they be the death of each other in the fourth Summer Sisters Tame the Billionaires book?

First Oram Productions Edition: April 2015

*Cover design by Jean Oram*

# Dedication

*To my grandmothers. For helping me rediscover Muskoka each summer.*

# A Note on Muskoka

Muskoka is a real place in Ontario, Canada, however, I have taken artistic license with the area. While the issues presented in this book (such as water shed, endangered animals, heritage preservation, shoreline erosion, taxation, etc.) as well as the towns are real, to my knowledge, there is no Baby Horseshoe Island nor is there a Nymph Island, or even a company called Rubicore Developments. The people and businesses are fictional, with the exception of The Kee to Bala and Jenni Walker—you can read about how she ended up visiting Muskoka in the acknowledgements.

Muskoka is a wonderful area where movie stars and other celebrities do vacation. Yet, having spent many summers in the area during my youth and adulthood, I have yet to see a single celebrity—though a man I presume to be Kurt Browning's (a famous Canadian figure skating Olympian) father did offer to help me when the outboard fritzed out on me once. Damn outboard.

You can discover more about Muskoka online at www.discovermuskoka.ca/

# Acknowledgements

Thanks goes to my readers the Jeansters for inspiring Evander. They requested a security, army hero who was wounded. I hope I did your request justice. (Don't tell the other heroes of the Summer Sisters series but Evander ended up being my all-time favorite hero—I may have developed a bit of a crush on him.)

Special thanks also goes to Evelyn Adams, Margaret Carney, Angelique Luzader, Erin Dixon, and Emily Kirkpatrick.

# LOVE AND DANGER

Aug 2017

To the Sylvan Lake Lib,

Thank you for all you do for small town readers.

Happy reading.

xo

Jon Oram

# Chapter One

*Daphne Summer pulled* her minivan down an unmarked, dead-end residential street in Port Carling, Ontario. She performed a quick U-turn and waited for the vehicle that had been following her while she did errands to come around the corner. Sure enough, the truck turned down the tree-lined road a moment later, slowing ever so slightly as its driver realized his error. As the Chevy rumbled past Daphne's van, she made eye contact with the man behind the wheel.

She knew that face. Evander de la Fosse.

Turning the steering wheel, she blocked the road's exit with her van. She got out, arms crossed, and waited for him to reach the end of the cul-de-sac and turn around. Grateful her five-year-old daughter was at a playdate with a friend, and not with her, Daphne prepared to give the man a piece of her mind.

The truck stopped and Evander cut its engine. He rolled down his window and licked his lower lip, resting one of his strong arms on the door as he leaned out to watch her.

Not a word.

The strong silent type, eh? Well, she had plenty of words to fill the silence. A bird whistled to her from an evergreen and the August breeze ruffled her cotton dress as she stomped up to the truck, feeling incredibly short as she gazed up to where the man was sitting.

She put her hands on her hips, well aware she was anything but threatening to the ex-marine looking down at her with mild interest.

"Evander de la Fosse, I presume?"

She caught the minuscule flicker of surprise on his usually stoic features. "At your service," he said with a brisk nod.

"Funny, I don't remember hiring you to tail me, and seeing as money's rather tight at the moment, I'm confident I'd recall ordering a shadow as I run about to grab the mail and a few groceries." Especially a man who represented everything she stood against.

He said nothing.

"So? At my service, huh?"

"Yes, ma'am."

"Don't call me ma'am."

"Yes, Ms. Summer."

"My name is Daphne."

He was starting to look uncomfortable, which she figured was good.

"So, being at my service would imply you are here to help?" She looked at him with big doe eyes.

"Yes."

"Good." Her voice turned firm. "Kindly take a hike."

"A bit warm for that today," he said, his eyes lifting to meet hers. He was so serious. Not even a hint of a smile, and his dark eyes held a hint of pain she figured must always be there.

"Don't get smart with me." Five years as a single mother had reduced her patience for sass to somewhere near nonexistent.

Evander's lips twisted slightly as though he was fighting the urge to smile.

"I know my meddling sisters and their billionaire hero boyfriends think I can't take care of myself. Poor little Daphne.

The clueless wonder who feels instead of thinks. But I *can* take care of myself. I don't need you tailing me and freaking out my daughter."

He studied her, his plump lower lip disappearing under a row of perfect white teeth. Nope, not perfect. The front tooth had a triangle-shaped chip and scarring ran down from his right ear to his chin, partially hidden by five o'clock shadow. He was not a man best described by light and love. He was large, capable and everything manly stuffed into one muscular package of testosterone-driven sexiness.

No, not sexiness. How could he be sexy? He was nowhere near her type. Then again, Daphne was used to men who claimed their lack of personal hygiene was a statement about their environmental beliefs rather than laziness. But this man right here knew his way around a washing machine and iron. His button-down shirt was as crisp as well-cooked bacon, and looked just as yummy fitted over his build.

What was she thinking?

She needed to get a grip. She was a mom. She didn't have time for drooling over a man who would be nothing more than a thorn in her side. And Evander was definitely a thorn. A thorn who was returning her heat and interest in his own gaze. It was as though his eyes were refracting the scorching summer sun onto her skin.

"What? What are you staring at?" she asked, shifting uncomfortably, wishing she could hide.

Again he said nothing.

"I know your type," she said, trying to be angry with him and failing. "I will not feel 'less than' just because you think we're in a staring contest."

"Okay."

She took a deep, cleansing breath and tried to channel joy and understanding for this man, who had obviously been broken during a battle somewhere.

"Take the day off," she said gently. "I don't need an ex-marine as my stalker."

"I'm not ex-marine. I'm Canadian."

She frowned, thinking through past conversations, her internal mother-detects-a-fib early warning system blinking. "You tell everyone you're an ex-marine—or so my sister Hailey told me."

"It's easier."

"Than?"

"Canadians don't know what JTF 2 is."

"Right." That was a good point, seeing as Daphne had no clue herself.

"Joint Task Force 2?"

She gave a shrug and he sent her a frustrated look, as though she should know this.

"It's like Britain's SAS," he prompted, and she shrugged again. "Special Ops. Always get the incredibly evil bad guys?" She gave another indifferent lift of her shoulder, enjoying how connected the movement seemed to be to his frustration level. "Coolest weapons? Top secret missions?"

"So you're a soldier?" she said simply.

"Formerly."

"Great. Well, you can go. I don't need a soldier following me."

"You've received threats," he growled from his position in the truck, evidently at the end of his rope.

"Not this again," she grumbled. "My sisters totally overreacted."

Ever since Mistral Johnson, her daughter's father, had popped out of the woodwork everything had kind of gone to heck and back. Sure, he'd said unkind things to her sister Melanie yesterday, but her sister had just served the man with legal action and had put several massive blockades between him and his company's planned resort. Of course he was going to blow his top. Who wouldn't?

But that didn't mean Mistral was a monster. Daphne wouldn't have spent an entire summer with him six years ago if he was. He was simply caught in a materialistic world, with unreal expectations placed on him by his father, and it was ripping him apart. She could help him, but acting afraid and having this brick wall of manhood standing between her and her life wasn't going to help anything or anyone.

"They did not overreact," he said, his brows pinching down over his eyes.

"Do you know Mistral?" When Evander didn't answer, Daphne demanded, "Do you?"

"No, ma'am," he said, his tone brisk, as though he was addressing a commander. "Not personally."

"Well, I do. And it's not ma'am. It's Daphne."

"Yes, Daphne."

Speaking to this man was like trying to train a cat. Or herd a five-year-old who was scattered and lively and utterly exhausting. Daphne needed him to go away and stop following her. It had to be bad energy, having him shadow her because he thought something bad was going to happen. She shivered, hugging herself through her thin summer dress.

"Mistral's my ex, and believe it or not, he is a kind and gentle man. He'd never do anything to hurt me."

"Isn't he trying to take your daughter away?"

Daphne gave the ex-soldier a look. "My, you are a real snoop, aren't you?"

"It's in the papers."

Right. She felt the familiar tightening in her chest. Her world was, quite simply, being upended like an unzipped purse, and given a shake to see what would fall out. She just needed to hang tight, think positively and let things unfold as they were destined to. The universe had a plan. She'd be okay.

"Mistral is under pressure. I'll talk to him soon."

"Soon?" Evander's body tensed and she could feel the air around them turn electric. Wow. That man had some serious energy going on.

She wanted to poke at him to get him to lighten up, but didn't kid herself. The truck's metal door between them was not protection; he could have that thing open and be out at her side, pulling her body against that tight, broad muscular build of his, in no time flat. Not that she wanted that. She might be hard up for a man, but she'd never be *that* desperate.

"We're going to discuss visitation."

"For Kim?" Evander's voice was so low and gravelly it sent tremors down Daphne's spine and between her legs in a way no other man's ever had.

"Yes. But everyone calls her Tigger."

"You should get a restraining order."

"Funny. Look at me laugh."

Daphne shook her head at herself. Sarcasm was not positive and it wasn't who she wanted to be.

"Is she safe?" he asked.

"Who? My daughter?" Realizing she was flapping her hands, Daphne stilled them. "I can take care of Tigger," she said quietly. "And her dad would never hurt her."

"Tristen said Mistral Johnson tried to take her during a picnic."

Not this misunderstanding again. Daphne sighed, her heart hitching, throat closing as she spotted the worry in Evander's eyes. She didn't know if her reaction was due to him, a stranger, looking so concerned over her daughter's welfare, or because she was letting the panic and fear of the situation slip into her mind.

"She's fine." Daphne struggled to keep her voice level.

"Abductions are more common than you think."

"I never pegged you as a man who would play the fear card to get what he wanted."

"It's my job. I look for what bad things could occur, then ensure they don't."

No wonder he had that crazy energy about him. Who wouldn't be affected by a job like that? It was impacting Daphne and she was only talking to him.

Running her hands up and down her sides, she breathed deeply, focusing on aligning her chi. It wasn't working. There was something about Evander's dark blue eyes that was causing interference and static with her energy field. His presence was making her heart hitch and her legs want to step closer to his truck. Her throat had turned dry, as though she was sucking desert air, and she tried again to steady herself.

"You have some strong energy, Evander de la Fosse. You need yoga. And Reiki."

His lips twisted in confusion. Right. She was being a hippie flake. She tried hard not to be like that around people who didn't "get it."

She closed her eyes, struggling to focus on the last things he'd said. *Tigger. Abductions.*

How dare he try to strike fear into her like that? Daphne didn't need him, and he was *not* going to scare her into changing her mind.

"Evander, sweetie..." she pushed patience into her voice "... children are more likely to be killed in a car crash than be abducted. We simply think abductions are more common than they are because we hear about every single one in the news. Reporters try to make it sound as though it was the kid next door, when it actually happened on a whole different continent. Tigger is safe. Thank you for trying to scare me, but it's not working."

"A man like Mistral—"

"Watch what you say." Daphne pointed a finger at Evander. "He's my daughter's father and you didn't see the caring side I did all those summers ago. I know him. He's scared, but he's gentle and kind. He's lost, but I can help him. I *will* help him."

Mistral's father was incredibly hard on him, and Daphne had a pretty good idea how much pressure he must have applied on Mistral, to make him give up not only Daphne and Tigger, but his own dreams of creating resorts that mattered, in order to follow in his father's footsteps businesswise.

Evander closed his mouth, his jaw tight. Although his arm was still draped on the truck's door frame, the stiffness in his shoulders belied the casual pose.

"Daphne?" Their eyes met, sending more chills down her spine. "Scared people act in unpredictable ways, and you have these men pretty darn scared of what you and your sisters are going to do to their bottom line. They're taking note of your actions, and I think in your case, you can never be too safe. In other words, I'm not going anywhere until this is over."


DAPHNE CONTINUED HER errands, keeping an eye out for Evander's black truck. Maybe he wasn't a cat, after all, and was trainable. Either that or she'd lost him. About twenty minutes ago she'd decided it was time to try and ditch him. She'd pulled into a parking lot and hung out long enough for him to get bored and allow his attention to wander—then she'd quickly sped off. *Special Ops that, Soldier.*

Once home, she'd parked the minivan and walked the few blocks to the island park in the middle of Port Carling. She waited on a bench for Mistral, keeping her eyes peeled for Evander to pop out of nowhere despite there being limited foot access to the island.

Six years ago, she and Mistral had had a summer to remember. And not just because she'd come away expecting Tigger. Mistral had been a ray of sunshine in the long tourist season of scooping ice cream at a local shop. While he'd looked like one of the rich "summer boys" her sisters always warned her about, he'd been different. One of the elite who vacationed in Ontario's cottage country, he could have easily acted as though he had the world in the palm of his hand, confident that everything would open up for him because of who he was, who his parents were, and how much money they had.

But as she'd handed him his mint chocolate chip ice-cream cone the day they'd met, he'd paused to look her in the eye—and had actually see *her*. And in that moment, she'd known. Mistral was just like her—struggling with life. Whereas she was wondering how she was going to afford entering the University of Guelph's environmental science program, he'd been struggling with having a large silver spoon force-feeding him his future. Mistral was in line to take over a very large share of his dad's business when he turned twenty-two that winter, but he'd been lost and confused.

On late-night walks they'd wander the town hand-in-hand, him encouraging her to change the world, adding layers and details to her dreams as though he was a part of their fabric and always would be. By the end of the summer they had decided they were going to create a sustainable, natural habitat with his money and her forthcoming environmental knowledge. Their little plot of land was going to teach people how to treat the earth, without major consumption and the destruction of the environment. Daphne had shown Mistral there was more to life than what his parents believed, and he'd shown her that some people with money could selflessly help change the world.

When the summer ended he'd gone home to Toronto and she'd stayed in Muskoka. They'd kept in touch for the first few months, emailing back and forth. Phoning. Texting. Planning their future.

And then she'd found out she was pregnant. Mistral slowly became more and more busy with his life in Toronto, shutting her out so thoroughly that he was gone by the time Tigger was born, leaving a gash so deep and wide Daphne wasn't sure how she'd survive.

The next summer, she'd seen him once, looking tired and drawn while crossing a parking lot. She'd had Tigger in her arms, and was still feeling fat from her recent pregnancy. Mistral had caught her eye for a split second, his gaze softening as he'd paused. Then he'd hurried on, forcing a laugh as he caught up with his friends when they noticed he'd fallen behind.

The first time he'd met Tigger was a few days ago, and Melanie's boyfriend, Tristen, had punched him.

Daphne rubbed her forehead, trying to remove the image of Mistral's bloody nose from her mind. Today she had to show him that they didn't need a lengthy, costly custody battle. They were adults and could resolve sharing Tigger like civilized grown-ups, because their daughter needed a father.

While Daphne had always kept the door open for Mistral to be part of their life, he'd changed so severely she barely recognized him as the man she'd once fallen for. The spark in his eyes was gone and he was acting uncharacteristically erratic. The old Mistral would have been the voice of reason, and remained levelheaded through something such as Melanie's fight against his resort. He wouldn't have issued threats, but would have sat down and thought of ways to work around the barriers, just as he had when they were planning their little nature reserve.

Daphne looked up in time to see Mistral come over the footbridge and onto the island—a park his company planned to turn into a parking lot. His stride was confident and spoke to who he'd become: a man used to getting his way, used to having crowds part for him. While she was pleased to see he'd found the self-assurance he'd been seeking, she knew he couldn't be happy or satisfied living under his father's thumb.

A chipmunk scurried past, one eye on her for snacks, and carried on, making her think of Tigger, who loved trying to tame the little creatures.

"Daphne," Mistral said with a curt nod. "May I join you?" He gestured to the bench where she was sitting, his pale yellow golf shirt making his dark skin almost glow. He'd always been handsome, but now his features were somehow more mature, more compelling. Her eyes swept over him, stopping at his bare ring finger.

She patted the vacant spot beside her and he sat.

"You never married?" she asked, feeling silly for how she phrased it. The man wasn't even thirty.

Mistral gave her a glance, but ignored the question. "My lawyer advised me not to talk to you without him present until things are settled. I'm curious about your message, though. And I like that you're willing to compromise."

Daphne knew lawyers would muddy the waters. And as much as her sister Melanie, her own lawyer for the custody battle, wanted to help, she'd want to do it an aggressive way that would alienate Mistral, instead of helping him find a way into their family, as Daphne wished.

"I think you and Tigger should spend time together before you decide how much time you want to ask for. Children are a lot of work."

If he asked for—and won—full custody, Daphne would be

done for. There'd be no point to her days. No joy and happiness in her life. She'd be completely lost.

Mistral was a busy man working long hours. There was no reason for him to ask for full custody unless it was a vindictive move to take Tigger away from Daphne. And even though the man had been acting erratically lately, she couldn't see him pulling a stunt like that—despite what the papers said.

"What are you saying? That she won't want to spend time with me?" Mistral glanced at a man who had appeared nearby. He was watching them closely and obviously waiting for Mistral.

"I'm not saying that at all. Just that kids take a lot of time and energy. Who is *he*?" Daphne asked, pointing to the man.

"He's my assistant."

"Well, he's staring at me as if I'm going to stab you." She crossed her arms across her chest, not liking that this was the second time in the past hour and a half that she was surrounded by negative energy. The way the man was watching them almost made her want Evander de la Fosse here, on her side. Almost.

A rustling behind her made her jump and turn, moving off the bench.

Evander.

Was the man a psychic with teleporting powers? Because Daphne was pretty sure she couldn't summon someone with her mind, and the fact that he'd suddenly appeared when she was thinking about him was kind of creeping her out.

"What are you doing here?" she asked.

"Who's this?" Mistral had left the bench, too, and was backing away, a hand laid protectively over his bruised nose, from when Tristen had slugged him only days before.

"You okay, Daphne?" The concern in Evander's eyes made her already galloping heart increase to a painful pace. When was the last time a man had looked out for her? Worried about her? She was always so busy being a mom, she rarely had anyone ask how *she* was doing. Even her sisters didn't think to do so, as they were always more concerned about the small human she was raising.

What was she thinking? Evander was a hired gun. A man who could escalate this situation in no time flat by bringing in the wrong kind of energy. He didn't care about the battles going on in her heart; he was worried about the possibility of violence happening.

"Evander, please go. This isn't about you."

Mistral smirked and Daphne resisted the urge to tell him off.

Evander crossed his arms, his massive shoulders bunching with the movement. "I'm staying."

"Are you trying to threaten me by bringing a bodyguard with you, Daphne?" Mistral asked. "I expected this of your sisters, but not from you."

"This man is not here because of me."

"Yes, I am," Evander said.

"I didn't hire you."

"You knew I was involved with Rubicore," Mistral said to Daphne, "and yet you stepped in anyway. You know how much pressure I'm under. You know how important this is to me. You know what the stakes are."

"I stayed out of that whole thing as much as I could, in case you didn't notice," she snapped. As she did so, Evander moved closer. Mistral's assistant followed suit, and Daphne began to wonder if the man's occupation might be more similar to Evander's rather than as "assistant" to Mistral.

She held out her arms to stop them. "Boys, enough. We're trying to have an adult conversation here about a little girl who needs her father in her life. Back off."

Evander halted, eyes wary.

"You need to park your nose in someone else's business,"

Mistral said to Evander. Or maybe it was to her. Daphne wasn't sure.

"Watch it, buster," her shadow warned, his body rippling with pent-up anger.

Daphne blinked, unsure about how to deal with the new sides the men were showing. She'd grown up in a household of women and had no idea how to put an end to this kind of posturing.

"It's fine, Evander," she said quietly.

"No, Daphne. It's not." He stepped in front of her, blocking Mistral's access. "He's threatening you."

"He doesn't mean it. My family's making things difficult for him. He's trying to prove himself, and he's just scared he's going to fail."

"You can think again if you believe I scare that easily!" Mistral shouted, his voice betraying him with a waver.

Daphne peeked around Evander to apologize. Mistral's moves were edgy as he shifted from foot to foot as though trying to decide whether to flee or fight.

"I knew meeting up with you was a bad idea," he said. "I'm glad I didn't tell my dad I was thinking twice about his advice."

"Mistral, hang on, okay? We really need to talk. Evander, go. You're making things worse." Daphne tried to push the man away, but his strength was impressive. There was absolutely no give when she pressed her weight against his chest, just 100 percent ripped muscle under his light jacket. She gave him another shove, her hand hitting something hard under his elbow. She gasped. "Are you *armed*?"

Oh, this just made things worse.

She went to pull at the gun, to try and hide it or throw it away, but Evander's hands were on hers, deflecting her. A second later, he'd shoved her behind him again in a move that left her stumbling. First she was in front of him, then—boom—back here wondering what the heck had happened.

She peered around him again, then ducked, holding in a scream. Mistral's bodyguard had a gun aimed at Evander, who already had his own drawn and leveled.

Daphne dived under the bench, arms over her head. Mistral was cowering behind it, knuckles white as he gripped the slatted back.

*Peace and light.* Everything was going to be okay. They didn't need her freaking out and adding chaotic energy to the situation.

Although she couldn't help but blame her sisters. They were being so pushy and aggressive with Rubicore. Sure, Daphne kicked hornets' nests all the time with her environmental protests, but this was different. This was trying to take down the whole company and kill their livelihood. It wasn't only about keeping them accountable in regards to the environment. This had become a fight to the death.

"Tell him to stand down, Mistral," she whispered. "Tell him."

"You tell your guy first."

"He's not my guy."

"What do you want, Daphne? Child support? Is that what this is about?"

"You know it isn't."

"Why did you bring an armed man to a chat about custody and visitation?"

She wanted to ask him the same question.

"Why do you want Tigger?" Her voice was quiet, and she hated asking, as it suggested that his intentions might be less than noble. But her sisters and Tristen had planted the idea that, due to the timing of his custody claim, Mistral might be using their child as leverage, and the idea wouldn't go away. Daphne's heart told her that him owning Baby Horseshoe Island—just across from her family's island—wasn't a coincidence, and that he wanted to be a part of their lives. But logic said his actions might only be those of a ruthless businessman.

"Why are you messing with Rubicore?" he countered.

"This is about family, not business."

But were they really that different now?

Sure, she thought Rubicore should clean up their act or receive a good smack upside the head for all they were doing. But the thing was…one of Rubicore's owners was Mistral. The father of her daughter. The truest, most precious thing in Daphne's life. She wasn't going to mess with that.

"Why are you ruining the island across from my family's?" A thought hit her and she gasped. "Are you trying to get *even*?"

"For what? You not knowing your way around birth control?"

"Hey! You were an equal participant, and here I am stuck holding the bag." She sucked in a breath. "I did not mean that. Tigger is everything to me."

"Ricardo? Is it safe?" Mistral called to his bodyguard.

Clearly it was not. The men were still having their testosterone-driven showdown.

"Do you want to be part of her upbringing, Mistral? Really and truly? Because she's a great kid. I'd hate to think…" *No, no negative thoughts or assumptions. Positive intentions only.* Daphne still believed if she could help Mistral get what he needed in his life, that little something so he could break free of his father, the man could really live the life he was meant to.

He snorted. "You don't live in the real world, do you, Daphne?"

"What's that supposed to mean?"

"Daphne, come." It was Evander, gesturing for her to get up. He was still pointing a gun at Mistral's man.

"No! You're *armed*, Evander. Don't you see that there is something wrong with that fact?"

Mistral scrambled out from behind the bench, giving Evander a wide berth as he scuttled toward Ricardo. Evander took out a second weapon, keeping one trained on each man.

She was definitely going to need a chakra cleanse after this.

Mistral ran behind his guard and the two men backed away.

When they were finally gone, hightailing it over the footbridge, Evander shifted his second gun to its leg holster and held out a hand to help her up.

Refusing his offer, she dragged herself out from under the bench, finding her cotton dress filthy with dirt.

Evander's eyes darted around the island. He waved a hand at her, hustling her along. "Come on. We're not safe here."

"Evander, stop. We're in *Canada*. They're just two scared men. They're not going to shoot me. Mistral's just… It's complicated." She brushed at her dress with brisk, agitated moves.

At least the press seemed to have decided to take the day off from their hounding about the legal action Melanie was taking against Rubicore. And, of course, the small fact that Mistral wanted custody of his and Daphne's daughter. The media showing up for this blowout would definitely not have worked in her favor. As an environmental advocate, she was generally a fan of the press—good or bad—seeing as it helped raise awareness. But this? This would have ruined her chances of keeping Tigger.

Evander's jaw tightened and Daphne vaguely wondered what sort of dental problems he might have as a result of the tensing he did all the time.

"I'd rather be cautious than find out what they are truly capable of," he said. "As I said before, scared men are unpredictable."

"Well, so am I!"

"No, you're not. You're along for the ride." With a firm hand between her shoulder blades, he pushed her out of the park.

"I resent that," Daphne muttered, allowing him to lead her to what he felt was safety. He kept his hand resting on the holster under his jacket, his body ever alert. While she fought the sensation of being taken care of, she silently reveled in the fact that someone else was in charge, if only for a moment or two, so she could collect herself.

# Chapter Two

*Evander felt alive* as he escorted Daphne Summer home from the park in Port Carling, where Mistral Johnson had blown his top and revealed more than he'd surely realized. When Evander had taken on protecting the single mom and young daughter, it was for the distraction of having a steady job to do—not for the money, seeing as he had more than he could spend in this lifetime. He no longer seemed to fit into civilian life, having lost some important synapse that connected him to humanity. To real life.

And anyway, field-testing new equipment in a low-risk, real-life environment was one of his favorite things to do, which made watching the Summers a perfect job. Perfectly boring. After less than twenty-four hours on the assignment he'd been wishing another G8 Summit would come to Gravenhurst and cause a fuss. That a prince would need Evander's former Special Forces training and protection services.

The job of watching Daphne, despite the verbal threat from her ex, had been so uneventful that an hour ago Evander had done the one thing a good soldier never did: he got cocky. He'd relaxed his guard while waiting for Daphne in that quiet parking lot. Sitting in his warm truck, he'd let his mind wander, until a flashback from his earlier life as a high-risk, elite protection agent had gripped him, and he hadn't fought it very hard. The flashback had washed over him, dragging him down like a determined undertow. It had been mercifully short—only about five minutes—but it had been long enough to allow Daphne a chance to slip away.

When he'd finally caught up with her again it was by sheer luck, or possibly good training. He'd spotted her flowered yellow dress in the park while he'd been driving over the drawbridge that separated the two parts of town. He'd barely got to her in time.

People didn't pay him ridiculous amounts to add a little extra safety to their lives. People came to him because they were serious. When Tristen Bell had asked him to watch Daphne instead of Bell's own girlfriend, Evander should have realized the stakes. And yet he'd made the mistake only a new recruit would make. Just because it was calm in the war zone, that didn't mean the war was over.

A single mother of one... He didn't want to consider what might have happened if he hadn't come along when he had.

He needed to pull himself together and focus.

But war had changed him and all he wanted to do was show Mistral and Daphne what a wonderful, healthy, vibrant little girl they had. Wanting to share a child wasn't something to get violent over.

Yet every day Evander saw individuals getting worked up over what he considered small things. If they looked beyond their sheltered and protected lives, they'd realize that good people were dying over things they regularly took for granted.

People—children, mothers, fathers, families, civilians and soldiers—were laying their lives down in the streets for the things they believed in. Big things. But back home folks were getting worked up because their expensive recording device didn't capture their favorite television show, or their neighbor shoveled snow onto their property. They were allowing small things to ruin their days, their lives.

Evander wanted to grab them and shake them, make them open their eyes. To let them know just how good they had it. Food. Democracy. Clean drinking water. Health care. Religious freedom. Public education. Safety. Nobody was going to get blown up on the school run here in Canada.

Realizing that his hands were in fists as he marched Daphne along, faster than she was likely comfortable going, he backed off, just as she wrenched her shoulder away. She wasn't out of breath from their brisk hike up the hill, which was good. In a foot race they'd probably do okay.

Always keep the weakest link in mind. Always know your viable exits.

"I can walk myself home," Daphne said. Her dress was no longer clean, after her dive under the park bench. She'd shown good instincts getting out of the way of the gun, which was something he could work with. Some people froze when faced with an armed attacker, making them an ideal target. That was tough, because it put Evander's own life at risk. And despite the number of times he'd thrown himself in front of things that should have killed him, he was quite fond of living.

He stopped when Daphne halted. He eyed their surroundings. He'd rather they kept moving.

She turned to him, hands on her slender hips. "I *said* I can walk myself home."

"Nope. Coming with you." He trailed behind her, giving her six inches of space, one hand on his gun in case her ex and his trigger-itchy buddy came by with a bright new idea.

Man, that civilian doofus needed to think again if he thought he could throw off a former member of Canada's JTF 2 simply by pulling a gun. There was something about having tanks, missiles, grenades, fire bombs, and land mines blowing up around you that made dealing with one gun look as basic as preschool.

Daphne tried to walk faster, to slip out from under the protective hand he kept lightly over her shoulder blade. *Keep her close. Know where she is at all times. Focus on possible threats and change in location.*

"What were you thinking, meeting him in the park?" Evander scolded. The slope had leveled out and the tangled shrubbery to their right had slowly morphed into trimmed yards, where hiding was more difficult. "Haven't you heard of coffee shops? Police stations or lawyer's offices? And why did you try to shake me off?"

"I told you to stop following me. It's not my fault you can't listen."

Her attitude reminded him of his old commander. The man had been a take-no-guff, tell-it-like-it-is, get-to-the-point type. "Keep it straight and honest and within the laws" had been one of his favorite sayings.

"You don't call the shots," Evander said, echoing part of the commander's welcome to JTF 2 speech.

Daphne whirled on him, her dress flaring out around her shapely legs. "It's my life."

"And I've been paid to protect that life. Those orders precede yours."

"I'll pay you to stop protecting me."

"You can't afford me."

"Yes, I can." A flicker of doubt crossed her face.

"You can't." He gave a small smile of satisfaction when her face flushed.

"How do you know? I might have tens of thousands of dollars stashed away."

"That's about what you'd need." She shot him a look of

disbelief, and he said, "I'm elite, and don't come cheap. Besides, I'm loyal to the one who hired me. He makes the calls."

"Loyalty among gunmen, great."

"It's what keeps us alive. Speaking of which, you really need to stop ditching me."

"I don't need protecting," she said quietly. He knew she didn't quite believe the statement.

"Did you notice your ex's bodyguard just drew a gun on you during conversation?"

"Yeah, because he thought you were drawing yours!"

"Because you touched my gun." Evander enunciated the words slowly, waiting for it to sink in that weapons being drawn had been due to her actions, not his.

"You didn't tell me you were armed."

"You never touch someone's weapon unless you plan to use it."

"Or throw it away so things don't get crazy."

Evander sighed. What was he going to do with her?

"It's your fault things went wonky back there," she insisted.

He sighed again. "Remind me why I took this job," he muttered. He paused a moment to settle his frustration, taking in the picturesque view of the north side of town, which was laid out behind Daphne. The Indian River cut through the small valley, creating a scenic backdrop for the woman, whose wild curls framed her delicate features, while the breeze pressed her thin dress against her curves…

"My eyes are up here, Evander."

"Your dress is dirty," he replied.

"Again…your fault." She brushed the garment with a long swoop of her arm and began walking again. He fell into step, positioned so that he could throw her down and shield her with his body at a moment's notice.

She halted suddenly and he slammed into her, wrapping an

arm around her, holding her tight so they didn't trip. Her body was warm and soft, and it had been too long since he'd had a woman against him. He allowed himself to inhale, to savor the unexpected treat.

"What are you doing?" she asked, wiggling out of his grasp.

He released her, hoping his expression remained blank. This was starting to look as though it was going to be a very long week in his life. Or however long it took to resolve this case.

"You're following me again," she stated, stomping away.

"My job."

"How do I ditch you?"

If she only knew the number of men trained in espionage that he'd managed to stay behind through gnarly Middle Eastern city streets, she wouldn't be asking that question. Then again, the single mom had managed to ditch him once. And there was the dead-end she'd trapped him in, too. He needed to get his head back on straight and start acting as though this was a critical matter—which he now believed it was.

"You promised you'd stop trying to ditch me."

"I did *not* make such a promise. Oh, and I was talking to Tristen earlier and we decided your services are no longer required. You are dismissed."

"You suck at lying."

Her jaw clenched and for a second Evander wondered if she was going to try and hit him. It wouldn't be the first time a peace-loving hippie had socked him.

"You're insufferable," she said finally, chin raised.

"That's what my mother tells me."

Daphne looked him up and down, then eyed the width of his shoulders. "You're a mama's boy?"

"Being on speaking terms with my mother does not make me a mama's boy."

Something niggled at the back of Evander's mind. His mom... something was up with her. He knew that she would tell him in time, but the feeling that something big was on her horizon kept bumping into his thoughts, distracting him.

"How do I get you and Tristan off my back?" Daphne asked.

A large truck rumbled by on the narrow road, close to the sidewalk. Evander placed his body between the vehicle and Daphne, shuffling her back a few steps.

"For starters, get a restraining order against Mistral and his bodyguard," he advised.

"I am not getting a restraining order against my daughter's father."

"Then you'll definitely be stuck with me for quite a while."

"Some of us believe that love changes people, weapons don't." She crossed her arms, scowling up at him.

"You love that man?" He struggled to say "man" instead of something derogatory. Mistral was not the one for Daphne, and Evander knew it without a doubt. Daphne's love, attention, and hopes were wasted on her ex.

"Whether I love him or not is none of your business."

"If you don't love him, then why are you defending him? Why don't you walk away and slam the door?"

"Do you have kids, Evander?"

Female version of a land mine. He needed to watch where he placed his size twelve feet. "No."

"Then don't pretend to understand." She turned and began walking once again. A few steps later, she stopped. It was going to take forever to get her back into the safety of her home at this rate. "How do I get you to stop following me? Besides a restraining order, what do I have to change in my life?"

"Tristen mentioned something about allowing your sister to

move in with you again. So you wouldn't be alone. The safety-in-numbers theory. That would be a smart place to start."

"Are you kidding me? This is about Melanie? Because I'll have you know she doesn't have the right to tell me how to deal with my daughter's father, as though she knows what it's like to be a single mom. And neither do you, I might point out."

Evander began herding her along, wishing they were less exposed. Going for a walk after having a gun drawn on you was not a bright idea. And as for the bit about her sister? If the two of them had been men they'd be well over it by now and enjoying a few beers, the water under the bridge having long ago reached the ocean.

"Add in handgun and training, as well as better security for your house. Those are the places I'd start."

Daphne let out a sigh so gusty he wondered how her lungs managed to hold that much air.

"You're making everything worse. More difficult," she said, not looking his way.

"The same could be said for you," he grumbled when she stopped again. "Keep walking, woman." He gave her a light poke in the back, but she didn't comply.

"You're armed."

"Yes, and that fact put luck on your side only a few minutes ago, might I remind you. Now get moving."

She gave a light laugh and the sound hit him in the sternum like an unexpected punch from a heavyweight. This woman was simply overflowing with life, which, instead of making him feel more empty, made him feel…well, he wasn't sure yet, but he liked it.

Daphne was everything he didn't have in his life, and never would again. Except for the danger part. He had that in spades.

"You have a nice laugh," he said, surprising himself.

"You carry a gun." Her breathing seemed a bit off as she added, "Two. Maybe more."

He stepped closer, infringing upon her space. "Does that make you uncomfortable?"

"Yes! You can't just walk around with weapons strapped to you. This is Canada."

He watched her closely so he wouldn't miss any emotions or internal truths she'd likely try to hide from him.

"How would you have felt if I hadn't been there and he'd pulled that gun?"

"It wouldn't have happened if you were off somewhere else, buster. You scared him." Daphne poked Evander in the chest, hard. He rubbed the spot with the heel of his hand, watching her, taken aback by her strength.

"The fact remains that you were meeting with a man who brought along an armed accomplice."

"Accomplice? How sinister." Her tone was flippant and sarcastic, but she wrapped her arms around herself and started walking again, brow furrowed, head down in thought.

"Do you see it yet?" he called.

"See what?"

"What you're up against?" This woman was so independent she'd stay clinging to a crumbling bridge, seconds from death, but determined to fix the structure herself even if there was a crane on shore ready to help.

She had stopped again, her eyes sliding away from his whenever she tried to meet them. "Rubicore is my sister's battle. All I want is a father for my daughter." Daphne finally met his gaze, her beautiful blue eyes flecked with green and hazel. "Can you understand that? I don't want a big mess, and with you here, a war is sure to break out."

"My dear Daphne, it already has."

EVANDER LET HIMSELF INTO his mother's house in Bracebridge and scooped up the orange tabby that was trying to make an escape. He called out, "It's just me," as he disarmed the home's security system. He scratched the cat behind the ears, careful of the right one, which would likely get him clawed, seeing as old Rudolph was working on getting over an ear infection.

"No going outside until you're all cleared up again," he murmured to the cat, depositing him on the floor, then picking up the potted geranium he'd bought on the way home.

The cat meowed at the door and Evander gently shooed him away with a foot. "I know, I know. You're ready to go on a mission and hate sitting on your paws until you receive the go-ahead. I get it, buddy. But there's no way I'm letting you out until you're through the twice-a-day meds. You're too unreliable." His life had boiled down to providing risk reduction to a feline since returning home late last winter. What a use of his skills.

Rudolph swore at him with a haughty flick of the tail and Evander scooped him up again, tucking him under his arm. He made his way to the back of the old Victorian, which had been rambling even before the previous owners had added to it, and found his mom sitting in a wing-back chair. Florence was watching the evening light change over the sloping yard, the sun's fading rays highlighting certain flowers in the garden just beyond the window. She was lost in thought, and looked up when he entered the room, but was not fully present, her usual buoyant self lost in untold secrets.

He plunked the cat on her lap and pulled up a tiny padded footstool, cramming his massive build onto it. He handed her the potted red flowers. "In case we get an early frost and the sunflowers don't make it to blooming. And you may have to take over Rudolph's ear drops."

The cat scrambled off his mother's lap and hightailed it out of the room.

Florence frowned after him. "He understands English, you know." She gave Evander a smile, her dark hair streaked with gray whisked back into a casual bun at the nape of her neck. She was tall and stately, but seemed wan. "You're lucky you weren't holding him or you would have got scratched. Again." She gave his hands a pointed look.

"The woman I'm watching needs more security."

"The single mom?"

"Someone pulled a gun on her today."

Florence's eyes widened and she sat straighter. "What are you doing here? You need to be guarding them."

"I was relieved by Chuck."

"Chuck?" She gave a scornful snort.

Evander chewed on his lower lip, then stood. Chuck wasn't the most attentive or well-trained bodyguard Evander's old buddy Tyrone Bellingham had working for his security company, and Evander had bitterly complained about that fact to his mother on more than one occasion. The only thing reliable about Chuck was that he was the weak link on any job. Which meant Chuck shouldn't be the one on night watch after what had gone on today. "Excuse me a moment."

His mom gave a nod and Evander pulled out his cell phone, moving into the next room, sending Rudolph scuttling from his hiding spot, belly low to the floor. Evander braced a hand on the oversize door frame and called his boss, Tyrone.

"Hey, it's Evander. We need better security on the Daphne Summer case."

Tyrone cursed under his breath. "What happened?"

"Nothing further." Thank goodness Tristen had had the

presence of mind to switch Evander from Melanie to Daphne that morning. "Have you checked in with Tristen?"

"Of course. As soon as you told me about what happened in the park. He says nothing happened over there today, but he's adding a couple of extra patrols around his house as a precaution. And word on the street is that the Hells Angels are watching out for Melanie." Tyrone gave a small chuckle.

"Good."

"I emailed the extra background checks you wanted about half an hour ago."

"Thanks. Is there security on their mother or the other two sisters?"

"None has been requested through my firm, so I can't say for certain. But last I heard, Finian and Hailey have their own private detail that's moving with them. No word on Maya or the mother, Catherine."

Last month, Daphne's eldest sister, Hailey, had needed Evander to help ward off the frothing paparazzi when she'd hooked up with the movie star Finian Alexander. Since then, the photographer had been on the road, with short stopovers to her home in Muskoka, and the star had been off filming and opening movies, meaning they had stepped beyond the local services Tyrone generally offered.

"Daphne needs twenty-four/seven security and you need to up her to a level four," Evander said. "You need someone better than Chuck."

"Four?" Tyrone protested. "Tristen's only paying for level one, man. Basic tailing and intervening as needed. We don't make those calls. Just deliver what they order."

"I know."

"She's not a dignitary."

"She's a mom, and she's in danger."

Evander had done a full dossier on the family last month when he'd covered Finian, needing to know what he was getting into. At that time he'd found pretty much nothing on the Summers, but since then things had definitely changed. In the past six weeks three of the sisters had hooked up with rich men. They co-owned a cottage that was about to go up for tax sale, and none of the Summers had much in the way of money. He was trained to look for connections, and these sudden hook-ups felt as though they went beyond simple coincidence. Something was at play here. Whether it might impact the case, he didn't know, but it was worth keeping in the forefront of his mind.

"We need to do some pretty serious paperwork," Tyrone said. "Permits, consent, release forms and more if we intervene at level four."

"She needs more than Chuck across the street at night."

Tyrone sighed.

"I'll pay the extra," Evander muttered.

"You're going to end up paying to work this job."

As an unannounced member of the billionaire boys' club, Evander didn't have a problem paying the bill in order to keep Daphne safe. She was a mom. In his mind, keeping her safe no matter the cost was a no-brainer.

"Fine. Whatever. I need the sanity the distraction will bring."

"The world's richest security guard pays to work for me so he doesn't have to think about the fact that princes don't pay him to get blown up any longer, and he's just a measly civilian like the rest of us. I should make that my company motto or something."

"Shut up. Talk to Tristen about my recommendations, and in the meantime, I'll cover any additional expenses." It wasn't as if Evander had anything better to do. He wasn't fit for the army or high-risk elite security any longer. His leg had healed well enough from the blast that had earned him the big payout from the

Middle Eastern prince he'd saved, but not enough for the work he used to do.

"Has your impartiality been compromised?" Tyrone asked.

"I don't have a crush on her, if that's what you're asking."

Him with Daphne? It was obvious that the two of them would never see eye to eye, nor get along. It didn't help that Evander was no longer made for real life, and everything about Daphne was innocence and genuine vitality—life itself. Plus, she had a lovechild with that prick Mistral Johnson, who had a friggin' silver spoon permanently welded in his mouth. That guy knew nothing about the struggles of the real world.

Assuming there still was one.

"Ever thought that maybe the police should be watching her?" Tyrone asked, and Evander knew his friend was going to approve upping the security on Daphne no matter what it took, but was checking him for emotional baggage attached to the case.

"Ever think maybe they don't have the manpower to do it right?"

"I hate it when you get like this. You know that?"

"You've hated me since boot camp, when I threw your ass over that wall when you couldn't make it on your own." Evander gave a smug smile, waiting for the retaliation he knew was coming from his longtime friend.

"Screw you. You had to throw everyone over that wall."

"That's all I get?"

"Kids are in the room," Tyrone muttered. When the man had finished his first tour, he'd come home to be with his wife and kids, opening a security business. But frankly, it didn't get a lot of action in the danger department and he was getting soft. The man was using his hard-earned skills to spy on unfaithful spouses more often than actually protecting anyone's life. Although some of those wives sure got dangerous when they saw photographic evidence that they were no longer honored and cherished by their husbands as the one and only.

"Don't let it get personal, man," Tyrone said. "Don't let her get under your skin and skew your judgment."

"I haven't gotten soft like you, Tyrone," Evander said, ending the call.

He thought about Chuck watching Daphne. The man was being paid to sit in a car across from the house, and was likely sleeping on the job. Any enemy worth his salt would take full advantage of that, and after what had gone on today, Evander knew he had underestimated the crazy side of Daphne's ex by at least a full point.

He rejoined his mother in the sitting room.

"Have you eaten yet?" he asked, knowing she hadn't. In fact, there was no hint of supper, despite it being after six.

"I was waiting for you."

She still hadn't moved from her chair, and Evander knew without a doubt that something was up.

"You okay?" he asked lightly.

Florence waved him away. "Just thinking."

He picked up a plate that was littered with the corner crusts from her morning toast. It was unlike her to leave them lying around. Pausing in the doorway, he watched his mother, feeling torn.

"I can hear you thinking all the way over here," she said, without turning around.

He took his spot on the stool again, placing the plate on the floor so he could grasp his mother's cool hands. They always felt so small in his and he stared at them in wonder. How could a woman who'd won boxing matches in her youth have such delicate fingers?

"What's wrong?" she asked.

He drew in a long breath. "Are you going to be okay on your own?"

"I have been for years."

He knew the comment wasn't intended to make him feel guilty, as his mother had always encouraged him to go out and see the world, even going as far as to join the navy. Still, the guilt he felt was uncharacteristically strong. She needed help, but obviously didn't feel she could ask, for fear of interfering with whatever he had going on. Which meant it was big. Frustration welled up inside him, threatening to burst out as anger.

"Go. She needs you," his mom said. "I'll hold supper."

"I shouldn't be longer than an hour or two, to get things sorted out. I'll bring pizza home if you haven't eaten by then." He stood and gave his mother a light kiss on the forehead, unable to dismiss the feeling that she needed him.

"Can you give Rudolph his treats before you go?"

The cat came into the room, meowing perkily, and Evander scooped him up, heading to the kitchen to doctor his ear.

With the cat fixed up and only one new scratch on Evander's hand, he unlocked the carriage house out back where he kept his gear, knowing that every moment he took to get ready was a moment Daphne was poorly protected.

It was time to move, move, move. The clock was ticking, and his nervous system tingled in anticipation, but he needed to get himself prepared. Take it slow and methodically. Think things through. Taking a minute now could save ten later.

He placed a GPS tracking button in his front pants pocket and double-checked the ammo clips for his holstered handgun, as well as the one strapped to his leg. Knife, present and sharp. He moved on, riffling through his meager gear with purpose. A lot hadn't come home with him from the Middle East, and he had been slowly restocking again.

He debated taking his entire duffel of supplies, but instead chose carefully. He didn't have permission to do any of the things he planned to do to the woman's house. He needed to be discreet. He didn't know Daphne well, but he knew she wouldn't appreciate having her house monitored, even if it was for her own safety. He held a bug in his fist, contemplating. He lowered his hand, dropping the bug back into its case, leaving it in the duffel. Later. Priority items first.

The monitoring gear he needed fitted in a large zip-top bag, and he placed it in his truck, wishing it had a backseat, before going to check on his mom once again. His leg was bothering him today and he kneaded the spot above his knee as he entered the house.

"Just me again!" he called, wincing as the security alarm went off. Digging through the pockets of his cargo pants, he pulled out his phone, silencing the alarm. If that app ever stopped working he'd be doomed.

He was getting rusty, fast. Just like Tyrone. He needed more discipline, as well as a schedule.

"You'd think this place was Fort Knox," his mom said from the other room. "But then again, you always liked your toys." She gave a light laugh, followed by a cough as he entered the sitting room.

"You sure you're okay?" The cold that had been wearing her down seem to be going on for much too long. "I can take you to the walk-in clinic tomorrow night after my shift."

"A woman is allowed to cough without dying, you know."

A feeling of dread settled deep within him. "Who said anything about dying?"

"It's just an expression, Evander."

Knowing he was less than square emotionally, he set out to put at least one aspect of his life back in order—Daphne.

# Chapter Three

*Daphne allowed her* sister Hailey to hoist Tigger out of the family's Boston Whaler and onto the dock at Nymph Island for the impromptu late-supper picnic. The four sisters—with no boyfriends in tow—had even managed to round up their honorary sister, Simone, to join them, making it just like old times. Single Daphne wouldn't be the third wheel at their jointly owned cottage tonight. She could sit back and enjoy the peace and her family. She'd be able to breathe and act as though her life was normal.

Evander, when he'd gone home for the night, had told her to stay locked in the house, and that a man named Chuck would be watching her from a car on the street if she needed anything. When Hailey—just home from Europe where her boyfriend was filming *Man versus War II*—had phoned, suggesting they all go to the cottage for a picnic, Daphne hadn't thought twice about leaving the house. Evander had told her there was safety in numbers, and traveling in a group was another form of following his orders. He couldn't get upset about that, could he? Just thinking about her afternoon made her hands shake, and she slowed her breathing, determined not to allow it to get to her.

Daphne unpacked bags of food from the boat, lost in her thoughts. The whole place, from the aging dock to the tip of the cottage's roof, needed so much work. Work her family couldn't afford to have done. In fact, if Daphne didn't somehow pull a miracle out of thin air, she'd be the one who lost their beloved island to the taxman in two short weeks. She'd asked her sisters if they'd consider asking their boyfriends for loans to make up the difference in what they had and what they owed. But all of them feared they might never be able to pay the men off again. This summer was the test. If they couldn't handle the taxes by themselves, then it was time to let go, because what would happen next year or the year after, if they borrowed money to get through now? They were in this situation because they hadn't been able to keep up with the payments for several years.

"I can't believe they're ruining Heritage Row," Melanie said, from her position on the end of the dock. "Termites. How stupid do they think we are?" She pointed to the charred remains of the cottage that had burned down only a few days ago. "And I know we're going to find evidence of arson with that one. Then we'll have Rubicore right by the—"

Daphne tossed a backpack at Melanie, distracting her from her rant.

"Mark my words, Maya," Melanie said, lowering the bag onto the weather-worn planking. "I'm going to save those remaining cottages."

"Didn't Rubicore buy the Fredericksons' place?" Maya asked.

"Where did you hear that?" Melanie's voice was breathless with outrage, and Hailey patted her on the back and gently guided her toward the cottage path.

"It seems like something they would do," Maya said to Simone, who nodded in agreement as she readjusted her shiny black locks into a fresh ponytail.

Daphne pretended to look for something in the boat as the other women trickled up the hill, still discussing the endless battle about heritage and Mistral's company. Her sisters knew little of real life. About real struggles and heartbreak. And the last thing Daphne needed after her day with Evander was the group of them ganging up on her and telling her how to run her life in regards to Mistral. Typically, if they talked about Rubicore long enough, her ex-boyfriend—one of the company's partners—would come up, as well as a lecture about how Daphne should deal with things.

She climbed out of the boat once everyone was well ahead of her. Her daughter was already halfway up the path, grinning from ear to ear, pleased to have her aunts together here, at her favorite place in the whole world. With a flounce of her party dress and a flash of bare feet, Tigger vanished up the last turn, Hailey hot on her heels.

On the cottage veranda minutes later, Daphne began unpacking the picnic, with Simone quietly helping. Soon a feast was laid out on the outdoor dining table, and they all sat down to eat.

Tigger, bouncing in her spot as she ate the last bite of her potato salad, asked, "Can I go work on my fairy houses?"

At Daphne's count, her daughter had built about fifteen elaborate fairy houses around the island. They were made of driftwood, leaves, pinecones, small pebbles and other natural treasures, plus coins her daughter had collected with the make-believe fairies in mind.

Daphne nodded permission, and Melanie pushed away from the table, saying, "I'll go with you, Tigger. I want to see the latest additions."

"Can I come, too?" Simone asked.

Tigger snatched her hand, pulling her from the table.

"Maybe the fairies need new dresses?" the woman asked, waving over her shoulder to the sisters left behind. She owned her own boutique in Port Carling and had begun to branch out, designing her own fashions, in particular 1950s-inspired sundresses that looked amazing on Melanie's curvy figure.

Daphne had been half hoping Melanie would stay at the table so they could resolve their recent differences over including Tigger's father in their lives. Instead, her sister had taken the first excuse to run off. While Daphne wasn't quite ready to allow Melanie back into her house, she needed Evander and all his intensity out of her space.

Tigger ripped up the hill, chattering a mile a minute, her excited voice fading as the three moved out of earshot.

Hailey and Maya exchanged a look and Daphne tensed.

This whole excursion had been a setup and she'd walked right into. Maybe she did need Evander in her life, if only to protect her from her sisters and their traps.

Maya cleared her throat. "There's no easy or gentle way to say this. But the upshot of it all is that we think Mistral is dangerous and you should avoid him. Get a restraining order."

Hailey added quickly, "He pulled a gun on you today."

"How do you know about that?" Daphne stood, palms flat on the table's cool surface. There was a chill in the air and it seeped into her bones. "Have you been talking to Evander?"

"This is getting out of hand," Hailey said, brows pinched together.

"No. Everyone's interference is getting out of hand. A simple, peaceable situation went south because Tristen's hired gunman, Evander de la Fosse, was there."

"Thank goodness he was," Maya said, arms crossed. "I can't believe Mistral pulled a gun on you."

"He didn't pull a gun on me." Shivers ran down Daphne's spine. "It was his *bodyguard*, and he only did it because Evander was there, minding my business and acting as though we were in the middle of a war, not peace talks. It would have been fine without him around."

"Why does Mistral have an armed bodyguard?" Hailey asked, eyeing her sideways.

"Because I have a big thug following me around scaring everyone. That's why." She sat, pushing her fingertips against her eyelids. "If Evander hadn't been there, then Mistral's guy wouldn't have gone off his rocker. Mistral and I could have sorted things out like two civil adults. It's a silly, exhausting, negative, expensive waste of time to tie up the courts with this."

"Civil adults don't draw guns when discussing the custody of their child," Maya stated.

"Is that why you were talking to him?" Hailey asked. "Didn't Melanie tell you to only talk to him through lawyers in court?"

"Melanie has very different views about how to go about this. It's my child, my life."

"We know you and Mistral had an amazing summer," Hailey said uncertainly, "and we all thought it would lead to you two marrying, but things…" She trailed off, eyes cast down.

"I was hoping to have a real conversation with him," Daphne said. "One where nobody else could meddle and push their own agenda. But thanks to Tristen, and probably Melanie, too, their nosiness just cost me and Mistral some major trust today."

Daphne felt the energy drain out of her, and realized that as forgiving as she was, it was going to be difficult letting this one go. She was mad at Mistral for allowing the situation to get out of hand. Mad at Tristen and Melanie for interfering and not consulting with her first. Mad at Evander for not telling her he was armed.

"Why couldn't you have had that conversation in a safe place with lawyers present?" asked Maya. "Mistral doesn't want Tigger as a daughter, he wants her as a pawn in this fight." She waved her hand in the direction of Baby Horseshoe Island, where his company was buying up land and planning a massive resort.

"Mistral reached out to me a few weeks ago about being in Tigger's life. I owe it to him to have a conversation without assuming he has less than honorable intentions."

"He reached out because we're attacking his company," Maya stated simply.

"Everyone assumes that they know Mistral better than I do. I know the real man. You don't."

If given the chance, Daphne knew that under all the trappings of money and success, she'd still find the man she'd fallen for all those summers ago—not for herself, but for her daughter. "Tigger needs a father."

"Finian adores Tigger," Hailey said of her boyfriend.

"And Connor, too." Maya nodded, eyes bright.

"A real father. A man who will be there always."

"They'll be there," Hailey said.

"Right. Where is Finian now?" Daphne asked.

"Well, he has his movie…" Hailey trailed off, looking to Maya for help.

While the sisters' new boyfriends had been amazing with Tigger, acting as surrogate father figures, the fact was they were influenced by new love, and it wouldn't last. They'd forget about her daughter and move on when they had kids of their own.

"Tigger needs a father of her own, someone who will be a stable, constant presence in her life. Of all people, we should understand that, having lost our dad. And right now her biological father is reaching out. That isn't something I can ignore just because the timing isn't convenient. I'm going to assume the best until there is a reason not to."

Her sisters opened their mouths to argue but she held up her palm, her body shaking with pent-up hurt and anger. Wordlessly, she fled to her bedroom in the cottage.

They didn't get it and never would. Mistral may not have proven himself in the past five years, but she at least owed him the chance to try.

It was easy for her family to think Mistral would use Tigger as a pawn in his company's fight against them, but Daphne knew him. She knew he was still the same man inside, wishing he could be more than a shrewd businessman, following the path that had been laid out for him by his parents. She believed in the old Mistral that she'd fallen for even if he hadn't shown that side to anyone else.

And the fact was, he had reached out first. Then the papers had caught wind of the news and twisted it into something negative and judgmental, trapping Mistral behind a wall of publicity he couldn't break through while still saving face. But if Daphne could find a way to be there…if she could get some positive press, then maybe he could find his way across to her. To them.

Her ex-boyfriend wanted and deserved to have the opportunity to be in Tigger's life in all the ways his own father hadn't been. Mistral could change the future. Their future.

But her sisters…how was she going to be patient with them until they saw what she could do?

DAPHNE PARKED IN HER driveway. She rubbed her eyes and stared at her small clapboard home until the minivan's headlights turned off to save battery power, plunging the yard into near darkness. While Melanie had lived with them for only a few days before their disagreement over Mistral, the house felt emptier without her, and Daphne wondered if they would ever manage to get back to the place they'd once been—close and tight. At the picnic last week, Mistral had been trying to befriend Tigger, but then Tristen had misunderstood the situation and ended up nearly breaking Mistral's nose. That had led to a difficult conversation with Tigger, where Daphne had tried to explain that the "bad man" was actually her father.

Contemplating spending the night in the van so she wouldn't have to disturb her sleeping daughter and go through the whole I-want-Auntie-Mellie-Melon-to-come-over-and-tuck-me-in fight that always broke her heart, Daphne continued to gaze at her house. How could she get her five-year-old into the house without waking her? When the child was smaller, no problem. But now? She was just too big. Daphne was going to have to wake her, then go through the whole crazy process of dealing with a kid who'd just had a power nap and was ready to take on the planet for another two hours.

Daphne wanted her own bed. She wanted peace. She wanted quiet. She wanted to not think about how muddled and messed up her life had become over the summer. Which meant that she'd likely stay up most of the night painting sunflowers to keep her thoughts at bay.

This summer she'd been selling quite a few of her paintings at the local farmers' markets and had earned over a third of what she needed for the cottage's tax bill in order to prevent it from being seized. She could pull an all-nighter at her easel, then if inspiration was thick, skip the protest on watershed issues she planned to lead, maybe even the Bala market, and paint through the day until it was time for work in the afternoon.

A dark figure rustled past a bush along the side of her house. The person was moving with confidence that didn't scream bad intentions, and Daphne quietly opened her van door. She slipped out, then locked it behind her. For a second she wished she had

Evander at her side. He was powerful and intimidating. Amazingly muscular and yet nimble.

Her mind drifted to the rippled skin that ran down the side of Evander's cheek. The scarring continued under the collar of his shirt and made her wonder if it was the reason he was no longer in the army. Undoubtedly it was responsible for that sharp, haunted look he carried in his hazel eyes.

Why was she thinking about him? He'd just escalate whatever this was into something awful. It was probably her neighbor wondering if Tigger had kidnapped his cat again to dress it up and have tea parties.

A squirrel raced across Daphne's path and she held in a startled squeak, snatching Tigger's Cabbage Patch doll from the lawn before sneaking around the corner of the house. The figure was gone and she let out an inaudible sigh of relief. She paused, listening. Nothing. She slipped off her flip-flops, the grass almost painfully cool under her feet.

Daphne held the doll by its legs, placing Maple's hard plastic head on her shoulder. Maple would make an excellent weapon if need be. Daphne had experienced that firsthand when she was still figuring out that sugar made her daughter go absolutely bonkers. She'd been in the wrong place at the wrong time when Tigger and Maple had been having a dance party on the living room couch. Daphne's cheek smarted just thinking about the way Maple had made contact with a bruise-causing crunch.

At the back corner of the house, Daphne took a quick peek, hidden by her John Cabot rosebush. Its soft fragrance filled the air as she watched an impossibly large man on the back step reach above the doorjamb, sticking something to the wooden clapboard. He stuck something else on the door itself. Leaning away from her, he arched his broad shoulders over the stair's metal railing and repeated the process with the kitchen's sliding window. Satisfied with his work, he turned, facing her from his elevated position.

"Hi, Daphne."

Darn.

"Um, hi, Evander."

"What are you up to tonight?" he asked.

"I'd like to ask you the same." She marched out of her hiding spot, still clutching the doll, although she allowed it to drop from her shoulder. She joined him on the cement step and reached above him to yank the thick sticker she wouldn't have noticed if she hadn't seen him apply it. She handed it back to him before turning to dismantle the rest. Evander caught her wrists in his hands. Not too tight, but enough to let her know she couldn't get away.

"What are you doing to my house?" she demanded. "Other than trespassing."

"Setting up a monitoring system to help keep you and your daughter safe."

Daphne's shoulders dropped, her righteous anger suddenly washed away. She was tempted to relax into his grip to see if she could borrow his strength for a minute. One of the hardest things about being a single mom was having to be strong all the time. And right now, the thought of being unsafe in her own home made every bit of bravado and strength she'd built up over the years slip away.

"I don't want to be spied on," she said softly.

He was still holding her wrists, his grip warm and reassuring. His hands were massive and engulfed her so fully he could have held her just as securely with one hand instead of two.

"It's not spying. It's a warning system that will tell me if someone disturbs your windows or doors."

"Spying," she said, unable to help chuckling when he gave her an exasperated look. A rich, deep bubble of laughter moved up through her body.

"What?" Evander asked cautiously, as her laugh ripped free.

"You know how many times a day I open and close windows and doors?"

"Well." He gave the house an uncertain glance. "I'm more concerned with disturbances at night, as I'll be with you during the day and see when you are disturbing the security points."

She pulled her wrists from his grasp, unable to argue with him no matter how uncomfortable the idea of being monitored made her feel.

"Why not get me an ankle thingy they put on people under house arrest?"

"I didn't think you'd go for that, but I have one in my truck. I can go grab it."

She couldn't tell if he was joking or not, but she had a pretty good feeling he was. She turned, feeling off balance. "I have a daughter who needs carrying to the house. You keep playing with your rescue hero toys. I have real life to attend to."

She left him on the porch, but was surprised to find him falling in beside her within seconds, a slight limp to his strides. Passing the front of the house, she propped Maple on the front step so she wouldn't forget to bring her in, and Evander caught the doll as it began a slow topple to the ground. He righted it, then followed her to the van.

"Why did you leave the house?" he asked.

The way he was watching the street with a frown was annoying. Why didn't he ever look at her? It wasn't as though danger was lurking on the quiet, small-town street, just waiting to catch them unaware. She'd like to be looked at every now and then.

She sighed. "Don't worry, safety in numbers."

"I believe I told you to stay put for the night."

"Yeah, and you also told me to hang out with large groups of people, which I did. So, fight your way out of that one." She hushed her voice, placing a finger on her lips as she pulled on the van door, wincing as the old metal panel slid open. Before she had a chance to unbuckle Tigger, Evander had the girl in his arms, her small head of curls tucked against his shoulder, her eyelids not even fluttering with the movement.

He was good.

Daphne unlocked the front door, expecting him to try and maneuver the girl into her arms. Instead, he crossed the threshold, barely making it through the doorway without brushing the top with his short, sandy hair. In the entry, he paused, angling Tigger's feet in Daphne's direction as if they'd done this a thousand times before. She slipped the girl's sandals off her grubby toes, completely in love with the perfect, clean imprint on her foot's sole where the sandals rubbed them clean with each foot strike. Trying not to appear too sappy, Daphne refrained from kissing the toes, and guided Evander to Tigger's room. He gently laid the girl on her bed, pulling up the blanket and tucking her in. He smoothed an unruly lock of hair off Tigger's face before stepping back.

Daphne, eyes blurry with tears of fatigue and gratitude, played with the collar of her dress, hoping Evander didn't see the emotions ruling her at the moment.

"Thank you," she said through a thick throat.

"All part of the service."

"You're a horrible liar," she said, and he smiled.

"It was my pleasure, Daphne." He gave a little nod and let himself out. Turning on the front step, he passed her Maple, but didn't release the doll until she met his eyes.

Feeling grateful for the gift of time alone to paint, she said softly, "Go ahead and rig the place up, Evander. Do your thing."

"Lock your doors and don't go anywhere until I'm back in the morning. Call me if you need to leave. You have my cell number as well as Tyrone's. I'm going to wait here until I see Chuck on the street again."

Daphne sighed. Give the man an inch and he turned into Mr. Bossy Army Pants who figured he had the right to rule her life as though he was the one in charge.

But she'd changed stubborn people's minds about the environment, and she could change his, too. She just needed to apply steady pressure and keep on smiling.

# Chapter Four

*Evander waited at the* stop sign behind Daphne's flower-painted van. The woman was something, that was for sure. She'd just led an early morning awareness rally about protecting watersheds as sleepy-eyed hydroelectric workers trickled past her and into their building, avoiding her and her gang of protesters. He'd never seen anyone come alive the way Daphne had, shouting and whipping up the crowd, spouting off facts that had even him looking sideways at the power company. That woman needed to find a bigger platform, because if she could get a man like him to care about fresh water, she could change the entire world.

Which made her all the more dangerous for a group like Rubicore and, therefore, meant she was that much more in need of protection.

He followed Daphne into Bala, mindlessly steering his truck along the town's curving streets. She hadn't tried to shake him off yet today and he took it as a good sign. Maybe having a few hours to think over what had happened yesterday had given her a much needed introduction to reality. Although, possibly, she was simply using him as a buffer between her and the reporter who'd been quietly taking photos of her all morning.

Evander visually swept the quiet streets for signs of danger. Did he have enough security on Daphne and the girl? Carrying Tigger into the house last night had felt so very real. In that brief moment he'd allowed himself to wonder if he could ever have something like that—the privilege of carrying his offspring into the home he and the love of his life had created.

Then again, who was he kidding? Having offspring would ensure he'd be in a perpetual state of alertness, everything becoming a danger. The kid would either have no life due to his restrictiveness or Evander would die of stress.

War had ruined him. He no longer had the little piece of humanity that would allow him to be a husband or father who reacted the proper way.

Shuddering, he blasted the AC, hoping to prevent a horrid flashback from his first tour of duty, where he'd seen children… no, don't let the memory in. Bury it. He was here. He was safe. That was in the past and he'd done all he could to improve the lives of others.

His head hurt as though rocked by an explosion and he lost the flashback battle, falling into a whirling pool of acidic horrors ranging across years of duty. He pushed his way out of it, his jaw clenched so tight his teeth were grinding together like broken rocks.

Evander unfolded his fingers from the steering wheel, regulating his breathing. The flashbacks were getting better. He hadn't lost sight of Daphne. Hadn't crashed his truck. He had to have faith that this wasn't just a quick reprieve before the flashback roller coaster dunked him under again, causing him to fight with everything he had in order to see the light, to breathe and stay alive.

Daphne pulled up at the Bala farmers' market, which hadn't yet started. He was no good to her in this state. He needed to get it together.

She put her van in reverse, preparing to back into a parking spot, and he sighed in relief. Good. Ready for a fast getaway. At least one of them was with it.

However, she continued backing up until she was in line with a row of tables. Evander, unsure what she was doing, stopped his truck next to her. He would have preferred if she'd placed her van closer to the main entrance, but they could discuss good parking habits once she was a bit more receptive. This was a fair enough start.

Evander leaped out of his truck and opened her van's side door, noting that his hands were still trembling from the flashback jaunt through Memory Lane's house of horrors. As soon as the door slid wide enough, Tigger bounced out. The girl was like a trick can. Open it and she sprang out.

"Thanks, mister," she said as she bounded over to stand by her mother.

Daphne opened the back of the van, unloading paintings that smelled of fresh paint. She was a vendor. Which meant he was losing his edge. This should have come up in his background search, shouldn't it?

He was stuck between worlds. No longer a JTF 2 with an edge sharpened to precision, ready to be used at a split second's notice, and no longer a civilian able to chill out and blend in.

He leaned two tall canvases against the side of his truck. "Are you selling these?"

Daphne nodded.

"You painted them?"

She nodded once more.

Again, shouldn't a hobby of this magnitude have come up?

"How do you find the time?" he asked.

She gave a wan smile and he gave her a closer look. He knew being a single mom was tough going, but today her weariness was similar to a heavy cloak pulling her down. It wasn't bags under the eyes or paleness like most people, it was a waning of the larger-than-life vitality he'd come to know as purely Daphne.

"I haven't been able to sleep much lately."

He felt conflicted. If she wasn't sleeping it could mean she was actually concerned about her welfare and might cooperate. However, he also knew sleep deprivation was an effective form of torture that he wouldn't wish on anyone, and could result in poor judgment.

"Mom, can I get some cotton candy?" Tigger asked, tugging at her mother's dress.

"No sugar this early in the morning. There are apples in the van."

"Do you have any candy?" Tigger asked Evander, a hopeful look in her eyes.

"Do I look like the kind of man who carries candy? That stuff will rot your teeth."

"No, it won't. I brush two times a day." She held up two fingers as though that would buy her a yes.

"Have the apple. It will make you feel better."

"I'm not sick. Who are you?"

"Evander de la Fosse." He held out his hand and she gave it a solemn shake. "You're Kimberly, right?"

She made a face. "Everyone calls me Tigger."

"Right then. Tigger. Nice to meet you."

Daphne was unloading paintings, not paying attention. He wasn't really sure what, if anything, she had told her daughter about him shadowing them, and was afraid he'd end up saying something wrong.

"Why are you here?" Tigger asked.

"I'm helping your mom." He turned to Daphne, arms outstretched. "Hand them here. I'll carry them."

Tigger, obviously knowing the drill, toted aluminum easels to a grassy area in front of the open van, not at all dejected from her sugar shutdown. "You were at our house," she said.

"Yes."

"Why?"

"I'm helping your mom."

"Why?"

"Because she needs help." Man. This kid was determined—just like her mother.

Evander faced Daphne. "Do you sell many?" He propped the paintings on easels, one eye on the reporter who was snapping the occasional photo. He'd talked to Austin Smith earlier and the reporter-photographer had been corporative, agreeing to keep Evander in the loop if he saw anything odd going on. The man had shown the appropriate amount of concern for Daphne and Tigger, making Evander believe he might actually be on their side.

"Sometimes I sell a few. I only just started trying to sell them," Daphne admitted, her lower lip tucked under her top teeth as she stared at one of her paintings.

Okay, so he wasn't that rusty at background checks. This was a new thing. He could work with that.

He followed Daphne's gaze to the painting, of a bright sunflower on an intense blue background. Stormy yet beautiful. She'd captured the ethereal light before a storm where everything is dangerous, the potential for life or death crackling in the sky.

He needed to have this painting. He opened his wallet and realized he didn't have enough on hand for something this incredible. Putting it away again, he lifted the painting off its easel, tucking it back in the minivan.

"What are you doing?" Daphne asked, drawing herself up. "Tigger and I are perfectly safe here in the crowd." She glanced at her daughter and lowered her voice. "You said so yourself."

"That one's mine."

"Oh." She came up short, surprise blanking her expression. "But you haven't paid for it."

"I'll pay for it tomorrow. It's mine."

"You don't even know how much it costs." She narrowed her eyes, arms crossed. "Are you taking pity on me?"

"No. And that one's mine. Have a problem with that?" He crossed his own arms and stared her down.

He'd never been an art guy, but that painting hit him in a place he couldn't explain. He needed to have it. It was that simple. His eye caught another sunflower, a smaller one. It had a red background, and streaks of pink in the yellow petals. "This one, too." He packed it away, knowing his mother would like it.

"You don't have to do this," Daphne said, unpacking the painting again.

"I'm not doing anything." He pushed it back into the van. "Is this how you treat all your customers?"

"You're not a customer, because you haven't paid for them."

He crossed his arms once more and sat on the bumper of the van's open hatch, not budging, blocking her access to the paintings he'd claimed.

"Fine." Daphne threw up her hands, not looking nearly as delighted as he figured an artist who'd just sold two paintings should look.

He thought he heard her mutter something about impossible men before turning back to her other paintings.

"Yeah? Well, they go well with impossible women," he retorted.

"I am not going well with you."

"You could say that again."

"Excuse me?"

"Hey, I'm just a friendly guy." Who was armed and lethally dangerous.

Always armed.

She snorted, heading to talk to an early customer, ending their fun banter.

The market crowd slowly began to ebb and flow around them and there was one man in a tan jacket who kept staring at the paintings, his mind obviously elsewhere. Evander watched him, his gut telling him the man was eavesdropping on Daphne. Evander moved through the paintings, circling around to stand behind the man. She was talking about things she thought a developer was doing wrong. Typical Daphne stuff, from what he'd learned.

He sidled up beside the man and cleared his throat, making him jump. Out of the corner of his eye, he noted that Austin had snapped a shot of the eavesdropper. Very nice. If Evander needed a photo to help identify the man later, he was set. Maybe there was a way to get the reporter on Tyrone's payroll. They could always use an extra set of eyes and this guy seemed to always be around.

"That one your favorite?" Evander asked the lurker.

Daphne, oblivious, chirped away with some scruffy, skinny hippie type. Another thing to talk to Daphne about—what she said where and to whom. The list was going to be endless by the time Evander got her back into the protection of her house at the end of the day.

The eavesdropper nervously glanced at the sunflower with the wilted petals. "Yeah. Yeah, I like it."

"Just bought two today myself. She's great. Shall I wrap this one up for you? I can ask the artist for a deal if you want to add in one of her framed sketches over there. They're a great gift for the woman in your life." Evander raised his eyebrows, waiting for an answer. He stood a little closer, well aware that he was intimidating the smaller man.

"They are very affordable," Evander continued. "I can tell you have exquisite style sense. Shall I package up both, or just this one?"

The man gave a wobbly smile. "Just this one."

Evander made the sale, winking at Daphne, who'd quirked her head at him. He would not be introducing this man to the artist. Making sure he kept chatting him up, Evander guided him away from Daphne's booth, handing off the painting at the last moment.

"Did you just sell the worst painting in the batch?" she whispered, coming up alongside him.

"Apparently."

Eyes twinkling, she gave him a tight hug that just about cracked a rib. "Thank you!"

He rubbed his side, reassessing the slight woman. Where on earth did she hide all that strength?

"Your hugs should be a weapon."

She gave a rich laugh that tickled him, almost making him want to smile.

He glanced around, tension seeping into his veins. "Where's Tigger?"

"I sent her to get pepperoni."

"What?" He clenched Daphne's shoulder, making her squeak. He quickly scanned the area, unable to spot the girl's pink party dress. "You need to keep her in sight at *all times*."

When would this woman get it through her head that she and her daughter were in danger?

"Evander." There was a warning in her voice, suggesting he was overreacting. He was *not* overreacting.

The eavesdropper would not have bought that painting had he not been trying to cover the fact that he'd been busted by Evander. Add in the gun incident yesterday, the custody battle, as well as how the sisters were attacking Rubicore's livelihood, and his blood boiled with danger in a way it hadn't in a very long time.

They were separated. Everyone was vulnerable. He grabbed Daphne's arms. "This is serious. *Never* let her out of your sight. Ever."

"That's no way to live."

"It's the only way to live right now, Daphne. The only way to ensure there's a tomorrow to live *in*." He gave her a brief shake, then released her so he could sprint through the crowds, hoping he wasn't too late.

EVANDER TOOK THE NARROW residential road to the beach's boat launch and park, uncomfortable with the sloping dead end that would have them pinned against the Indian River with no escape. There was one exit. One. And anyone could easily block it.

He'd found Tigger at the farmers' market pepperoni stand and had whisked her away, ignoring the unimpressed look from both Summers when he'd sat them side by side and told them to never leave his sight without permission. Ever. Again.

His growing sense of unease was not helped by the fact that he was certain Daphne had tried to shake him en route from Bala to Port Carling. She had some good moves, but there weren't a lot of places to shake him between the two small towns had made it futile. That and the fact that he had hours of training, whereas she had none. Something was up, but he didn't know if it was her feeling ticked for him telling her off or if she was planning to do something he'd dislike.

His gut told him it was the latter.

The effects of his earlier flashback were catching up with him and he yawned, wishing for a nap. Just before the boat launch he spun his truck around, parking it along the edge of the grass to ensure it was aimed up the road. He got out and made a twirling motion with his finger, telling Daphne to turn around as he had. She rolled her eyes, but laughed as she complied, her good mood from selling three paintings at the market keeping her buoyed. He was not that easily fooled, though. She'd tried to ditch him, and her body language didn't have its usual lightness. It was as though each movement was carefully thought out ahead of time so as not to reveal what she was hiding. It was a basic interrogation skill—watch body language for tightness. He'd just never thought he'd be using it in a domestic matter.

*C'est la vie.* Real life.

With a practiced eye, he scoped out the playground, park, boat launch, river, and treed residential area for places someone could hide—friend or foe—as well as possible escape routes. He held out a hand to help Daphne out of her van, then unleashed Tigger, who had been struggling with the door. The girl burst forth, sprinting for the play equipment shaped like a fortress. He would have loved playing here with his brother when he was a kid, but instead he'd grown up in the city, where things were busy, sterile and a whole lot less fun.

"You don't have to stay," Daphne was saying. "I'm sure you have lots of things to do today. We're just going to hang out and play for a while."

He stretched and ran a hand through his hair. "A man can always use more vitamin D."

She was definitely up to something.

Daphne leaned into her van and looked at the dash clock. She stared at it as though contemplating something, her lower lip pinned between her teeth.

There was no way he was going anywhere but where she was.

And if she thought she could outwait him, good luck. He'd spent twelve days in scorching desert heat waiting outside an enemy bunker for just the right moment. This would be nothing.

"Hungry?" Daphne asked, tossing him an apple.

He caught the red delicious and took a large bite before saying, "Thank you."

She took a bite of her own, watching him as his gaze flicked from her to their surroundings, then back again.

"Are you always thinking of ways to escape?" she asked. "Always on the lookout for enemies that might need a weapon waved at them?"

"It's my job." He gave her a cold, steely glance and with satisfaction saw it hit home, making her shiver. "Have you noticed you're being followed by a reporter?"

Daphne glanced around, her eyebrows puckered over her bright blue eyes. Her face relaxed when she spotted Austin. "That's Austin Smith. He's paparazzi."

Now Evander was ticked off. The man hadn't been fully honest. Reporters and paparazzi were two entirely different things. Plus, Daphne knew more than he did. That small fact was becoming increasingly familiar. And not a good kind of familiar.

"He's an old family friend," Daphne said brightly, and Evander was certain she knew just how much this was bothering him. "Rick Steinfeld might come around soon, too. They're trying to help."

"In what way?"

"Melanie convinced them to help with the publicity angle. To help Mistral see that I'm not a threat." She waved her hand dismissively, not expanding on what was going on.

"More info, please."

"Oh, you know. Just some positive press to combat all the stuff in the papers. They haven't exactly been kind or honest. It's making things worse for Mistral instead of easier."

The crease between Daphne's eyebrows had reappeared and he figured it was best to change the subject for now. He had enough to mull over.

"Is she always like that?" He gestured to Tigger, who had already made a few friends and was in the middle of a battle with a group of boys over who got to be on the top of the play structure.

"Gregarious? Yes. Full of energy? Yes."

"They should bottle that."

"She's actually part of my grand scheme on how to take over the world."

Evander gave an amused chuckle. "She's a good secret weapon."

He turned his back to the river, figuring a flank attack was less likely than one from the road. He kept his eyes peeled, waiting for whatever Daphne didn't want him to be there for.

But every once in a while, he found himself becoming involved in the antics of the children. They were boisterous and so full of life and innocence. Everything he had gone to war in order to protect, right there. That was the reason. And it made every bit of loss and destruction worth it so they could have a real childhood.

He seemed to have caught the attention of a few boys, who edged closer. Finally, they summoned their courage and came right up.

"Are you a bodyguard?" asked a kid with dirt smudged on his nose.

Evander loosened his posture, realizing that with his sunglasses and firm at-ease pose he must look like a member of the Secret Service.

"What happened to your face?" asked his buddy.

Evander debated ignoring them, but figured that wouldn't help his case with Daphne, seeing as she was listening in.

"Yes, I am a bodyguard. And I got blown up protecting a prince." He sighed to himself. That information was way too interesting for young boys. He should have said no, that he had been born with the scars that ran down the side of his face and torso.

"Did it hurt?" asked the first boy.

"Like a son of—" He caught himself in the knick of time and glanced at Daphne for her reaction.

She looked just as interested as the kids.

"Do you have a gun?" asked the second child.

Beside him Daphne flinched. "You should show them some soldier moves in the woods. He was in the army," Daphne told them, her eyebrows raised, obviously trying to convince the kids to gang up on him.

That was unfair. Offside.

Clever, too.

"I'm pretty sure your parents wouldn't like an armed stranger teaching you how to be a soldier in the dark and scary woods." Evander could teach these kids stuff that would turn their heads inside out. Without even touching on the amphibious assaults he could coordinate along the water's edge. They'd never see water the same way.

"Our parents won't mind," one kid said quickly. That was followed by a chorus of head nodding.

"The woods aren't scary," Daphne added.

"I need a push!" called Tigger from the swings.

"I got this," Evander said, eager to get away. At the rate they were going they would have national secrets exposed within seconds.

Daphne was following him across the sandy play area. "You don't have to push her, I can."

"What? You don't trust me?" he challenged.

She looked momentarily taken aback and he used her hesitation to reach Tigger before she did.

"Maybe you could go get us ice cream," Daphne suggested.

Setup. One hundred percent. He'd been tailing the two long enough to know that Daphne almost always said no to anything with sugar, and there was no way she would introduce sugar-induced chaos into her world midday. Especially after a late night of painting that had obviously led to her energy levels taking a hit.

"Ice cream!" Tigger squealed.

"Only if Evander gets it," Daphne said. "I need to stay here with you."

"We can all go!" Tigger said.

"Great idea," Evander said. "When can we go?" Daphne scowled at him, but he kept a straight face. "What? We're not going?"

"Aw," Tigger complained.

He gave her a light push on the swing. "Hey, I met your Cabbage Patch doll last night. What's her name?" His brother, Kyle, had wanted one of those as a kid—until a neighbor kid had laughed and called him a sissy. Evander had given the neighbor a black eye for that, then saved up his allowance to get Kyle the doll. But by then the damage had been done and his brother had decided the safe place for him and his sexual preferences was the closet.

One day his brother would open that door, and until then Evander would be there, letting him know he was still loved, no matter what.

"You met Maple? Push higher!" Tigger demanded.

"Nice name. Very Canadian." He gave her another push, this time a little harder, worried he would knock her right off the swing if he wasn't careful.

"It's my favorite ice cream."

"Oh."

"Higher!"

"Have you ever killed anyone?" asked one of the boys. They'd crept closer while Daphne fumed at him for foiling her plans.

"Where are your mothers?" Evander asked.

"We're old enough to come here on our own," the kid said.

"Well, I think I hear someone's mom calling," Evander stated, avoiding meeting their gazes.

"Higher!"

"Do you want an under-duck?" he asked.

"What's that?"

"A monster push where I dive under you while letting go at the last minute."

He glanced at Daphne questioningly, wondering if the running push would be too much for the girl. Daphne gave a small nod, her arms wrapped around herself as though warding off a chill. A moment ago she'd seemed ticked, but now she looked defeated. He watched her for an extra second, trying to figure out what had changed, and nearly got knocked by Tigger as she swung back toward him.

He moved so he was in front of the swing, wondering if the running push would send the little girl flying. "Are you sure about this? You're wearing a dress."

She carefully let go of one of the chains and he felt his heart stop for a second, worried she'd fall. She lifted the hem of her dress, revealing a pair of shorts. "It's okay, I'm prepared for play."

"A girl who is prepared for play. I like that. Too many kids spend all their time inside these days. Do you have a tree fort? Secret club?"

Tigger gave him a frown. "Nobody will make a fort with me."

"You have a good tree?" He realized that by going down this conversational road he was, in a little girl's world, practically offering to build a fort for her.

He was getting in too deep. He was going to lose objectivity.

"There's a big tree at the cottage. But it's too hard to get tree fort stuff there because it's on an island. And the generator isn't good enough anymore to run power tools. That's what Mom says."

"That's a pity." Tigger needed a man in her life who could step in and resolve these petty issues.

"Under-duck?" she asked.

"You bet. You ready for this? Hold on tight."

Without looking at Daphne, he grabbed hold of the swing and gave it a massive push. As he let go at the last second to duck underneath, Tigger's face flashed a look of fear.

Too high, too fast.

What kind of bodyguard was he?

Again, *not* equipped for real life.

The girl squealed and he spun, preparing to dive and catch her before she plummeted to the sand-covered earth.

Tigger was holding on for dear life, her grin wider than the Grand Canyon. He glanced at Daphne, worried she was going to yell at him for pushing her little girl so high.

Instead, the mother threw up her hands with a resigned smile. "Well, I guess that gets me off the hook from now until eternity. There's no way I can top that."

He smiled internally, proud of himself. This was feeling pretty close to real life, and it felt incredible.

That was, until he spotted a man who stopped him cold.

DAPHNE RECOGNIZED THE two figures that had caused Evander to tense and act as though he was mentally prepping for a takedown. Every fiber of his awareness was directed at the pair, even though he continued to push Tigger on the swing as if on autopilot. What had felt like a quiet family moment seconds ago was shattered.

This was where things got tricky and Daphne got to practice her juggling skills. She needed to change everyone's points of view, but she couldn't do it when they were in the same space, breathing fire at each other.

Then again, what did it matter? Neither she nor Mistral had kept their word today, putting them off to what was surely to be a bad start.

"Daphne," Evander said carefully, his tone quiet and dangerous.

"Oh, Mistral is here," she said lightly, stepping away from the swings. "Great."

"Did you arrange this?"

"Yes. I have to set things right between us." Evander wasn't supposed to be here and neither was Mistral's man. She chewed her bottom lip, which was feeling tender from all the attention it had been receiving from her teeth today. She needed to chill out with a few candles and some good old-fashioned meditation.

Energy fizzed off of the bodyguard. Tigger continued swinging, blissfully unaware.

"What is it going to take, woman?" Evander snapped, moving away from the swing.

"This is my life, my family. *Please* follow my lead and try not to do anything stupid today."

"Such as saving your life?" He stood toe to toe with her, his minty breath hot on her face.

For a moment she had trouble reminding herself that he was

the one increasing the complications in her life and upsetting things that had nothing to do with him—such as her discussions with Mistral. Daphne was going to be a full year older in a week's time and was no closer to having the life she wanted, and she couldn't figure out why. She tried, she really did. And yet…it just never happened.

She turned as Evander held out a hand as though stopping traffic. Mistral and his bodyguard had advanced on them quickly, but stopped when Evander directed them to. Already taking charge.

"I asked you to follow my lead and not get into a competition with Mistral's assistant over who has a bigger penis, and what are you doing? Taking charge."

Evander's eyes narrowed. "I create the boundaries to keep you safe. You can be as stupid as you want within those bounds, but only after I say you can."

"You don't trust me."

"You have yet to give me a reason to." He brushed her aside, placing himself between her and the men.

She fumed silently. He was such a big, fat, pushy blankety-blank. She needed to do like the heroine in the movie *Tangled* and hit the man upside the head with a cast-iron skillet to show him not to turn his back on her or to take her for granted. She could take care of herself just fine, thank you very much.

Evander lumbered toward the men, his body moving as though he was a beast at the top of the food chain and on the prowl. Shivers ran up her spine, but it wasn't from fear. There was something so primal and intense about him that made her skillet idea fall away. He left her off-kilter, her core tightening with a strange mix of longing and resentment.

She needed to get him out of her life.

"Are you armed, Ricardo?" Evander asked the bodyguard, and

she blew a sigh into her curls. Direct route to getting off on the wrong foot. Lovely. Had the man heard of social etiquette?

The bodyguard flashed his piece and Daphne closed her eyes. Great. Now she'd never hear the end of this. Another armed meeting.

Evander's massive hands closed into fists, the muscles and veins in his forearms bunching. Strength, power, and not afraid to use it. This man was everything she stood against.

"I thought you said you were going to leave him behind," Daphne said to Mistral, pushing past Evander, who didn't budge, causing her to bounce off him. "No weapons. No trigger-happy bodyguards."

"I think it's a good thing he came." Mistral gave Evander a pointed look.

"I tried to ditch him," Daphne said quietly, hoping the other two wouldn't hear.

"Got a permit for that?" Evander asked Ricardo.

"Evander, enough," Daphne said. The other bodyguard smirked and she glared at him as she drew Evander aside.

Tigger had slowed on the swing, her feet dragging in the sand, her eyes wide and wary.

"Can you support me on this, please?" Daphne asked Evander. "Without violence."

His large hands were cupped together; his legs were apart. He might be "at ease" but his eyes belied his body's stance.

"I need this, Evander." She rested a hand tentatively on his forearm and he flinched, his gaze dropping down to hers in surprise. Hadn't anybody ever touched this man? Then again, most people likely took note of the keep-away-or-I'll-break-body-parts-you-didn't-even-know-you-had vibe and stayed far, far away.

Lucky people who had the choice.

She touched him again, this time with no apparent impact. "Please?"

"Why?"

Answering the simple question would open a can of worms she preferred to keep stashed away. It wasn't as if he'd understand, anyway. Just like her sisters. They thought no father was better than Mistral. But she had to give him a chance, didn't she? It wasn't her right to prejudge his parenting skills and discount him accordingly.

"Trust me?" she asked.

"You should be applying for a restraining order, not meeting with him. These men are not as safe as you think."

"And they're not as scary and evil as you think they are." She called to Mistral, "What do you say we have our bodyguards sit at a picnic table so they don't interfere with our conversation this time?"

"Sure." He gestured for Ricardo to go to a nearby table and, like an obedient dog, the man complied. She wondered if Evander would do the same.

With reluctance, Evander joined Ricardo at the picnic table, but didn't sit down, apparently finding it more comfortable to cross his arms and scowl at her.

Daphne called to her daughter. Tigger somberly slipped off the stopped swing. She meandered over, her bounce gone, her gaze flicking to Evander several times as though seeking support. When she approached, Daphne knelt beside her, her nerves getting the best of her. Evander was acting as though he was a puffed up guard dog and Mistral was avoiding looking at their daughter.

"Tigger, honey," Daphne said gently. "I'd like to officially introduce you to your father, Mistral Johnson."

Tigger folded herself against Daphne's back, nearly knocking her over onto the grass. "He's the bad guy," she whispered.

Daphne's cheeks flushed, and she hoped Mistral hadn't overheard. "No, no," she replied. "That was just a misunderstanding. He's your…he's your dad."

This was supposed to be the moment where her daughter jumped for joy and skipped off into the sunset, hand-in-hand with her father.

Why was everyone looking so uncomfortable?

Daphne darted a glance at Evander, who seemed pained. Okay, so she could have prepped Tigger a bit more, but that would have meant a morning of endless questions and Evander becoming more interfering—just like her sisters—as he grew more and more suspicious that Daphne was leading her own life without his input.

Mistral held out a hand to shake Tigger's and the girl tried to disappear into the folds of Daphne's dress. Gently, she tried to coax her daughter to stand up. Wasn't this the moment she'd been waiting for? Tigger had been dreaming about her father for years and making plans around meeting him and spending time together.

Maybe Daphne just needed to give Mistral more space so he could step up as a parent. So Tigger could stand on her own and they could develop a relationship without waiting for her to determine it all. Rising, Daphne stepped back, pushing Tigger forward.

Father and daughter had their heads cocked the same, watching each other. Awkward silence stretched between them and Daphne bit her lower lip, wishing she could create a dam against her emotions. Their first meeting was supposed to be amazing…not this.

"Hi," Mistral said.

"Hi," Tigger echoed back.

More awkward silence.

"Why don't we take this over to the swings?" Evander said, coming to crouch beside Tigger. "Do you want another underduck?"

Daphne didn't know whether to be angry with him for butting in and for Mistral allowing him to take the lead, or to be relieved at how Evander was ensuring her daughter had someone to help her break the ice.

Evander began striding away and Tigger hurried ahead to whisper something to him.

"Sorry? What was that?" he asked, with an uncharacteristic gentleness that rocked Daphne, who had been trailing behind them.

He got down on one knee like a quarterback about to start a play. Tigger cupped her hands around his ear and whispered loudly enough for Daphne to hear, "I don't have a father."

It was as though someone had stabbed her in the heart. Daphne reeled, trying to remember to breathe, trying to stop the pain and horror as it struck her full force.

Mistral's expression didn't change, but she noticed that Evander had to brace himself so he didn't fall over. Clearing his throat, he stood, taking the girl's hand. He led her to the swing, his strides so long and fast that Tigger had to skip and jump to keep up.

Evander plunked her on the swing and, with his head bent close to hers, said something that made her smile. Daphne's heart hitched and she raised a trembling hand to her lips. For all his guns and gadgets, Evander was an incredibly decent man—even if he likely had some definite darkness to his aura.

The next time he glanced her way, his brows pinched and

furrowed, she mouthed, "*Thank you.*" He gave her a curt nod, the tension in his expression easing.

"What's your favorite color?" he asked Tigger, giving her a push.

"Pink, purple, yellow, green. But not puke green. That's gross."

Evander, still pushing Tigger, asked Mistral the same question.

He thought for a moment and Daphne worried he might not play along with the ice breaker. "I don't think I have one."

"It's black," Tigger said shyly.

Nobody said anything as they watched Mistral battle an internal argument over the supposed favorite color.

"Why do you say that?" Evander asked Tigger.

"He's always wearing it."

Mistral's bodyguard laughed, holding a hand over his mouth as though nobody would notice the mirth bubbling forth. "She has a point," he said, when everyone continued to stare at him.

They all looked to Mistral, who was decked out in a tailored black suit despite the heat of the August afternoon.

"Where would you like to travel to?" Evander asked, picking up the game again, and Daphne sighed. He was making the questions too complex. Her daughter was only five.

"Disney World," her daughter replied without a pause.

"Good pick." Evander addressed Mistral, "And you?"

"Been there."

"Well, la-di-da-da." Evander flopped his hands and bobbed his head in a haughty dance that made Tigger giggle.

All right, this was a whole new aspect to the special ops ex-navy man, and Daphne wasn't quite sure how to take him. She knew children often brought out the real side in adults, but that was often the cranky, generous or impatient side. Not a huge-hearted, gentle, silly persona from a man with muscles on his muscles and a glare that cut holes through steel.

If she wasn't careful, she was going to hold this man as the new ideal for a father for her little girl. And that was Mistral's job.

"Mom and my nanny took me," her ex said.

Evander raised his eyebrows at Tigger, who giggled.

"Do you know how to build a tree house?" Daphne blurted to Mistral.

He gave her a puzzled look. "Um. No. Do you?"

She shook her head.

"Me, neither," Tigger said with a heavy sigh. She slid off the swing and came over to take Daphne's hand. "Can we go home now?"

Usually she had to bribe her daughter with everything under the sun to leave the playground. Daphne glanced at Mistral and Ricardo. Her ex was checking his phone and easing toward his black, unmarked car.

Her heart sank. He was done already?

Her sisters could not be right about this. He wanted to be a father. That's what he'd said over the phone. Their daughter was amazing. Quick-witted, fun, and vibrant. Couldn't he see that? Didn't he want to be a part of her life?

Daphne freed herself from the girl, hurrying to fall into step beside the retreating father. "You're leaving? Already?"

She hated the desperate whine in her voice, but couldn't help it. She'd hoped for so much. She'd expected him to want to make up for the way his own father had been painfully absent in his upbringing. All those years ago he'd spoken as though he wanted to change the past. And here was his opportunity.

"You can change it all," she said breathlessly. "You can stop the cycle right here and be a present father who is loving and caring and spends time with your daughter. There's no reason another child should grow up without the love of their father."

Mistral looked at her with surprise, then glanced back at Tigger, who was getting a ride on Evander's shoulders.

That was supposed to be him, didn't he see that? That man could be him.

"What are you talking about?" he asked. His phone was vibrating in his hand.

*Baby steps,* she reminded herself. *Don't overwhelm him with changing the world before he sees how he can make small changes in his own life.*

"I thought you wanted to get to know Tigger before arranging visitation, and before we settled on custody."

"Why do you call her Tigger?"

"She's bouncy."

He gave the mellow child a doubtful look. "I think we did well today," he said with an easy shrug. He held up his cell. "I have to take this."

Daphne grabbed the phone, surprising him when she didn't allow him to raise it to his ear. "Don't you want more?"

He paused, staring at her for a moment. "I'm not sure I can have it all, Daphne. Your dreams are too big." He gave a helpless shrug.

"I meant more time with Tigger. To get to know her."

His phone began buzzing again in their shared grip. "I'm sorry, Daphne. Today's gone sideways on me. I wish I had more time, but I have a business to run and my dad needs a proposal from me ASAP."

There was hurt in his eyes as he walked away, phone at his ear, shoulders hunched forward in defeat.

Moments later, Mistral paused, then turned back. "Daph, the kid and I'll spend time together. I'm here for the rest of the summer, off and on." He came closer, voice dropping. There was a hint of the young man she'd once loved hiding in his wistfulness.

"We'll get to know each other. Okay? Plenty of time."

Summer ended in less than two weeks.

"You'll see her again?" Daphne asked.

Mistral paused, watching Evander and Tigger goof around. "Call me."

DAPHNE HAD TO REMIND herself that just because she was ready to move faster, it didn't mean Mistral was. She had a habit of looking far into the future and wishing for too much, and this time she needed to allow it all to happen as it was meant to.

He would see their daughter again. That should be enough for now.

She turned to find Evander behind her, teeth clenched so tight he was going to need cranial sacral massage to align his body systems again.

Reaching up, she gently placed a hand along his tense jaw. "You're going to pull yourself out of alignment."

He blinked at her as though not quite sure who she was or what she was saying.

"It's time to get home," he said.

"Fine." She'd lost brownie points with Evander today, while he'd earned a stack to last him a lifetime—or, in his case, until tomorrow at least. The idea of losing points with him bothered her even though he was a bossy grump. For some dumb reason she wanted the big lug to think highly of her.

It was almost as though she'd developed a crush on him today. The idea tickled her mind and she began laughing. How ridiculous! Evander? Not on your life.

"What?" he snapped.

His frown made her mirth all the more contagious and it spread through her body until she was bent over double, helpless.

"You've finally cracked. Well, can't say I didn't see it coming." He put his hands on his hips, looking so stern and serious that her laughter took out her knees, dropping her to the ground, where she let it take full control.

"She gets like this," Tigger said, giggling.

Daphne sat up, holding her gut, trying to stop the laughter. "I'm sorry, I really am. This is all just so ridiculous all I can do is laugh."

Tigger bounded away, chuckling to herself.

Evander yanked Daphne to her feet, his glare as deadly as a sharpened blade. "Just because nobody pulled a gun today does *not* mean we can laugh and have a merry time."

Daphne did her best to try and quell the riot of giggles expanding in her chest.

Under his breath, Evander muttered, "What went so wrong in your life that you want your daughter spending time with a man who has an armed bodyguard with an itchy trigger finger lurking behind him at all times?"

Her amusement ceased as though someone had pulled the emergency brake.

"I don't judge your life, you don't judge mine." She went to gather Tigger, who was sitting under a picnic table, picking dandelions and singing softly to herself. Daphne glanced back at Evander, who was waiting, arms crossed.

How was she going to deal with him following her around for what would likely be days or weeks?

And yet...if it hadn't been for him today, things probably would have belly flopped hard enough to leave her stunned and breathless. She had expected him to make things worse by escalating the men's worst sides, but instead he'd helped her daughter. He'd stepped up as the father figure Daphne had been seeking for her little girl. The fact that he was the one who had put Tigger at ease and looked out for her, instead of it being Mistral, was like a pebble in Daphne's shoe.

The universe obviously had a cruel sense of humor. Evander was not going to be the girl's father figure. End of story. Mistral was.

The universe was simply teaching Daphne patience.

She just wished the universe would pick up the pace a bit.

She crouched by the picnic table. "Come on, Tigger, time to go."

"Home?" the girl asked. "With you?"

Daphne bit her bottom lip to hold in the pain. Just like that, her daughter's world had changed enough that she no longer trusted that she would always be with her mother.

"Yes, with me."

"Evander, too?"

"Yes, I expect that he will follow us as usual."

"Can I ride with him?"

The question set Daphne back. The man had definitely left an impression today. On both of them.

"I think you should probably ride with me."

The girl crawled out from under the table, grass stains rubbed into the hem of her dress. Without a word of argument, she climbed into the minivan.

Evander was talking on his phone, and Daphne felt so exhausted that even though she knew this was her chance to shake him, she couldn't bring herself to do it. Instead, she waited outside her van, intrigued by the way his forehead was scrunched and lined. Phone still to his ear, he raised a hand, placing a thumb on one temple, his index finger on the other. Yup, definitely pulling things out of alignment with all that stress he kept bunched up under his skin. The man could use some serious yoga, too.

"Mom, are you sure you can wait that long?" he said into his phone.

Mama's boy.

"No, I'll be there in twenty. Time me."

Daphne tried not to show her surprise. Just like that he was ditching her? What had happened to all the safety stuff he was so keen on? Had the meeting with Mistral convinced him that the danger was gone? The idea both elated and disappointed her in one mixed-up swirl of confusing emotions.

Evander looked up at Daphne, and she felt the power of his gaze hit her hard in the chest. Something was wrong in his world. Something big. Realizing that he, indeed, was human shouldn't be so shocking to her, but the idea was foreign and new.

"That's for me to figure out, Mom. Just sit still. I'll be there soon."

Evander turned off his phone, eerily silent for a moment. His shoulders were hunched forward, his eyes screwed shut. She watched as his hands flexed tighter and tighter around his cell. Afraid he was going to break it, she gently tried to loosen it from his grip, hoping not to disturb him. His fingers tightened instinctively and she lightly rested both palms around his fist. She wasn't afraid, but she felt the need to move slowly and carefully.

"You're going to break it," she whispered, tugging on the phone. His fingers released immediately and she took the warm case from him. "Are you okay?"

He remained silent, not moving.

She pushed him toward her van, her mind made up. Time to earn back some brownie points, or at least repay a favor or two. "Where are we going?" she asked. She had him in the van's passenger seat before he realized what was going on, and began blinking and shaking his head. She shut the door on him, not knowing whether he would stay put or not.

She climbed into the driver's seat and pulled out. "Where to?"

"Bracebridge," he said finally.

"Buckle up, then."

They were on the main road out of town before he began protesting. "I can drive."

"We're already on the road."

"I should drive."

"You're in no condition to do so."

"You don't have enough gas."

"Sure I do."

"The gas light is on," he said, his voice hollow.

"I can get to town and back on that."

"You should always keep in the top quarter."

"I'd always be at the gas station."

"Stop taking risks." He turned to her with haunted eyes. "What if you had to evade someone and ran out of gas?"

"Evander…"

"Promise me you'll be more careful."

"Shut up and let me drive," she said, already regretting the good deed.

# Chapter Five

*Evander was out of the* van before Daphne had pulled to a complete stop in front of the house. He didn't even remember getting into her van. He bounced against the front door and it shook and creaked in protest. Right. Unlock it first. His fingers fumbled over the security code and the dead bolt finally released, letting him in.

His mother was waiting in the entry, sitting on a stool, face pale, fingers trembling as she tied the laces of her running shoes.

"There you are," she said, as though everything was normal.

But nothing would be normal ever again. Florence had been hiding a massive secret from him. They had been living in the same house, and even though he'd been trained to spot irregularities, he'd missed the fact that his mother had cancer.

She patted his arm and said, "Now, now, you're blaming yourself for something, aren't you?"

"Why didn't you tell me?"

She sighed. "Let's talk about that later."

The home's security alarm began screaming and he wished there was something he could smash to make it shut up. Couldn't it see they were in the middle of a crisis?

"Where's your phone?" Florence asked.

Evander patted his large pockets, finding the gadget. He

turned off the security alarm, and with his pulse still racing, swept his mother into his arms and out the door.

"Oh, for heaven's sake, put me down." She gave his shoulder a swat. "I can still walk, you know."

Daphne's eyes were as round as saucers as he strode up to the van. She scooted around the van to open the passenger side door, and Evander placed his mother inside, buckling her in. She gave him an exasperated look.

"I haven't turned into an invalid, you know," she said sternly. "And don't forget to lock the house."

He shut the van without a word and returned to the house to do so. He needed to get an app for that, too.

When he got back to the vehicle, his mother and Daphne were commiserating. He could tell by the way they shut up when he entered the van.

He turned to Tigger, who was silently regarding his mom. "They were talking about me, weren't they?" he asked.

The girl sat up straighter, as though trying to keep the secret inside.

"No, it's okay. You can side with your mother," Evander said. "I know they were complaining. It's what women do about men."

Daphne giggled and pulled out, taking them to the medical office as per his mother's directions. Evander's right foot kept pressing into the floorboards, wanting them to go faster. Didn't she know his mother wasn't well? They needed to get there ASAP.

"Let me drive," Daphne said calmly.

"I didn't say anything."

"You didn't have to."

Florence chuckled in the backseat. "You didn't tell me Daphne was so lovely."

Daphne laughed. "I think it's beyond his capacity to see that."

The amusement in his mother's voice allowed some of the

tightness in his chest to ease off. If she still had a sense of humor... No, that didn't work. Soldiers had joked in his arms as they drew their last breath. He needed to pull himself together. He would be no good to his mom if he allowed the fear to take over. Gripping the door handle, he got ready to leap out as soon as they stopped.

A few minutes later, Evander was sitting beside his mother in the doctor's waiting room, tapping his foot.

"Are you okay? How are you feeling?" he asked again.

Florence sighed, a hint of exasperation darkening her expression.

Daphne and Tigger sat on his opposite side. This was not how he'd envisioned his day going down. He was supposed to keep work and life separated. Not this. The fact that Daphne was doing more of the take-charge and take-care role than he was didn't help. She'd been the one who'd thoughtfully fetched his mother a cup of cold water from the waiting room's cooler. She'd been the one who had lowered the room's blinds so they no longer let the early afternoon's sun stream into her eyes.

He rubbed his mouth, hating the way his stubble felt against his hand. He needed a shave. He needed to get control. And the more he was around Daphne, the less he seemed to have.

"You look tired," his mother said.

"So do you."

"Yes, but I have cancer. It's a good excuse." She gave him a beatific smile that nearly stopped his heart.

"Tigger, stop it." Daphne grasped her daughter's arm, keeping her from restlessly tapping the table with the flat of her hands.

"How old are you?" his mother asked the girl.

"Five. How old are you?"

Daphne reprimanded her. "You don't ask adults their age."

"She asked me first."

"That's fine." Florence smiled. "I'm sixty-three."

"That's pretty old," replied Tigger.

"It is. Come over here and I'll show you something I'm working on."

Tigger was at her side in a second flat, taking the free chair to her left. His mom slowly pulled her knitting out of the shoulder bag she'd brought along. Her movements were slow, another hint that she felt worse than she was letting on. Evander reached over and helped settle the ball of yarn on her lap.

With a calm and even voice, Florence began telling Tigger the story about how she'd learned to knit, and what she was making.

"Can you make blankets for fairies?" Tigger asked.

His mom paused thoughtfully. "I don't see why not. Although I think you would need special yarn. This is too thick and wouldn't cozy around a fairy in the right way. They are much too delicate. But I have a yarn…yes, a very thin, fine yarn that just might be right for fairies."

"Really?" Tigger's eyes were glowing, and she seemed enthralled with his mother. Something pricked at the backs of Evander's eyes and he breathed a silent prayer that whatever deity or power ruled the planets would spare his mother. Not just so she could be this amazing person for Tigger, but for his own children one day. Now there was a thought that hadn't struck him since leaving the army. Where had that hope come from?

"About how tall is your fairy friend?" Florence asked.

Tigger placed her palms a few inches apart. "I think they're about this tall. It's hard to tell because they're so fast and secret and magical." She clasped her hands together, squeezing her shoulders toward her ears as though trying to hold in her exuberance. Cute. That's what Tigger was. A real-life rocket launcher in human form.

"They live on Nymph Island. I made them houses."

"Did you know your mother is a woodland nymph?" Florence asked.

Tigger's eyes grew round and Evander held in a groan. His mom was going to get carried away and the girl was going to be sorely disappointed when the truth hit her.

"It's true," Daphne said. "I was named after a woods and plant nymph. All of my sisters were. Hailey is named after the water nymph. Maya is a celestial nymph—stars and such. Melanie is, well, Melanie."

"She's not a nymph?" Tigger asked.

"She's an earth goddess."

"I miss Auntie Mellie Melon."

Daphne studied her hands and Evander wondered just how long the two sisters were going to fight.

"Is the doctor ready yet?" he asked, shifting forward. Maybe he should remind the receptionist that they were waiting.

His mother pushed him back in his chair, barely pausing in her knitting. A headline from a newspaper on the table caught his eye. He picked it up. The story was about Rubicore, the municipality and the legal action Melanie had started against them. Which got Evander thinking.

"Where did Austin go?" he asked Daphne.

She gave a shrug.

"I asked him to help keep an eye on you today."

Another shrug.

Civilians. So reliable in their unreliability. It looked as if it was all on him when it came to watching Daphne and Tigger.

His mother's name was called, and while she refused his assistance down the long hall to the exam room, she let him guide her past the reception area. Then she paused, hand on his forearm, eyes meeting his.

"You need to keep that family safe, Evander."

He nodded in reply.

"You need to bring them home, to our house."

"I'm not bringing them home."

"How are you going to keep them safe if you aren't with them? You need to keep them together and you need to be under the same roof. Our roof."

"I understand that, but I'm not bringing them home."

"You have the place so rigged up I'm half afraid to move and half afraid not to for fear some sensor will tell you I've expired." She gave a wan smile.

He'd never been a fan of gallows humor and especially not now.

"Maybe that's a good thing," he growled, wishing he was like any regular man right now. At home. In front of a game, rum and Coke in hand. "And they are *not* moving in with us. That's final."

His mom patted his cheek and smiled as though she knew something he didn't. He hated it when she did that.


EVANDER WIPED HIS EYELIDS with the tips of his fingers and sighed. His mom's appointment had revealed that she was dehydrated—something that scheduled home care could have prevented if his mother hadn't been trying to hide her cancer from him.

They'd given her fluids intravenously in the doctor's office, then Daphne had helped take her home. Once Florence was settled, Daphne gave him a ride back to his truck in Port Carling, making him feel about as useful as air-conditioning in the Arctic.

"Why would she try and hide that from me?" His fists were clenched over his knees and he willed himself to open his hands flat.

"Well…" Daphne said, casting him a glance. "Maybe she

worried you might try and take over?" There was doubt and hesitancy in her voice.

"But wouldn't that make her feel better? Knowing someone else was taking care of the details so she could focus on getting better?" The fact that he hadn't noticed how ill she was made him feel like the world's worst son. She'd already started radiation and had gone to numerous appointments without him knowing. The fact that she didn't trust him to know of her illness was the worst part.

She didn't trust him.

"I thought old age was setting in rather rapidly." Man, that sounded lame. "She told me it was a cold. I should have known. She normally bounces back from something like that within days."

"You can't blame yourself. She's an adult and makes her own choices for whatever reason." Daphne's voice had an edge and he knew she was thinking about her own life.

"When was she going to tell me?"

Before he'd left, he'd called the neighbor to look in on her, even though he'd be gone less than an hour. His mother had protested about bothering their neighbor, but all Evander could think as they drove farther away from her was that he should be there with her.

Daphne pulled up alongside his truck and he faltered. He couldn't leave her and Tigger unprotected. Coverage wasn't coming to sit outside their house for another hour. But he needed to get back so he could arrange for home care to do regular check-ins on his mother, as well as live-in help until she got the all-clear. He pinched the bridge of his nose as emotions overwhelmed him. She'd better get the all-clear.

His mom had assured him that radiation would be done in another week and this blip was likely the worst of it all. Then she'd have a scan to see if the treatment had worked. Meaning she would likely try to railroad his attempts to help, since she figured the end was in sight. But she hadn't reached it yet, which meant she needed help and support. Help and support he wasn't there to give.

He followed Daphne back to her house, needing to see her tucked in until someone came to relieve him. Thank goodness she'd gone with the flow this afternoon. He'd been so taken aback by his mother that he hadn't even thought to call Tyrone to get someone over to fill in for him so Daphne could go home.

He phoned Tyrone now, and slapped a GPS locator on the back of Daphne's van as he ushered the two Summers to the front door. With his mind in two places he was going to need as many gadgets on the job as possible.

"I'm going to double-check the sensors," he told Daphne, shutting the door behind them. He checked the house, and when he'd decided all was still okay, went to the front door.

Daphne opened it on the first light knuckle rap, not checking the peephole. He knew, because he had his thumb over it, testing her.

"Use your peephole," he said.

"I knew it was you."

"No, you didn't." He handed her a wad of cash he'd pulled out of his wall safe back in Bracebridge. "For the paintings."

Not counting it, she shoved it in the pocket of her cardigan, and he found himself wondering if she had a wall safe of her own or would like him to install one.

"I was watching you from the window," she said, "so I could answer before you rang the bell and woke Tigger—she totally crashed on the couch. What did you put on my van when we were coming inside?"

"A locator. That okay?"

"Other than it being utterly ridiculous?"

"Yes."

She chewed on her lip for a moment. "I don't like it."

"I know."

"It represents everything that's wrong with this situation."

"Tyrone, my boss, will be on watch tonight, other than for a few hours—that will be Chuck, okay?" Evander didn't like the fact that Chuck was still on the job, but Tyrone was short staffed tonight, to the point of needing to fill in himself to reduce the amount of time they had to lean on someone like Chuck.

"You're going home?" Daphne hugged her sweater around her, even though it was a warm August evening, and he stepped closer, worried that she was having a tougher time than she was letting on.

He waved his cell phone, wanting to thank her for all she had done that day, but unable to find the right words without showing her his cracks. "I'll call if I sense any disturbances. You can also call me if you need anything. Do you still have my number?"

She shook her head and, with a sigh, he pushed past her, inhaling her fresh scent. He'd given her his contact info after the Mistral incident, and he'd had a feeling she'd crumpled it up. But things must be changing if she was receptive to having it now. Or at least letting him barge in to give it to her again.

Either way, he'd take it. It would be easier to keep her safe if he had her participation.

In her kitchen, he scrawled his name and numbers on a notepad. "Put this in your phone. Leave it in your van, your house, work. Everywhere. I'm never farther than a breath away, but I want you to feel safe. Know I have your back, Daphne. Even if I'm not on your doorstep."

She held the small piece of paper, staring at it blankly in the early evening light. Finally she looked up, brushing a mess of curls off her forehead. "Do you live with your mom in Bracebridge?"

"Yes."

She swallowed hard and he knew she was thinking that being twenty minutes away wasn't exactly next door if she was having an emergency. Normally, he'd find a place closer, but with his mom…

"Chuck and Tyrone will keep you safe."

Her lips parted and Evander resisted the urge to kiss her.

Strange. He wasn't one to get involved with his job. And that's what she was, a job. Plus, she wasn't his type. She'd take him to task on every thing in his life, and he didn't have the energy to battle that on a daily basis. Nor a desire to. The woman of his dreams would take him for who he was.

"I'm out," he said, striding through the small house, which was warm and friendly—just like Daphne and her daughter. "Call if you need anything. Any time of day. If I call, pick up." He held on to the door frame. It was now or never. He swallowed hard. "Thanks, Daphne."

"For what? Not busting your balls?" She gave him a light shove, her hands warm on his chest, and he once again had to rein in the urge to kiss her.

"Yeah. And for today. Appreciate it."

She nodded and he closed the door, calling through it, "I want to hear those locks click into place, Daphne."

He could hear her sigh from the other side of the door, but the sound of metal on metal made him smile.

"See you in the morning," he said. With one last check on her place using his app, he waved to Chuck, who had finally arrived, yawning and holding up a Big Gulp. Evander headed home to take care of his mom and present her with a painting he figured she'd enjoy staring at as much as her garden.

# Chapter Six

*Daphne sat up in bed* and checked her bedside clock. Who was calling her cell at two in the morning? She fumbled for her lit-up phone, trying to clear the sleep from her voice before answering. Pulling an all-nighter yesterday had not done wonders to her ability to wake up in a flash.

"Hello?"

"Daphne." It was Evander, his voice low and urgent.

She was out of bed before she processed a thing, hurrying to Tigger's room, heart pounding.

"Where's Chuck?" Evander asked.

"Chuck?" Who was Chuck?

"Can you see him on the street? No, don't go to your window."

Daphne froze, unsure what he needed her to do.

Evander swore under his breath and she could hear clanking in the background, a door slamming, an alarm going. Another curse and a "Hang on a sec." A truck started up. "Stay on the line." Another phone chimed as it powered up.

Heart pounding, Daphne climbed into bed with Tigger, careful not to wake the girl. She placed her back to the wall, eyes on the doorway.

"What's wrong?" she whispered into the phone, listening for any sounds in the small house. She found herself wishing Melanie still lived with her. Technically, she'd kicked her out only for one night, but her sister had stayed away longer. Right now, Daphne wished she had someone bigger and bolder to lead a charge against whatever was going on that had Evander flipping his lid.

She eyed the bedroom window, wanting to escape, believing the wide-open yard would offer better fleeing options. At the same time, she was too freaked out to move. Was Evander overreacting to a tripped sensor?

"There's been a disturbance to one of your windows," he said, and she could hear his truck picking up speed in the background.

"Sometimes they rattle during thunderstorms," she replied, eager to dismiss the fear coursing through her nervous system.

"It's been opened."

Daphne held in a terrified gasp.

"Have you heard anything?" he asked.

Her old house creaked, but she couldn't tell if it was a late night breeze or someone inside.

"No, I don't think so."

"Hang on, okay? I'm right here if you need me."

She overheard Evander giving Chuck heck over voice mail, on what must have been the other phone she'd heard start up moments ago. A moment later he was talking to the police.

"Do you have a grip on the wheel?" she asked, envisioning him with a phone in each hand as he stormed the curvy road between the two towns. He didn't answer, although she could still hear the hum of tires on asphalt. So he was still moving, still right side up, still on the road. All good.

Daphne wrapped Tigger in her blanket and carefully lowered the sleeping girl to the floor, then slid her under the bed, joining her a second later. In the movies, they always hid under the bed or in the closet. And they were always found.

"Daphne?"

"Yes," she whispered, afraid to be overheard.

"Do you have a weapon?"

"No." Her voice quavered.

"Stay where you are. I'm on my way and so are the police. Stay...stay hidden."

He'd save her.

But he was still at least ten minutes away. Anything could happen in ten minutes.

"Hurry," she whispered, and curled tighter under the bed.

THE HOUSE ROCKED AS the front door banged open, and Daphne held in a squeak, squeezing Tigger close, her own back to the room as she wiggled closer to the wall, trying to flip the edge of the blanket Tigger was wrapped in over herself for more cover. The little girl moaned in her sleep and stretched her arms, knocking the underside of the wooden bed frame.

"Shh," Daphne begged.

There were shouts, the thumping of heavy feet, the slamming of bodies and more shouts. Daphne could barely breathe, and tears trickled out the corners of her eyes.

*Please, Evander, please.*

The house grew quiet around her. Then the bedroom light flicked on.

"Daphne?" It was Evander.

She pulled her head out from under Tigger's blanket, body still curved protectively around her daughter, then craned her neck to look behind her, counting feet.

Two very large black army boots were in the middle of the room. Just Evander. She sighed in relief and Evander's face popped into view, his shoulders bulging as he watched from a plank position. Slowly, he lowered his chest to the floor, his biceps rippling under his T-shirt in a way that would have left her in awe if she hadn't been busy losing her mind with fear.

He cautiously extended his hand, as though to a feral kitten. "Are you two okay?"

She gripped his fingers, snatching them to her as she rolled to face him, placing her back to her still-sleeping daughter.

"Is Tigger in there?"

"Asleep," Daphne whispered.

"You okay?" He pulled on her arm, gently tugging her out from under the bed as though reeling in a fish. Once she was clear, she threw herself at him, collapsing onto his chest and knocking him onto his butt. His arms wrapped around her as he squeezed her close, his breath ruffling the curls that had fallen over her forehead.

"Everyone accounted for, Evander?" asked an officer from the doorway.

"Yes, sir. Everyone is fine." He tipped her chin up. "Right?"

She gave a tiny nod, her mouth trembling. He pressed her to his hard chest so she wouldn't wake Tigger as sobs broke free.

"We'll give you a minute," the officer said. "Meet us outside when you're ready."

"Roger that," Evander said.

Daphne burrowed deeper into his arms, protected by his strength.

"We caught the man who broke in," Evander murmured. "He was riffling through papers in your living room. Came in through the kitchen window."

Daphne shuddered. A man had broken in, unbeknownst to her, while they were sleeping. What would have happened without Evander and his gadgets?

He stroked her hair and her hiccupy breathing slowly worked its way back to regularity, with only the odd hitch here and there.

"How'd you get here so fast?" she asked.

He ignored the question. "He wasn't armed and the police have him in custody. I'm sorry, Daphne." Evander sounded so grim.

"Why?" She looked up, amazed at how angular his face was from this viewpoint. All sharp lines, but soft, too. Caring. Warm. Safe.

Ridiculous. He was an army man who had served several tours of duty. And his scars? You didn't get those by sitting behind a desk. This man wasn't here to comfort her, he was here to take care of problems. She pushed herself out of his arms, feeling small and alone.

"I should have been here," he said.

"Chuck was on," she replied, wiping her cheeks dry.

As if feeling her need for space, Evander stood, moving to the doorway. "He was at the local convenience store. He's been dismissed." Evander ran a hand briskly down the scarred side of his face. He spied the cardigan she'd left on Tigger's dresser during story time. "You need a wall safe."

Daphne stared at the sweater, which she'd been wearing when he'd paid her for the paintings. There was a lot of money in its pocket at the moment. "Do you normally have that much cash on hand?" she asked him. She knew he hadn't been to the bank between buying the paintings and paying her.

"I was trained to be prepared for anything."

He was watching her in a way that made her feel nervous. No, not nervous, just…inspected. He was trying to figure something out about her and she wasn't sure if he was drawing positive conclusions or not.

"The army had a pretty big impact on you, didn't it?"

"Yes," he said awkwardly. "But this is…this is real life. It's good to have money on hand in real life, too."

He moved to sit on the edge of the bed, making it creak with his size. Daphne had a momentary vision of it collapsing and her daughter being squished. Evander clasped his hands together, elbows on knees.

"What did he want?" Daphne asked, sitting on the opposite end of the bed. "The person who broke in?"

"He was eavesdropping on you in the market today while you were talking to that hippie guy about your plans for the development. You need to start watching what you say and where. Tyrone and I have ideas about this guy and we're confident someone from Rubicore sent him."

"Rubicore?" A cold dread settled deep in Daphne's gut. "It wasn't Mistral."

"What are you not telling me, Daphne?"

"Nothing. I just know Mistral, and that you and everybody are going to assume it was him. He's not like that. He wouldn't do this."

"Well, we'll put a tail on this guy once he's released from custody, and find out for sure."

"They're going to let him out?"

"Probably."

"But he just broke into my house in the dead of the night and you saw him spying on me."

"Yup." Evander's hands were clenched together, his knuckles turning white, and she got the feeling he was fighting back something dark and sinister.

"I let you bug my house because I felt…and now it just…" She bit her knuckle, her breath hiccupping again.

Evander, with fluid, easy moves that came from using his body in unpredictable, real life settings rather than in a regimented gym, had an arm around her in seconds. She pushed him away. If she let herself collapse into his strength she'd never be able to stay strong on her own, and would turn into a blabbering puddle of desperate tears and wails, dependent and needy.

"You can't be a passive participant in your life any longer, Daphne. You have to take action."

She nodded, not following his logic.

"I mean it. You need to take action like you do with your environmental protests."

The intense look in his eyes made her throat catch.

"Nobody can stop you when you take charge. But with this whole thing going on, you've been allowing yourself to be the passive recipient. It's real, Daphne. It's very real. Take charge. Take the reins. Take control. This is your life. *Yours.*"

Her lower lip started to tremble, but he didn't come to her this time. She breathed through the upset, imagining being wrapped in peaceful, loving light, and positive energy.

"I am taking charge," she said finally. She'd arranged to meet with Mistral several times and could have simply run away after the gun incident. But she didn't.

The break-in wasn't about her and Mistral. It was related to the battle her sisters were having with Rubicore.

"You need to step it up. Your ex…" Evander paused and glanced toward the underside of the bed, as though on the lookout for a girl eavesdropping on them "…is working with men who just had someone break in to find out what you have planned against them."

"Custody and Rubicore are unrelated."

"You need to take this seriously. You owe it to her—" he tipped his head "—to act as though this threat is real, and to keep yourself and your daughter safe."

Daphne swallowed hard. "I can't be like you."

He lowered himself onto his knees, joints popping with the controlled effort, and took her hands in his. His eyes were dark, but in this light she could see flecks of copper running through the dark blues, their star-shaped pattern feeling familiar.

She withdrew her hands from his. "I'm about peace. Harmony. Mistral and I can talk through all of this. Weapons and fights aren't the way, Evander."

"I know."

She looked at him in shock.

"But sometimes you're working against someone who is operating on a different plane, Daphne, and you need to protect yourself accordingly."

"I can't arm myself."

"I'm not asking you to."

"Then what are you saying?"

"You need to move somewhere more secure. You need to let me watch over you and your family. For real. Twenty-four/seven."

"I can't be around that kind of energy. Not for all hours of the day." She wrapped her arms around herself, imagining him putting her and Tigger into a bunker.

"Was today really that bad?" he asked, the corners of his lips turning downward.

She had to admit that today had been okay, and he'd been helpful at both the market and the park. She'd seen a different side to Evander even before the issue with his mother.

But she couldn't reconcile the man who'd escalated a conversation to drawing weapons in a public park, with the one who had been so tender and caring toward her daughter, then nearly out of his mind over his mother's illness. Add in the fact that he'd come here at high speed to rescue her, and then held her tight. There were many sides to Evander de la Fosse, several that she quite liked and admired, but she couldn't forget that he was trained to do things she couldn't even imagine one human doing to another.

"Put better locks on the windows, Evander, or whatever you need to do, but I am not leaving my home. I have my own life and I am going to live it. Alone."

# Chapter Seven

*Evander hadn't slept* after Daphne's break-in. With reluctance, he'd driven away last night, only after ensuring that several patrol cars would remain watching the home. He'd had to build a sufficient case to the chief of police that Daphne could still be in danger, and that had not helped him sleep. Not that he'd even tried.

He'd gone straight home to order several new security items for Daphne and her house. Then he'd gone to the garage where he kept his gear and dug through his duffel, mentally counting gadgets and forming plans.

The second problem he needed to solve was his mother. A day nurse wouldn't be able to come in for another twenty-four hours, and the idea of his mom being home alone was not an option he was comfortable with.

He needed to get Florence and her care squared away so he could focus on his job. Having his mind in two places when things were escalating was not safe.

Evander set down a tracking device and punched in a familiar phone number. "Kyle? We need you back home."

"Evander?" His brother's voice was groggy. "It's five in the morning and you're not calling me Brick."

It didn't seem the time for nicknames. And besides, the name had never suited his brother. If anyone was a brick in the family, it was Evander, and everyone knew it—hence the ironic nickname for Kyle. It had bothered him at first when the kids had started using it, but his brother had liked it, so Evander had gone with it until it stuck.

"Time for you to get up and book a flight. Mom's got cancer and is undergoing radiation. I need help. How fast can you get here?"

"What?" There was panic and pain in his brother's voice. "Mom's sick?"

Shoot. He hadn't handled that one well, had he?

"Yeah. Sorry, man. It's been a long night. She's doing okay, but I can't get a nurse to come by until tomorrow, and I'm on a sticky job. I need someone I trust here to watch her and make sure she's okay."

"She's not okay?"

"Well, she has cancer."

"I'll be there as soon as I can." His voice tight with held-in grief, his brother said goodbye and hung up.

Evander kicked himself for being an insensitive jerk. This was that take-charge side that bothered Daphne, too. He sighed and turned his phone over in his hand, contemplating calling his brother back, but deciding against it. Evander needed to get more things solved, and his brother could talk the ear off a brass monkey. Best to keep moving forward.

Giving the duffel's zipper a sharp tug, he decided to take everything he had with him, and went to load up his truck in the early morning chill. He locked the vehicle and garage, then headed to the house. The sun's early rays were just reaching the white clapboard as he let himself into the silent house, turned off the security alarm and checked the time. He had to take over Daphne's security in one hour.

Enough time to make his mother breakfast and get her set up

for the day. The neighbor would look in on her again, and hopefully his brother would be able to get an early morning flight from Nova Scotia and be here by lunch. No, too far a drive from the airport. He'd be lucky to get here by supper.

Evander picked up his phone and redialed his brother.

"Oh, Evander. This is just so—" Kyle's voice broke off.

"Did you get the time off work? Can you leave today?"

"Yes."

"Good. I'll send a private plane. Get on it and you'll be here by noon. I'll make sure a car is waiting for you at the airstrip."

"I just can't believe it. I need more time to process it all, and Mom…how's Mom?"

"You'll see for yourself at noon." Evander paused for a split second. "Thanks, Brick."

He hung up, breathing deep and slow. He hated cutting off his brother, but he had too much to do and not enough time.

He booked his brother a plane while wondering what would taste best for breakfast to a woman who wasn't feeling well. He tested a honeydew melon for ripeness and carved balls out of the tender fruit, placing them in a bowl along with banana slices. If she ended up having chemo she would need more potassium, so he may as well start ensuring she was getting some in her diet already.

Chemo.

He braced his hands on the counter.

Radiation.

He let out a jagged breath.

Cancer.

Righting himself, he swung at the air, hitting nothing and feeling no better for the physical outburst.

She had to beat this.

End of story.

With a focus of purpose he hadn't experienced since his army days, he slapped pieces of buttered toast beside the bowl of melon and carried the tray upstairs. He rapped lightly on the door. He'd forgotten water. She needed water, lots of it.

Maybe a sports drink with electrolytes added to it.

He swung the door open.

"Good morning," he said. His mother was sitting up, looking thoughtful. "I brought you breakfast."

"And it's not even Mother's Day," she said, her voice its usual chipper tone.

He stared at her for a moment. She had cancer. And yet she looked normal. He half expected to see it gnawing through her body.

"How are you feeling?" He set the tray on her lap and gently pinched the ends of her fingers to check for dehydration. The skin puffed back out, her fingers pads rounded again. Good.

"I'm fine. A good night's rest was all I needed."

"And intravenous fluids," he scolded. "Stick out your tongue."

"Evander, I will not."

"I'm not leaving until you do."

She darted her tongue out quickly, like a child hoping not to get caught by an adult. The color had returned. It looked as though the intravenous fluids had worked. One less thing to worry about. For now.

"Evander, really. I am fine." Her tone had a sharp edge to it, which he ignored.

"I couldn't get home care to come in today, but the neighbor will stop by to check in on you."

"And how will she get in?"

"Are you not able to get to the door?" He hadn't taken that into account. Could he trust the neighbor with the code to their home? He needed someone nearby who could get in. He should have done a background check on the people next door. He didn't have time this morning, but maybe Tyrone could get one done on the double.

"I was joking about the security alarm. Never mind. It wasn't that funny."

Rudolph leaped onto the bed with a "hello" meow and strode straight toward Florence, tail up, a cat with a purpose. She tucked the feline against her as he stretched to sniff at the tray.

Evander took the cat from his mother and got a claw dug into his knuckle for the effort. "Do you remember how to turn it off? I printed out the instructions. Do you still have them?"

"Evander, relax. I was kidding."

"Not funny."

His mother sighed. "Did I hear you go out last night?"

"Sorry, I didn't mean to wake you."

"Girlfriend?" She raised her eyebrows in jest.

"Daphne's house was broken into."

"Oh, no. Is everyone all right? I told you they needed to move in here."

"Good luck convincing Daphne of that. She asked for more security on her home, at least. And yes, they're fine."

"Who's watching them right now?"

"The local police."

His mother relaxed, her body sinking into the pillows she'd propped up behind her.

"Don't worry, Mom. I have everything under control."

"I have no doubt about that." She began poking at her breakfast, nibbling at the toast.

"Make sure you eat the fruit, too." He wanted to stand over her, to make sure she ate more than just her toast, but he needed to get moving. "I'll bring you water. Do you think you'll get out of bed today?"

"Don't be ridiculous. Of course I will."

He stood in the doorway, the cat held too tight against his chest. He let go of the furry beast and it skittered out of the room. "Mom, why didn't you tell me?"

"Well, at first they didn't think it was anything." She toyed with a melon ball, idly chasing it with her spoon. "I figured there was no reason to alarm you. You were just getting settled back into civilian life. Then…" She gave a small shrug. "It became hard to tell you. You don't have a lot of friends or a support network, and I didn't want to lay something on you that you might not be able to carry on your own."

His mother didn't have faith in him. That hurt. He turned and left.

Florence called after him, "I'm sorry, Evander."

He came back to the doorway. "I told Kyle. He'll be here by noon."

"I'm not on my deathbed." There was a sharp brightness in her eyes.

"No, but you need help."

"I'm not an invalid."

"If you'd have told me sooner, I could have scheduled my work around helping you." He'd done his research last night and knew that in a few weeks the radiation was going to catch up with her and lay her low. She might not need help today, but she was sure as heck going to need it soon.

"I don't need you altering your life just because I'm having a health bump."

"Then what the hell is family for?" He resisted slamming the door, his muscles trembling with the effort of holding in his anger.

*A health bump?*

Health bumps didn't get much worse than cancer. And she'd

just proved yesterday that she couldn't do this on her own. She needed help. She needed support.

And he would find a way to be there without letting Daphne down.

WHEN EVANDER PULLED up to Daphne's house, Tyrone was waiting for him.

"Hey, man," Evander said, shaking his hand while slapping him on the back. "Police are gone already?" You couldn't trust anyone to do a good job these days.

"I told them they could take off."

"Oh. All right. What brings you back here so early?"

"I figured you'd want to beef up security on the house." He gestured to his unmarked van sitting in the driveway.

"What did you bring me?" Evander opened the side door, eager to rifle through the man's gadgets.

"Pretty much everything I have."

Evander picked up a toy walkie-talkie. "I didn't realize these were the up-and-coming model. What's the range on one of these things?"

His boss snatched the toy, tossing it on the passenger seat. "Sorry, man. Nothing is sacred when you have kids. They're going through a spy phase."

"You let them in your van?" he asked with surprise. Tyrone used to be incredibly finicky about his space, always going on about boundaries when he was in the navy. Although, come to think of it, it wasn't easy sharing every inch of space with a roomful of alphas ready to piss on anything and everything. You had your own bunk and a foot locker and that was it. Messing with someone else's stuff was grounds for a fight that would send you to the infirmary for a few stitches, if nothing else.

"I have kids," Tyrone said simply, running a hand through his short, tight curls. "Now, what do you want? I have to get Vanessa to gym camp in forty minutes."

"The sensors I placed on the windows worked well. Maybe something else, though. Security cameras? Better locks on the doors and windows for sure. Panic buttons." He glanced toward the house. Daphne was watching from the front window, but allowed the curtain to drop back into place when he gave her a nod.

Today was going to be interesting.

Tyrone held up a lawn ornament. "One of these?"

"Tyrone. Focus, man."

"No, really. It's like a nanny cam for your yard." He turned the gnome so Evander could see the camera hidden in the small man's eye.

"Does it send a signal?"

"Of course it does." Tyrone gave him a look of disgust.

"Great. How many do you have?"

"Two. Put one in the front yard and one in the back."

"Did they come with instructions?"

"Instructions? Are you freaking kidding me?"

Evander grinned. "Just messing with ya. Plug and play, right?"

He tucked the gnomes under an arm, snatched a few other fun items from Tyrone's treasure chest and set to work. "Thanks, Tyrone."

He waved as his friend drove off, wondering how he'd managed to find his way back into real life with such apparent ease. Was it because Tyrone had a wife and family waiting for him back home? Was it because he had never gone into private service and gotten himself blown up? If Evander had left the life sooner, would he have been okay?

When would asking himself a million what-ifs change his past?

Never.

He needed to look forward, move past it and settle in where he was now.

After installing the last gnome, Evander picked up his insulated coffee cup and took a long swig. Then, feeling properly braced to face Daphne and her quips about his gadgets, he knocked on her front door. She'd been peeking out the windows here and there, but hadn't stopped him, nor asked questions.

The woman was a puzzle. She'd freaked out over him being armed, and yet was trying to arrange for her daughter to spend more time with a man being protected by a trigger-itchy, rap-sheet-carrying baboon. Yes, Evander had found the skeletons in Ricardo's closet pretty darn quick after their first run-in. So why wasn't the peace-loving hippie scurrying the other way? She'd been a single mom for five years already. Why bring in a father now?

Daphne opened the door. "Good morning."

Evander tipped his insulated coffee mug toward the cup she had clutched in her hand. "Good morning. Sleep well?"

"Ha. Ha." She gave him a nasty look, which tempted the corners of his mouth to lift into a smirk.

"Humorless in the mornings, eh?"

"You are way too happy today, putting all your gizmos around my yard and on my home. You live for this, don't you?" She crossed her arms, holding the half-empty cup against her chest.

"Us gun-toting, fear-mongering heroes like a little action every once in a while."

She began to close the door and he placed his boot between it and the frame.

"I'm going to install better locks, so you may as well leave it open."

The way she bit her bottom lip, her brows arching in worry, made him feel bad for approximately one second. That's how long it took to remind himself that at least now she'd take things seriously and he could finally help without her blocking him.

"How's the kid?" he asked. She'd had a big day yesterday. And while it seemed as though she'd slept through the entire ordeal last night, he was certain she'd be intuitive enough to pick up on her mother's vibes. "Does she know about last night?"

"No. Please don't tell her." Daphne headed back into the house, and Evander set about improving her front door's security.

As he finished with the windows an hour later, Daphne walked by in a red sundress, looking as lovely as ever. She had a picnic basket slung over one arm, and if she'd been wearing a red hood he would've called her Little Red Riding Hood.

Tigger, following her mother, spotted Evander and asked, "Are you coming to the park for a breakfast picnic with us?"

Evander raised an eyebrow at Daphne. They still needed to talk about scheduling her days and giving him heads-ups, obviously, as this whole being-out-of-the-loop thing was starting to really piss him off.

"I resent that look," she said.

"I would love to go on a picnic," he said to Tigger. "Thank you for inviting me."

He handed Daphne written instructions on how to set the alarm he'd installed.

"You installed a security system? My landlord isn't going to appreciate this."

"I'm sure your landlord will love the upgrades, especially since he doesn't have to pay for them."

"Do I have to pay for them?"

"No. It will go on Tristen's bill." The man had been more than willing to pay for more protection on Daphne, especially when Evander had called him from the road this morning, bringing him up to speed.

"I can't believe you did all of this without asking."

Oh, here they went again.

"You said last night you wanted this. So I did it." He kept his tone light, but left no room for argument. "Now, let's go have a lovely picnic out on some exposed rock, shall we?"

Daphne glared at him and he had a sneaking suspicion she blamed him for every problem in her life at the moment.

He helped them into the minivan, then gestured for Daphne to roll down the window. "I'll follow you in my truck. Where are you going?"

"Just down the road to the park. The same one as yesterday."

Something was up. Why would she drive to a place so close? Fear? Plans to ditch him?

"Why are we driving?"

"I have to work later. I'm driving so we can leave directly from the park."

"We need to talk about your schedule."

"Fine." She bit out the word, then threw the vehicle in reverse and backed up so quickly she nearly ran over his toes.

Evander hurried to his truck, catching up with Daphne a short way down the road, disliking the fact that she was so in love with a park that had so few escape routes.

It was still early enough that mist was hanging low over the cool, damp grass in the park and wisps of it drifted and disappeared on the river as the sun came over the trees.

Evander stretched, on the lookout for changes in the park since yesterday. After walking the circumference of the playground, he sat on a bench, not caring that the dew was seeping through his clothes. It was going to be a long day and any chance to sit and take a breather was a smart idea.

He watched, a twinge of envy weaving through him, as Daphne pushed her daughter on the swing, smiling and chatting. Only yesterday he'd been in her place and feeling more real and alive than he had in ages.

The two Summers were happy, free, and innocent. And it should stay that way at all costs. Crossing his arms tightly across his chest, Evander glanced around the park again, hating the way the tall wooden forts and play structures made it hard to spot anyone sneaking up on the oblivious duo. They were too exposed. He resisted the urge to pace the perimeter like a caged panther.

Earlier, the break-in had given him greater focus, but now his protective instincts had reared up, and the way they were raging against what Daphne wanted for her life made it difficult to sit there and respect her wishes to engage in normal daily activities.

Evander dragged a hand over his mouth. In his haste, he'd forgotten to shave this morning and the stubble bothered him.

He checked his phone for the time. His brother should be in the air by now. Tyrone should be working on finding a suitable replacement for Chuck. The neighbor should be checking on Florence.

Things were taken care of, but Evander still felt ill at ease.

The park was filling up with the occasional mother and child, the kids buoyant, the moms clutching their coffee cups with a need that rivaled addicts.

Daphne was laughing with her daughter, living a life where everything was seen through rose-tinted glass. There was always a bright side. The glass was half-full, even if it contained poison.

He admired that about Daphne, even though it suggested she had her head stuck in the sand.

A child in one of the forts screamed and Daphne jolted, her face paling.

Good.

She was on edge. That probably meant she wouldn't try to slip away from him today.

He stood, checking the perimeter of the park once again. A cloud passed in front of the sun, giving the air an extra chill.

Someone tugged on his pant leg and he frowned down at the little person. "What?"

It was one of the kids from the other day.

"Are you in the army?"

He'd grown out his buzz cut to a length he could finger comb. He wasn't wearing fatigues.

"No. But I was," he admitted. "The navy. And JTF 2."

The boy gave him an impressive salute.

"At ease, soldier," Evander said, shaking his head. Where was this kid's mom? He was a distraction.

"What's J-something-something-2?"

"Special soldiers who do secret stuff so you and your parents can sleep safe at night."

Unlike Daphne. He needed to get her out of that house. She was too far away. Too unsecured. Too unpredictable.

"Did you kill Osama Bin Laden?"

"Go play."

"Are you Tigger's dad?"

Evander's gaze flicked to the little girl who was smiling on the swing. His mind went blank for a moment, refusing to kick into motion.

He didn't believe he was cut out for real life, but he was starting to wonder how many people actually were. In fact, he kind of wondered if he might do a better job of providing a stable father figure in Tigger's life than Mistral. Namely because Evander would actually try his best.

"No. Go play."

"Do you have a gun?"

"Yes. Now go play before I shoot you."

"Awesome." The kid vanished into the fort, and about twenty seconds later Evander was surrounded by a crowd of boys all about nine years old.

Weren't kids supposed to sleep in and play video games during the summer holidays?

"Can we see your gun?" asked the first boy.

"No. Go play." He kept his hands behind his back, eyes sweeping the periphery.

"Please?" One kid clasped his hands under his chin and batted his eyelashes.

"That only works on mothers. Go." Evander tried to shoo the boys away, but they squealed and moved like marbles on ice. This way, that way, too slippery to catch.

Realizing they were distracting him, egging him on to play, he shook his head, trying not to smile. "You kids are little punks, you know that?"

They laughed and scattered, heading back to their fort, knowing the gig was up.

"The surprise of the week—you're good with kids," Daphne said, coming up beside him.

He hadn't even seen her leave the swings with Tigger. He took a deep breath to keep from imagining all the things that could have happened in his moment of distraction.

"We need to discuss a schedule, as well as what's safe and what's not." He glanced around at the playground. "Let's go." He almost added, "It's not safe here." But he knew that was likely a lie.

He just wanted to get her somewhere that offered better protection.

"Piggyback?" Tigger asked him hopefully as she joined them. She smiled up expectantly, and the longer he paused, the sadder her face got. Jeez, the kid was a killer. She could teach those boys a thing or two. Grumbling, he lowered himself into a squat. "Fine. Climb on." He caught sight of her fluffy party dress ruffling in the breeze and stood, causing her hands to slip off his shoulders.

"I wasn't on yet!"

"You can't get piggyback rides wearing a dress."

She glowered at him in a way that made him chuckle. So serious. This girl would laugh at the concept of a glass ceiling, then go ahead and smash it.

He glanced at Daphne for help, but all she did was give him an infuriatingly serene look. He was on his own. He jerked the cardigan that was slipping off Tigger's shoulders into place, zipping it up. "You're going to catch cold."

Humanity. Right there. He'd just proved he had some, hadn't he? And here Daphne had the gall to think he didn't have any just because he'd served their country, protecting her and others from all sorts of evils she couldn't even begin to comprehend.

"I'm wearing shorts underneath again," Tigger said, revealing a flash of pink as she pulled up the hem of her dress. She didn't thank him for zipping up her sweater.

He sighed and squatted once more, pressing his fingers into the sandy ground for balance. The girl climbed on, clinging so hard he figured he could scale the Himalayas and not lose her.

"Ready?"

"Yep!"

"Then let's go." He began walking up the slight hill to where Daphne had parked her van.

"You're helping my mom save the whales. Can you help me, too?" Tigger whispered in his ear, and he frowned.

"The whales?"

Daphne shrugged, giving him a small smile.

"Right. The whales," he said. If the girl knew how hard the navy could be on whales in the middle of a war, despite precautions, she'd hate him forever.

"Can you teach me kung fu?" she whispered.

"Why are you whispering?" he asked softly.

"Mom thinks I should solve everything with light and love and forgiveness and understanding," she said loudly.

Oh, boy. Where to start on that one?

Daphne called back, "Violence is not the answer." She gave Evander a preemptive dark look and he refrained from letting out a weary sigh.

"Can you?" Tigger urged.

"Dunno. We'll see." He took a few steps, thinking. "Is someone picking on you?" He pointed at a woodpecker sporting a crown of red feathers to distract Daphne. She slowed to watch the bird, chatting to herself about how free and pretty it was.

"A boy at the babysitter's pushes me down when the adults aren't looking. I asked him to stop and he won't. He just pushes me harder."

"Right. I can help with that." Evander caught himself. "Maybe." It wasn't his place to teach someone else's child self-defense, but the idea of someone bothering the girl made him want to send heads rolling. He could probably come up with a compromise. He could teach Tigger some moves that would protect her and help her stand her ground, while being relatively nonviolent. With Daphne still hot and cold about allowing him into her space, even despite the threats, he didn't want to push things too far.

"Horsey sounds," Tigger said, bucking against his back.

"No."

*"Please?"*

"No."

Daphne smiled and he figured she knew something he didn't.

His phone began ringing in his back pocket and he had it out in a flash. "Hello?"

"Evander, it's Mom."

"Are you okay?"

"I can't find Rudolph for his eardrops." She sounded worried. More worried than she should about the cat.

"I gave him his drops before I left."

"Who is Rudolph?" Tigger whispered in his other ear.

"Quit eavesdropping," he grumbled.

"Rudolph from Santa's Village? Can we go? Please, Mom, please?"

Evander lowered Tigger to the ground, having to give her a shake so she'd let go. He gave Daphne a grateful nod as she pulled the girl farther away.

"What's wrong?" he asked his mother. It had to be more than just the cat.

"Nothing. I just thought that you'd forgotten to give him his drops."

He watched Daphne and Tigger hop from foot to foot as they made their way to the van. Daphne had let her guard down, her shoulders relaxing into their usual fluid, graceful moves.

In fact, she was more at ease with him than he'd seen yet. She was letting him in, one small step at a time.

That was promising.

But would she let him in far enough, fast enough to match the speed with which Mistral and his men were escalating things?

"Are you sure you're okay?" he asked his mother. "Kyle should be there in three hours. Maybe less. Has the neighbor checked in?"

"Yes, she has, and I'm fine. I was just worried about Rudolph."

As he hung up he wondered if the cancer suddenly felt more real to his mother now that her kids knew. It had likely released all the worries and fears she'd been keeping hidden from herself.

"Is Florence okay?" Daphne asked as she closed Tigger's van door.

"She probably wouldn't tell me if she wasn't."

"My mom's like that, too."

"Did you tell her about the break-in?"

"Why? So she can worry about something she can't help with?"

So his instincts about Daphne had been correct. Strongly independent, often to her own detriment. She kept things close to her chest when life went wrong instead of reaching out and causing drama like so many women did.

"You can lean on me," he said, not quite understanding why he felt the need to tell her that.

She watched him quietly for a moment, her slender hand resting on the driver's side door handle. "Yeah. Okay," she said softly.

"Promise?"

"Promise."

Baby steps. They would just need a lot of them in rapid procession for him to keep her safe.

# Chapter Eight

*The whole Evander* business was getting ridiculous. She'd been letting the man into her life little by little and it wasn't healthy. It shouldn't feel normal to have a bodyguard at one's side. But there was something about him that made him feel more like a friend today. Which was silly. He was still worried about safety all the time and definitely still bossy.

Daphne crossed her arms and glared at Evander, who was trying to convince her that him coming to her workplace with Tigger was a good idea.

"Tigger and I will hang out in the back room while you're at work. We'll stay out of the way. It'll save you on babysitting costs and I'll be right there if you need me. We'll play."

His idea of play was probably teaching her how to clean a gun and throw knives. No, thank you.

Daphne shook her head. That wasn't fair. He'd proved he was awesome with Tigger and could be a silly, fun playmate. He was also gentle and caring with her, but a mother had to draw a line somewhere, and he wasn't going to become the girl's babysitter.

Evander finished filling her van's gas tank and pushed the button for a receipt.

All she wanted was to go to work as though everything was normal, and all he wanted was to act as though she was going to be kidnapped if he wasn't within arm's reach to prevent it.

They'd just been to the police station to fill out some paperwork, and the officers had assured her that the man had broken in only to look at her plans against Rubicore, and would remain in custody until his hearing in four days. She was safe.

Life went on.

Tigger, who had been drawing happy faces into the dust on her van doors with a wet squeegee, came up to Evander.

"Done?" he asked, before tossing the girl into the van as though she weighed nothing. Tigger giggled and tried to crawl out so he'd have to do it again.

He gave a shake of his head and closed the door.

"You need to go home and take care of your mother," Daphne said. "That's what you need to do. I have this covered. Everyday life is back in progress. The police said that the man will remain in custody, and that Mistral's assistant, Aaron Bloomwood hired him. Not Mistral."

"Aaron works for Mistral."

"Mistral doesn't give him every little order, you know. Aaron is trying to become a partner in the business and he's his own man. The sooner we act as though everything is normal, the sooner it will be. Go to your mom."

"My mother is fine." Evander's jaw clenched, causing a muscle to flicker below his ear.

"She needs you." Daphne stared him straight in the eye, but his gaze kept sliding away. She was right and he knew it. She pressed her palm against his forearm. "She needs you more than we do."

"You're forgetting that your home was broken into last night."

"I wasn't hurt. They wanted plans. They saw them. They're in jail. End of story. This isn't a big deal, but the bigger deal we make of it, the bigger deal *they* will make of it. Do you like it when things escalate in war? Because that's what you are doing in my life right now."

She wrenched open her door, but Evander gripped it, not allowing her to climb inside and make her escape.

"You're being a fool," he growled.

"And you're being a warmonger. I don't know what reality your head is stuck in, but this is real life. In real life…" She paused, looking him over, wanting him to hear what she had to say, but knowing there were scars below the surface that would deflect her words to protect his internal beliefs. "…we don't act this way."

His grip on the door loosened and she took advantage of it, slipping into the seat. Evander wouldn't let her close the door, however, and the next driver in line for the pump honked his horn.

Evander glanced back, but didn't move.

"I'm going to tell Mistral's partners I'll cooperate. We can work together. Compromise."

"You're selling out?"

When he said it like that, his brows pinching over his dark eyes, it felt as if she was doing more than just reprioritizing her life.

"It's just one more development. I don't have to fight them all. It's over." She ignored the tightening in her chest over all the environmental wrongs that Rubicore would be getting away with.

"It's not over."

"Evander, don't make a federal case out of this. You're being hired to protect me. You should be happy I'm not stirring the pot like Melanie is. You should be happy you no longer have to sacrifice anything in order to protect me, because once I talk to Mistral you can quit."

He gently shut the door. "Come on, you'll be late for work."

Daphne hit the power locks and spun away, leaving him behind on the large square of asphalt, looking stunned. Okay, so she was heading for work and he knew where that was, but it didn't mean she couldn't have five minutes to herself without him breathing down her neck.

As she turned the corner to head to the highway, she saw him hightailing it to his parked truck. Instead of taking the main highway, she spun onto a side road, hoping to extend her Evander-free time a tad longer.

Talking to Mistral and his partners would not be selling out. She was settling the disagreement, taking things down a notch. She could take her own voice out of the battle without undermining her sisters, and everyone could get what they wanted if they listened to her plan.

"Mom," asked Tigger from the backseat, "what about Evander?"

"He's taking his truck, honey."

Pulling onto the country road outside of town where the babysitter lived, she dropped off Tigger, surprised not to find Evander on her tail. Had something happened to him?

Before climbing back into her van, she circled it, wondering where he'd placed the locator. She'd seen him put it along the back somewhere, but still hadn't discovered where the snoopy device was hiding. Checking the road for his truck, she wondered if he'd decided to shadow her from afar.

Back on the highway, she headed for work, happy to have her life feeling closer to normal. Cranking up some old Van Halen, she sang along, unwinding.

Today was going to be a good day.

As she drove through the striated rock cut that towered over her van, she began planning out how she was going to present her plan of cooperation to Mistral. She hadn't dared call him that morning for fear of Evander, who had been working outside her home, interrupting and giving her a hard time. Now he knew her plans and could get over it.

In fact, now would be a good time to try Mistral at his office. They'd discuss ways to work together and create a compromise, then she'd present the plan to her sisters, informing them that she was the new go-between. Melanie would probably be upset, but then again, she likely didn't realize just how much she was messing with Daphne and Tigger's life by taking Rubicore on the way she was.

Daphne's cell rang, and hoping her Bluetooth was working properly, she hit the connect button.

"Daphne Summer," she said. She always felt a bit silly talking alone in the van, as people passing by might think she was talking to herself, and therefore a little off her rocker.

"Daphne! It's Nate Rockerfield from Environment Canada. How are you?"

"Oh, Nate. How are things with the oil sands?"

He groaned. "Don't ask."

The man had wanted to leave a legacy, but energy resources were always a tough battle. Again, finding balance between two parties and their disparate needs.

Daphne checked her rearview mirror for signs of Evander. It wasn't as fun evading him if he didn't put an honest effort into catching up again. She took a side road, leading to another highway. Ten minutes until her shift: she had time to extend the game. In fact, Evander could already be outside her place of work, arms crossed, scowl in place, foot tapping at her delay.

"We were wondering if you would be interested in coming in for an interview?" Nate asked.

"Job interview? As in nine-to-five for the government?"

He laughed. "What you do for the environment on your own is unprecedented."

"Aw. Thank you."

"We offer pensions, health plans, child care, family days, the works."

But she'd be stuck behind a desk for very regimented hours.

"Signing bonus?" she asked. The idea of a regular, decent paycheck was tempting.

"We're not a big department. Taxpayers pay our wages."

"Is that a no?" she teased, turning onto another secondary highway. Almost there. A Hummer had been following her and she slowed to let it pass. She hated it when vehicles blew past on a solid line. It seemed as though everyone was in a hurry these days and didn't pause to think of the safety of others, just themselves getting ahead.

"I can ask," Nate said. "Remember, we hold a different form of clout than private firms. We can extend our influence internationally. I think you could make a real difference working with us rather than a private firm."

"When do you want me to come by?"

"Next week?" The hope in his voice made her feel pretty darn good. Environment Canada wanted her. Her!

"Sounds good, Nate."

He gave her the date and time. Her birthday, the appointment time within an hour of her birth. It had to be a sign. Her life was about to pull into focus and order. Maybe a real job would be okay, after all.

Feeling jazzed, she hung up and pulled over, allowing the Hummer to pass as she stopped to dial Mistral. Ensuring her Bluetooth was still working, she pulled out again.

"Mistral Johnson, please," she said when his secretary answered.

"One moment, please."

There was a series of clicks and then Mistral was on the phone.

"Hello." His voice was crisp and professional.

"It's Daphne."

"I know, my secretary has caller ID."

Well, that was probably a good thing. The secretary knew to let her through. Things were progressing in the right direction there, at least.

"I'm sorry about last night," he said, sounding rather grim. "I heard the news."

"About the break-in?" she clarified.

"Yes. I've talked to Aaron. I think the man is feeling rather desperate after what your sister threw at us. Any chance to figure out what your next move might be."

See? It wasn't Mistral. It was Aaron. It was her sisters. She was on the right track. Meaning Evander was wrong. She stuck her tongue out at her rearview mirror, even though it was only the Hummer behind her and not Evander.

Wait. The Hummer was back?

"Actually, I'm calling about the development," she said, feeling distracted. "You don't know anyone with a gold Hummer, do you?"

"No, I don't think so. Why?"

"No reason. Anyway, I was thinking we could figure out a way to work together with that development."

Mistral sighed. "I think we have very different ideas on what should be done on the island."

"True. But I also believe we can work together. And let's be honest, if it isn't us giving you pressure about the environment, then it's going to be someone bigger, such as Environment Canada. So who would you rather have? Us or them?"

"Are you threatening me?" His voice had a steely edge.

"No, I am being realistic."

"Really? Because it sounds as though you're saying if I won't work with you, you'll go tattling to Environment Canada."

She almost laughed. She was going to *be* Environment Canada. Possibly.

"I want you to succeed, Mistral, and I know how important this development is to you." She refrained from saying how this whole project was an obvious cry for approval from his father. "I think you could create a nature preserve like you used to dream about."

"Daphne, I grew up. I know now that a nature preserve would be a money pit."

"So, money is everything?" She knew it was an unfair jab, but he had it coming. He'd been adamant when he'd told her only a few years ago that he never wanted to become that man where money was everything. And now he was. It made her angry. The man had no backbone of his own.

"Daphne, you don't understand."

"And what is it that you've learned in the past five years that I am unable to comprehend?"

"Don't pull the past into this."

"You can have it all, Mistral. You *can* have it both ways."

Something slammed on his end of the phone and she imagined him smacking his desk in frustration. "No, I can't have it both ways. I tried and I failed. And now I have to live with that. Out here in the real world we have to make money, and so that's what I'm doing."

She fought to stay calm. "I believe you can have your development, stay within environmental protocols, as well as preserve the environment. Your development could be a nature preserve. A nature retreat. A green vacation spot. Eco-tourism. It's the wave of the future. Don't you want to be the one to start the trend here in Ontario?"

"There's no money in it."

"Then maybe you need to start talking to me."

He gave a derisive laugh. "And you suddenly know about money?"

"I guess that's for me to know and you to find out. Are we on to meet up with Tigger again in a few days?"

"I'm pretty busy."

Daphne bit back her disappointment. "You said you wanted this, Mistral."

"I do, but I'm tied up."

"You know where to find me."

She fumbled for the button to end the call, but Mistral said, "Do you really think you could get your sisters off my back?"

"Everything except the legal stuff Melanie started against the municipality for failing to follow protocol, but everything else, yeah. I think so. We could create a solid compromise that's fair to both sides."

"Fair for both sides?"

"Yup." She could almost hear him thinking how unlikely that was.

"Let me think on it, but this sounds incredibly unrealistic." He let out an uncertain laugh. "Daphne, as crazy as it is, I still trust you. I know everyone's telling me not to, but you're still the same woman you always were. You haven't changed despite everything. I'd like for some big pipe dream to work out, but I can't help but feel it's highly unlikely."

Daphne sighed. Same old Mistral. All talk and dreams, but no balls to take action.

"If anyone can bring a pipe dream to life, it's probably you, Daphne."

They said goodbye, and while Daphne knew that changing Mistral's mind was still a long shot, she felt better about where the two of them stood than she had in a long time. Smiling, she turned up the music and concentrated on the Hummer, which was finally pulling out to pass once more. Panic reared up like a wild horse as she realized the vehicle was passing on a solid line, with a ten-foot-high rock cut coming up fast on either side.

She tapped her brakes to let the Hummer get by safely, but it dropped back alongside her. When she waved at the driver, the vehicle just crept closer to her van, and she laid on the horn.

Daphne finally slammed on the brakes, and the Hummer zipped on ahead. She drew a deep, calming breath That had not been someone simply forgetting to shoulder check after passing.

On the other side of the rock cut, the Hummer was waiting, and Daphne had to swerve to avoid a collision. Panicked, she sped on past, pulling visuals on her location. She was only a minute from town. One long minute. Then she could find Evander and have him help her figure out what was going on.

When she checked her rearview mirror again the Hummer was back on her tail, following too close. She sped up, freaked out.

"Call Evander," she said, slapping off the radio and hitting the Bluetooth button.

"Look up colander, is that correct?" her phone asked through the speakers.

"No." She kept an eye on the vehicle behind her, keeping her speed constant. They wouldn't hit her. They were just trying to scare her. It would be okay.

"Call Evander," she repeated to her phone.

The Hummer slammed into the back of her van and she screamed, fighting to control the vehicle as it swayed and swerved.

She heard a dial tone, then ringing through her speakers.

She glanced behind her, expecting another hit. The Hummer was gone, replaced by Evander's truck.

Blinking, she looked back again, not believing her eyes. The man must have superpowers.

Slamming on the brakes, she went to pull over, never so relieved to see the muscle monkey in all her life. Evander came up fast, waving at her to keep going. She could see him mouthing, "Go, go, go." Or maybe that was him through her phone, which had finally connected.

"Don't pull over," he commanded. "Go straight to the police station."

"I have to go to work."

"Don't start with me, woman. That was not a friendly bumper tap. Get your ass to the station or I swear I'll run you off the road myself."

DAPHNE MADE IT ALL the way to the police station before breaking down. But as she turned off her Caravan, Evander's black truck stopping beside her, she lowered her head to the steering wheel and let it all out. Great big van-shaking sobs.

What if Tigger had been with her? What if the Hummer had succeeded in knocking her off the road? As the what-ifs flooded her, she gave over to the terror.

Her door opened and Evander was there, talking to her in a calm, low voice as though she was a spooked animal.

"It'll be okay, Daphne," he said.

She lashed out, trying to hit him with her left hand and failing. "This is not my world, Evander. Not my world! Mistral's a nice guy. He has to be. I let him in. I let him be the father of my baby girl."

Evander shushed her sobs as he eased her out of the van. A police car sailed past, sirens and lights going, and her legs grew weak with the severity of the situation.

"You okay?"

"No." She let out a small sniff, laughing at herself and the truth. She was not all right. She turned into Evander's warm strength, hugging him.

"I'm sorry I ditched you," she muttered.

"I'm glad you did. If you hadn't, how would I have been in position to knock that guy off your tail?" With an arm around her shoulders, he guided her into the station. The officer seemed to know Evander and they began discussing the incident as though she wasn't there.

She had no control over her life any longer.

She stood. "I need to go get Tigger. No, I need to get to work. I need to…" She swallowed hard, feeling dizzy.

Evander caught her, lowering her into the chair across from the detective, pushing her head between her knees. Moments later, the officer handed her a cup of ice water.

"Shock," he said.

"This is not my life!" She tried to stand again, but strong hands held her head down. "I need to get Kim—my daughter—Tigger." The hysteria in her voice was unnerving, even to her own ears. They were going to give her a shot of something to knock her out if she wasn't careful, then make decisions that weren't theirs to make. This was *her* life, and as Evander had said, she needed to be the one in control of it.

She pushed the ice water away and shrugged off Evander's hand, which was resting at the nape of her neck, way too powerful to feel as comforting as it did. "I need to get my daughter."

"A patrol car has already been dispatched," the detective said. "In case."

"I need to tell my boss I'll be late."

"I've already called," Evander said.

There was nothing left for her to do. To take care of. And that's what she did. She took care of things in her life. And they'd taken it all away from her.

All of it.

Even her freedom. A sob escaped her chest, pulling the muscles tight as she fought it with all she had.

Everything had gone chaotic. And not in a, "it will all work out if I give it space" sort of way like usual. It was a destructive energy. Negative, toxic, and contagious.

Everything happened for a reason. So why was this happening? Why had someone tried to push her off the road?

She looked at Evander, who was calmly sorting things out on her behalf.

*Everything happens for a reason.*

Hailey burst into the large room, her boyfriend, Finian, two steps behind, and was pulling her out of the chair for a hug in a matter of seconds. Daphne felt like a teenager whose parents were about to fuss over her, then scold the heck out of her.

"Thank goodness you're all right." Hailey smoothed Daphne's hair, looking around. "Where's Tigger?"

"They've gone to get her."

Her sister sagged. "Thank goodness she wasn't with you."

Next, Maya and Melanie came blasting in. More hugs, a few more tears.

"I'm sorry for everything. I really am. I'm so sorry," Melanie said.

"Why? Did you plan this?" Daphne joked.

Melanie paled. "For starting everything. I should have kept my mouth shut. I'd rather have Rubicore's nasty development across from the cottage than lose you." She gave Daphne another squeeze, then let out an "oomph" when she squeezed back. "Forgive me?"

Daphne nodded.

"Does Mom know?" Maya interrupted.

"She's going to panic!" Hailey said, clapping a hand to her mouth.

"I don't even know how *you* know," Daphne said, wiping at her eyes. Connor and Tristen, who'd come in behind Maya and Melanie, were looking as though they were ready to rip someone apart on Daphne's behalf. She'd never felt so loved as she did in that moment.

"Evander called," Maya said.

Daphne turned to him. "Thanks."

"You're going to be stuck with these sisters nagging you now, too, I hope you know." There was no way she was getting her family off her case now that they knew just how bad things seemed to be getting.

The detective took down Daphne's side of the story, shuttling everyone else into a private waiting room down a short hallway. When she finished, an officer came in with Tigger, who had a huge, dripping ice cream cone grasped in her sticky hands. She was grinning and looking immensely pleased with herself.

"Mom!" She came running over. "I got to ride in a police car. I asked for an ice cream and he said yes!"

Daphne laughed, hugging her daughter tight.

"Oof! That was a big hug, Mom."

"Does she know?" Daphne asked the new officer, as he led them to the room where her sisters and the men were waiting, Tigger bouncing along ahead of them.

He shook his head. "I told her it was a surprise field trip. I hope that's okay?" He opened the door, where everyone but Evander was present, all leaning forward in case there was news.

"Was the man in the Hummer…?" Daphne began.

"Still working on that. Hey, Tigger. Want to see the holding cells?"

"What's that?"

"The jail."

"Cool!"

"Don't worry," the officer said to Daphne, "they're currently empty." Before he closed the door behind him and Tigger, he leaned in to say, "Take as much time as you need."

A moment later, Evander joined them in the room, saying, "They arrested him."

"They just took Tigger to go see the jail!" Daphne stood.

"It's okay, he still has to be processed and interviewed first. It'll be a while before he makes it as far as a cell," Evander assured her. "The man driving the Hummer works for Aaron Bloomwood. Apparently no connection to Mistral."

Daphne shut her eyes. "I was just talking to Mistral before the incident. He swore he had nothing to do with the break-in, and he said he talked to Aaron. I don't get it." Tears threatened to fall. She still wanted to believe that Mistral had nothing to do with this attack, but how could he be that clueless about what his project partners were up to? Was everything he said to Daphne just a lie? Or was his life so out of control that he thought he was telling the truth?

"The break-in?" Her sisters stood as though connected by a string, their heads turning to her.

"When?" Maya asked.

"Are you okay?" Hailey asked. "What happened?"

They crowded around and Daphne sighed at letting that tidbit slip.

"Her house was broken into by a man sent by Aaron Bloomwood," Evander said. "He was looking for any plans you might have against the Baby Horseshoe Island development."

As the women gasped at the news, their boyfriends stepped back, heads down.

"You told the men, didn't you?" Daphne asked Evander, staring at Finian, then Connor, and finally Tristen. They knew and had obviously kept it a secret from her sisters.

Protection. Keep the women in the dark. Alpha male crap.

Daphne stood. "I'm so tired of this." She slammed her foot into the side of the metal table, making a loud enough clang that an officer poked his head inside the room to make sure everything was okay.

"We are *not* a bunch of stupid females." She swiped her arms through the air. "Enough secrets. Enough."

"You knew?" Hailey asked Finian.

Evander pinched the bridge of his nose, his shoulders rounded.

Finian nodded, saying, "Evander told us. We, the three of us, agreed not to tell you, as you'd worry. We've all upped security, though."

"You men need to stop making decisions that affect my life without talking to me—and my sisters first. Do you understand? All this covering it up isn't making anything better. It's making it worse."

The men looked sheepish as she collapsed into a chair, feeling drained. She turned to Evander, the one person she felt she could trust to keep it all together for her. Which was silly, seeing as he'd helped the guys keep secrets from her sisters, and tried to run her life. But then again, she doubted that he'd ordered the men to keep things from Hailey, Maya, and Melanie. Evander was all for everyone knowing what they were up against. Even when she didn't want to listen to what he had to say.

Daphne looked around the room. Each of her sisters had

someone who was helping her through this, so she didn't have to face it alone.

Funny how none of them believed in the magical power of Nymph Island, and yet look at what the island had done for them this summer.

Daphne believed in the island's magic, and where was her man? It definitely wasn't Mistral, given his inability to follow his dreams and be himself. And it was certainly wasn't Evander.

But for the moment, he'd have to fill the role. "Take me home," she whispered to him, knowing she was too shaken up to drive herself safely. Too afraid of what might be out there waiting for her and her daughter if he wasn't on hand as her shield. Because as much as she wanted to blame him for everything, that was incredibly unfair and she'd done it for too long. She had to start taking responsibility that she was, in fact, a big part of why this target was painted on her back.

Holding her elbow, Evander led her to the door.

"Wait," Hailey said. "We need to sort things out." She left Finian's side, touching Daphne on the wrist. "Don't leave."

"Why were you talking to Mistral before the 'accident'?" Melanie asked.

"I have an idea regarding the island." Daphne added carefully, "I don't think we should give up what we're trying to accomplish, but I think there's room for collaboration with Rubicore in order to meet in the middle."

The room grew quiet.

Evander gave her a nod, as though to say this was her moment to step up and take charge.

"I know Mistral. I know his dreams. And I think I know a way that we can meld his need to prove himself to his father and our need for a good neighbor who honors the environment."

Daphne turned to Evander, expecting him to recommend a restraining order again, instead of more talks.

"I think that's a good idea," he said, placing a hand on hers.

"Thank you."

"He's going to railroad you," Maya warned.

"Mistral threatened you, Daphne," Melanie said. "When I filed suit against Rubicore and the municipality, he made verbal threats. He said you're going to pay. That you knew he was Rubicore."

Daphne sighed. Everyone kept getting hung up on that outburst, didn't they? And while she understood where they were coming from, the man didn't seem to be frothing at the mouth to have her killed. His business partner, however, seemed to be a different story.

"It's okay, Melanie," Daphne said quietly. "We've all made mistakes when the heat is on."

"What do you think?" Connor asked Evander, drawing Maya closer to his side.

Evander paused, and for a second Daphne thought he was going to side with the majority. Instead, he looked her in the eye and said, "I made a promise to protect Daphne. She's made it clear that doing it my way cramps her style, and I think she's right. Things are escalating instead of improving." The muscles in his jaw flexed, his collared shirt stretching and pinching over his crossed arms. He drew his lip under his chipped tooth for a moment, watching her. "I think she has good instincts. Even in war there are peace talks among countries. She needs to give this a try. If anyone can take the threat out of this man, I think it's Daphne, if she's willing to step up."

"I am." She reached over and squeezed his hand in gratitude. Go figure, that the army guy would be the one to understand what she was trying to accomplish.

"Can you keep her safe?" Tristen asked.

"I will do my best." Evander turned to her. "As long as Daphne tells me her entire plan and allows me to help."

She couldn't meet his eyes, due to the shameful way she'd made it so hard for him to do his job for the past three days. But she'd finally learned her lesson. She wasn't going anywhere without Evander until this whole thing was over and done with.

"Thanks," she said to Tristen, her hand on the doorknob.

"For what?" he asked.

"For Evander."

Tristen smiled. "Sometimes I get things right."

"Wait." It was Melanie stopping Daphne this time. "Where are you staying?"

"Toronto's only a day trip if I have to go down to his offices to chat. But he's been here a lot this month so maybe we could meet up somewhere nearby."

"No, I mean you can't stay alone in your house."

"I've been staying with Connor lately," Maya said, "and I'm giving up my rental at the end of the month, but for the next week you and Tigger could crash there if you want." She frowned. "Although that's still living alone."

"She's staying with me," Evander stated.

"No, I'm not." Daphne gave a laugh of disbelief. Her? With him? "I have no desire to live in your bunker, thank you very much, army man."

"It's not a bunker."

"Nope." She crossed her arms. "Not happening." She might see that it wasn't wise to leave his side, but she wasn't upsetting Tigger's world by moving them in with a man they barely knew.

Evander gripped Daphne's arms, lowering himself so he could give her what she figured was his best listen-to-me glare. "You've seen how poor my relief staff is. What if Chuck had been on today when you'd decided to ditch the bodyguard?"

Daphne sucked in a breath, visions of the morgue floating through her imagination.

"And you were right, Daphne. My mom needs me. But so do you. So does Tigger. It's the only way to solve this problem."

Sometimes being a mom trumped everything else, didn't it?

"I don't want to hide out." She really didn't. She wanted Mistral to stop all this and protect his daughter. Because when it came right down to it, he was on Rubicore's side and that side was against her and her family. He was choosing money over what should be his family.

Mistral's father had raised him to be just like him despite Mistral's contrary wishes. And the sad thing was it looked as though his dad was succeeding. Mistral had wanted to live a life that truly mattered, with people who knew how to share and spread their love, without limitations or conditions. Yet he was still living under his father's thumb. She'd thought he'd been reaching out for help, but now she wondered if that had just been her own hopes clouding her judgment.

"If you'd be more comfortable with someone else protecting you we can make that arrangement," Evander said. "Just say the word."

The idea of someone else armed and watching her didn't sit well. Evander was real. She trusted him and he was incredible with Tigger. If anyone was going to have their back she wanted it to be him, even if the idea of him being armed at the breakfast table didn't particularly line up with her family values.

"I can keep you safe." His tone was gentle now. Giving. "Do you trust me?"

She nodded, wishing he'd hug her or something. Crush her against that big chest of his and allow her to borrow his strength and determination for a moment. Today had proved that she couldn't do it on her own, that she needed Evander.

"Can I continue to help you, Daphne?"

She nodded again. "Please."

"Settled," he said, stepping back. He addressed the room. "You all have my contact info if needed, and I recommend tightening your security where you can. Be vigilant until you hear otherwise from me. In the meantime, you can find Daphne and Tigger with me."

# Chapter Nine

*Evander parked the truck* in his mother's driveway and turned to look at Daphne and Tigger. How was this all going to work out? In the police station it had seemed like the no-brainer answer to a multitiered equation. But now he looked at the quiet old house and thought of all the complications that could arise. Daphne still had a job to go to, his mom still had radiation treatments, his brother was visiting and Tigger was one big ball of energy. There were going to be times where he'd be needed in more than one place. Never mind that sometimes he liked a little space and solitude to think. It was going to be similar to living in a submarine, but he'd been there, done that. He could do this.

"Right." He opened his truck door, watching them exit the other side, thinking his mother would have his head for not going around and opening the door for them if she happened to peek out the window. He pulled the bags they'd packed back at their house out of the truck's box and herded the Summers into the house.

He paused in the doorway, watching them take off their shoes.

He'd never had to protect a woman before, let alone a single mother, and his instincts to destroy anything in her way that could cause anything from a frown to an outright cry was alarmingly strong.

Still holding their bags, he wondered if he should teach them how to disarm the security system. Maybe show them where he kept his weapons. How many ground rules should he set? Should he tell them to stay out of his mom's sitting room, so she'd have more space and quiet in the house? When he'd called Florence, she'd been elated at the prospect of them coming to stay, even teasing him about bringing home strays, something he used to do frequently as a kid.

"Evander?" Daphne lightly touched his arm, giving him a shock. "Are you sure it's okay we stay here?"

"Of course. Plenty of room. Doors and windows are alarmed at all times. Kitchen is at the back. Your rooms are upstairs." He glanced at Tigger, then crouched beside her. "Are you okay staying here and helping my mom? She isn't feeling well and could really use your company."

"I'm a good helper."

Daphne stroked the child's curls and nodded. "Very good helper."

What on earth were they going to do, cooped up together for days on end? The kid was going to go bonkers from boredom and his mother was going to be worn-out in about five seconds flat.

"She's sick, though, so she might need quiet times."

"Okay," Tigger whispered.

"I told your boss you were staying home for a few days," he said to Daphne, leading them up the staircase while carrying their bags.

"Okay."

He turned, having expected a fight.

"What?" she asked.

He said nothing, but pointed to the end bedrooms at the top of the stairs. "These are your rooms. I'm in this one." He pointed to the room next to Daphne's. "That one on the other end is my mother's."

His brother was going to have to stay on the basement pull-out bed. Was he even here yet? The house felt awfully quiet.

"Is your mom here, Evander?" Tigger asked, rolling up onto the balls of her feet.

"She should be downstairs." He leaned over the small railing and hollered, "Mom? Are you home?"

"That's not quiet time!" Tigger exclaimed.

"Down here," Florence called. "Brick phoned. He'll be here shortly."

"Who's Brick?" Daphne and Tigger asked at the same time.

"My brother, Kyle."

"Is he like you?" Tigger asked.

"Not in the least."

"Well, I should like him tremendously then," said Daphne.

He glanced at her in surprise and she rewarded him with a mischievous grin.

"I want to see Granny Flo's fairy yarn!" Tigger said, disappearing down the staircase in a flash, her bare feet slapping the wooden stairs.

"Is that okay?" Daphne asked. "Does your mother need quiet?"

"She'll tell us if she does." Probably. But he was going to have to come up with diversions so the girl didn't overwhelm his mom. He paused, unsure whether he should take Daphne's bags all the way into her room. A good host would, but in his mind the bedroom was already her space.

He entered the room, placing the bags on the floor by the far wall where they would be accessible, but out of the way. "Do you need anything else?" he asked, feeling awkward as he waited by the bed, unable to leave without pushing past her in the small room.

She was chewing on her bottom lip.

"Do you still have alarms on my house?" she asked.

"Yes."

She nodded, thinking.

"A tracker on my van?"

"Yes."

She stepped closer. "So then? What took you so long to get to me today?"

"My GPS doesn't show all the roads. I had to take what turned out to be the long route."

"Oh."

She was so close her soft skin was brushing his, and he took her chin between his thumb and index finger, tipping it up so he could see her face. "Are you okay?"

She let out a shattered sigh and a tear broke free.

He pulled her to him and she collapsed against his chest, sucking in strength from him.

This? It felt real. The most real thing since before his army days. Even his mother's cancer didn't feel like this. Scary, but not truly real. Holding Daphne felt genuine and he wasn't sure why.

He gently stroked her hair as she hiccupped into his chest, trying to hold whatever it was inside.

This woman, with the world wrapped around her finger, needed someone to keep her safe. She was a seedling standing her ground in a raging storm. She needed a hand cupped around her, protecting her so she could grow and change the world, make it pure and full of light again. This was a job only he could do. He was made for it, and he'd do the best job he could.

"I'll keep you safe, Daphne," he whispered.

Her body shuddered in reply and he held her close, feeling her arms tighten around him. They could barely reach around his chest, and she lowered them until they were wrapped around his waist. He kept stroking her curls, wondering what she was thinking, what she was feeling, what she needed. Her arms pushed between them, moving up his chest as he let her go, his hands reluctant to leave her welcoming warmth. Her palms drifted up to his face, the dark circles under her eyes enhanced in the dim light of the room. She cupped his jaw, her fingers tracing the scars that extended down the side of his neck.

Her lips parted to ask, and he pulled her hands away. "I was blown up. It doesn't hurt."

"Was it the war?"

"Afterward. Protecting someone. A prince."

Her eyes darkened and she pulled away, horror flashing across her features.

"Daphne, I've been in many dangerous situations, and I've always known what I was getting myself into before taking a job. This situation is nothing like any of those, but I still know what I'm getting into."

"You would allow yourself to get hurt protecting someone else? Someone who isn't any more special than you are?"

He almost laughed at the idea of being more special than a prince, but stayed serious, drawing his spine straight as though about to salute an officer. "Yes."

Her slim hand rested tentatively on his chest. "For me?"

"Yes." He wasn't sure he liked where this was going.

She sprang on him, her feet leaving the ground as her legs wrapped around his waist, her arms hooked tight around his neck. Her lips landed hungrily on his and he caught her waist, holding her against him as she kissed him with tremendous need. He squeezed her to him as he instinctively turned to lower them onto the bed.

Her kisses lit a fire within him and he wondered why he'd

never thought of the protecting-scared-women angle before. It was hot.

Invigorating.

As close to real as he could wrangle.

But Daphne. She was in a bad space and would regret this. This was a Molotov cocktail of emotions, adrenaline and fear. It was nothing more than those reactions spurring her forward, seeking a sexual outlet to ease the unfamiliar and overpowering emotions. He knew sex was a temporary stopgap and she'd feel uncomfortable around him if he let this go any further.

So why wasn't he stopping?

He stole one more starved kiss, then, ignoring his own need and his ready cock, gently pushed her off him, his lips unwilling to break the connection. She tasted sweet and delicious. Pure. He pushed her away again and she sighed.

There was a fire between them that was still burning as they stared at each other from across the bed. Then she lunged at him again and he caught her, rolling under her slim form. He caressed her back, trying to find the strength to push her away once more as they kissed, his hands finding their way under the hem of her dress, her legs straddling him as her tongue dipped into his mouth.

He flipped her over so she was pinned under him, her thigh caught between his legs, pushing against his erection. He stroked her curls off her face, knowing that with every kiss, he was getting in deeper.

The sound of small feet on the stairs gave him what he needed to break away.

He sent Daphne one last hungry look before rolling off the bed, taking a moment to catch his breath before going to douse his desire in a freezing shower.

EVANDER PUSHED TIGGER on the rope-and-board swing he'd made for her in his mother's rambling backyard. She and Daphne had been living with them for less than twenty-four hours and he was already wrapped around Tigger's finger. Although, he reminded himself, the swing had been his idea as a preemptive measure to keep the girl from wearing out Florence who, so far, seemed perkier from having her light up their home.

He eyed the ropes as the child swung back and forth. If he added a rubber strap he could give the swing a little bounce, which would appeal to Tigger's nature.

He added rubber straps to his ongoing mental shopping list, then visually swept the yard's perimeter for safety breaches. He needed a better detection system than he currently had. As well as more lights and possibly a pack of vicious dogs that snarled and frothed at the mouth.

Daphne joined them on the lawn, smiling, seeming not at all shy despite the way she'd attacked him with her lips last night. She moved with grace and simplicity, a compelling figure of femininity, and he wanted to hold her, inhale the scent of her hair while falling into her warmth.

Thinking that way was a direct route to mission failure. Women were almost always the biggest distraction for soldiers. He needed to stay focused. Stay impartial, objective, removed.

He turned his back to Daphne, giving Tigger another push.

"Look what Evander made me," the girl said to her mother.

"A whole swing just for you?" There was something wistful in Daphne's voice and he caught her hugging herself in his peripheral vision.

"Take over," Evander said, directing her to step in and push Tigger. He needed to go check the feed from Daphne's yard gnomes. Maybe he could ask Brick to help out. His brother had arrived, distracted by grief to the point of being more of a hindrance than a help last night. This morning he seemed better, but he needed purpose to help keep him from dissolving into worst-case scenarios. Plus, once the press caught wind of what had happened on the road yesterday, and where Daphne was hiding out, Evander would surely need a bit of help with crowd control.

At the edge of the yard, he turned, checking on the mother-daughter duo. It wasn't smart spending this much time in the open backyard. There was a fence along the alley, plenty of large trees, lots of coverage, but it was still open if you knew where to peek in—and there were plenty of places to do so and not be noticed. The swing had been a bad idea. Tigger would want to spend too much time out here.

Evander knew he needed to focus, but he was so damn tired of it. He wanted nothing more than to sit back and laugh while watching the kid bounce around the yard. He wanted a life where he had nothing better to do than worry about her happiness.

But he had to be the man he was trained to be, because Aaron Bloomwood wasn't in custody even though the Hummer driver had pointed his finger at him, and Daphne's little chats with her ex weren't leading to progress.

It was up to Evander to be vigilant and keep them safe at all times.

His mother called from the back door, "Rudolph got out."

The cat pranced past him in the grass, legs extending as he upped his pace to stay out of range.

Tigger, out of nowhere, pounced on the feline, rolling him over to rub his belly.

"Oh, not a good idea," Evander warned. "He claws." He swooped the cat off the ground, and like sharpened steel on silk, those claws sliced through his skin.

"He liked that," Tigger protested.

"Cat's don't like having their bellies rubbed," Daphne said, backing him up as she directed Tigger to the swing again. She was being careful not to allow her daughter to bother Florence too much, and Evander appreciated the effort.

He passed the cat to his mother.

"Lunch?" she asked.

"That time already?"

"I can make quiche," Kyle said, appearing behind her, his face covered in some sort of green goop that made Evander think of women in spa commercials.

"That would be lovely, dear," Florence said.

"Consider it done," Kyle said with a graceful bow.

Florence cuddled the cat to her chin, still standing in the doorway. "You looked like a family out there."

"Mom," Evander warned.

"I like having kids around." She gave the cat an extra squeeze. "And you seem different with them here."

"Yeah, super worried they're going to be hurt," he grumbled, familiar anxiety rising within him. He turned to face the yard. "Time to come in!"

"Aw," protested Tigger. Daphne began ushering her off the swing. At least the woman was listening to him now. Although he wasn't sure if she wasn't just going with the flow and taking the path of least resistance. Either way, today he'd take it.

"I meant you seem relaxed," his mom said. "More alert and worried, but relaxed somehow."

"That makes no sense," he said over his shoulder, hurrying to where Tigger had stopped to peer into the lush lawn, Daphne crouched over her, her back to Evander.

"Come on," he said, glancing at the ladybug that had delayed them.

Daphne jumped, hand going to her throat. "You scared me."

He placed a palm on her shoulder, guiding her to the house. "Didn't mean to sneak up. The old lady wants lunch, Tigger. Let's see what we can make her. My brother wants to make something that I'm sure will take five hours, and you probably won't like it, anyway. If we beat him to the kitchen we set the menu."

Tigger skipped to the house, then, seeming to catch herself, slowed her pace to a walk. "Florence isn't old," she said. "Old people have candy."

"Oh, she has candy. And I know where she keeps it."

"No sugar before lunch," Daphne said, frowning.

"Yeah, yeah, yeah. That's what all the moms say." Evander shot Daphne a wink and she shook her head in warning.

"Mom says it makes me bouncy!" Tigger added an extra bounce to her step, landing on the back step.

"Even more than usual, huh? I'd pay to see that."

"Oh, you'll pay all right," Daphne muttered as he held the door for them.

He paused to reset the alarm and throw the dead bolt behind them, trying to be subtle about it.

"Tigger," Florence called from the front room. "I made something for you."

"Goody!" The girl bounced off, disappearing around the corner, her party dress swinging.

"Your mom's going to spoil her," Daphne said with a sad smile.

"I can talk to her." He moved to the kitchen, Daphne following.

"No, it's fine. Tigger loves her. She's going to miss her, that's all."

"She's not dying." He cleared his throat, hoping it wasn't a lie. He braced himself against the open fridge door, pushing back the insistent hollow ache that threatened to turn the bright day gray. He slapped a brick of cheddar on the counter, then added a pound of butter and a carton of milk beside it.

"I'm sorry," Daphne said carefully. "I didn't mean to imply that she was."

"It's not terminal," he said, swallowing hard. "And I'm sure she'd love it if you and Tigger stayed in touch. After. She used to be a kindergarten teacher and she misses kids." He pulled a package of whole wheat elbow noodles from the cupboard, then handed Daphne a large pot. "Can you fill this with water?"

Without a word she filled it, then set it on the stove, lighting the burner beneath it. "How long before you think it'll be safe for us to return home?"

"I don't know."

"We're in your way, Evander."

"No, not really."

"Cramping your style at least?"

He let out a sigh and gave her a dry look. "I have no style to cramp."

She glanced at his ironed shirt and raised an eyebrow.

"Army habits." Yeah, so a T-shirt might not need heat to flatten, but the action was soothing. A hot blade running across wrinkles, making everything smooth and perfect in one stroke. It was easy to get lost in the meditative rhythm of ironing.

"If we're making it difficult for you to parent your daughter," he said, "tell us."

"It's fine. Really."

He gave her a stern look and she laughed, tossing up her hands in what may have been delight.

"This is the best thing to happen to her all summer." Daphne's smile fell and she wouldn't meet his gaze as she busied herself grating cheese with too much vigor.

They worked in steady silence, but finally he had to ask, "How come?"

"Family is good for her."

Family? Was that what she thought this was? He tried to argue, but found his mind stuck on the word, his throat seized as though in the solid grip of an enemy commander.

"Hey," Kyle said, entering the kitchen, his face washed from the earlier green mask, "I said I'd make lunch."

Evander pushed the jug of milk into his hands. "Take over. Mac 'n' cheese."

"But I was going to make quiche."

"Plans change."

# Chapter Ten

*Daphne clamped her mouth* shut so she wouldn't argue with Evander. Tigger was happily learning to knit in the other room, completely enraptured by Florence and her ability to create gorgeous fairy blankets. Kyle, who'd barely left his mother's side since his arrival, was helping by untangling the balls of yarn. He was so unlike Evander, with his slender build and feminine gentleness, that Daphne could barely believe they had the same parents.

Outside the large kitchen window chickadees were eating at a bird feeder, their black caps bobbing as they pecked at the seed. Another movement caught her eye, a streak of faded orange fur. Rudolph. She stood to try and warn off the birds, but they were already gone, and Rudolph moodily stalking away at the missed opportunity.

"Are you listening?" Evander asked.

"I don't know. Are you still lecturing?"

He gave a disgruntled snort at her flippant dig.

She'd been carefully following his directions and advice in hopes that he'd take his tension down a notch. If he said it was time to come in from the yard, she came in. No questions asked. But he'd been on a tear since she'd announced wanting to go back to work. She'd had to remind him that even though she was living here she still had expenses.

She took a seat at the kitchen table, cupping a mug of coffee in her hands. While she'd seen a new side of Evander by sharing his home for the past day and a half, his being on edge was getting to her. Yesterday he'd all but stormed out of the kitchen while they were making lunch, leaving her and Kyle to finish the macaroni and cheese.

"Have you heard any more about the guy in the Hummer?" she asked him now.

"There's no new information," he said. "Have you talked to Mistral?"

"Do you think I should?" She found it strange that Mistral hadn't called her cell. He had to have heard what had happened.

"I think you should be an active participant, Daphne."

"What's that supposed to mean?"

His voice took on an edge that she didn't like. "You have a habit of sitting back and allowing your life to steer itself, or letting others make decisions for you."

"Fine. I can move out. I thought this was the safest option, but if you'd rather I stand up and make a big choice about it all I'll go pack my bags."

"Hear me out before you go twisting your panties in a knot."

She stood up. "You really don't know how to be civil, do you?"

"You can't let everything flow by you, Daphne. Being one with the world is not a life plan." Evander punctuated his sentences by slapping the back of one hand into the opposite palm, like a politician making an important point.

She'd never liked politicians that much. Too many seemed to be on the take or didn't have the balls to make the big changes the planet needed, for fear of ticking off their constituents.

"You need to be an active participant in keeping yourself safe. Don't wait for everyone to make your decisions without you."

"And what do you know about my life?"

"A lot more than you seem to." His eyes were flashing as she dropped her hands onto her hips to glare up at him.

"I doubt anyone like you could *ever* understand someone like me."

"For all your acceptance," he said, stepping close enough that his body heat scorched her skin, "you sure as hell don't seem to accept me and where I'm coming from. I'm putting my life on the line to save your skin. In fact, how many times have I bailed you out in the past five days and you can't even find it in your big, generous heart to grant me a sliver of understanding?"

Daphne felt as though he'd not just turned the tables on her, but that he'd pushed one against her, pinning her in a corner.

Her voice wobbled as she said, "You know what? You showing up with your testosterone hanging out, and waving that gun of yours around like a big ol'—"

"Oh, no you don't." He was so close now that she could barely think, only feel desperation and anger and something else she most definitely didn't want to feel anywhere near this man. "You don't get to blame the gun thing on me. Do you even know who Mistral's bodyguard is?" Evander pressed closer. "Do you?"

She slowly shook her head, her curls tangling as they brushed over her shoulders.

"The man you want your daughter hanging around employs a man with a rap sheet longer than my tibia. Ricardo's been arrested for assault several times. Is that in line with your family values?"

She really wanted to slap him. At the same time everything Evander was saying was slamming kernels of truth into a tender place she'd tried to keep buried inside.

She closed her eyes, willing herself to be strong enough to take what he was saying. He was pointing out all these things because he believed it was best for her and her daughter. She knew that, but it didn't make it hurt any less.

"Okay," Daphne said, giving in, hoping he'd just stop talking.

He gently took her arms, his large hands covering so much of her skin that she leaned into his touch, wanting more. She wanted to have a long nap in the shelter of his protection, then wake up and find her life fixed again. Instead, she had to be strong. As strong as this man who was telling her she had to be even stronger. She had to be a mother. She had to do what was best for everyone, even if it wasn't the best thing for her.

"Okay what?" Evander asked.

"You want me to accept you?" Her voice shook, so many emotions battling within her she was surprised she didn't burst at the seams. "Then let me in."

She needed him to break down the wall that always seemed to come up whenever she saw glimpses of the real man. The more she got to know him, the more she saw snippets of realness, but she needed *something* to show her that he was feeling the same attraction she was. She wasn't even sure what it was exactly, but she needed to know if he felt it, too.

"You want to know why I went to war?" Evander said finally. "Because of love."

She twisted out of his grip, laughing as she ran a hand through her hair, fingers catching in the fine knots. "To get in some girl's pants? I didn't expect that."

Evander ignored the joke. "I know that what you do comes from here." He touched his chest above his heart. "Everything in your life is guided by love. But what if someone or something was threatening that?"

Daphne blinked hard. Someone *was* threatening it.

"Sometimes in order to protect love so it can grow and spread throughout the world, you have to crush those who are trying to destroy it. Those who are so ruined they can no longer see the beauty in this world and only want to break it. You can't talk to people who have gone that far into the pain. They only understand fighting and weapons."

She didn't want to believe him, didn't want to grasp his rationale, but his argument made perfect sense.

She didn't want there to be people who understood only fighting and weapons, and not love. She didn't know how the world had become so broken, but war never fixed things. Nothing seemed to. Not even love.

Evander swallowed hard, fighting some emotion she wasn't familiar with. He'd seen things she never could and he was closing up before her.

"I went to war, Daphne," he said, glancing up, his eyes dark and chilling. No, he wasn't closing up, he was letting her in. He was showing her what she was seeking, baring himself so that she could understand. "To protect love. To make sure it had a place to grow—even in the unlikeliest of places."

She shivered despite the warmth of the morning sun. His gaze softened and he extended a hand to her. She hesitated for a second before reaching out and placing her palm in his large one.

"Let me protect you, Daphne. Let me give your love the shelter it needs so it can grow and change this world."

She folded herself into his arms, nodding, mute with the shock of having someone so different finally understand and accept where she was coming from. Evander was quickly becoming the man who was everything that had been missing in her world.

DAPHNE SHOOK THE TENSION out of her hands and released a gusty sigh. The way Evander had revealed himself in the kitchen had been unexpected. The fact that he went to war for the same reasons she lived her life was unsettling. How could they both be driven by love? It was incongruent having a gun-toting, knife-throwing hunk of muscle going to war to preserve love in the world. What had set them on such separate paths if they had similar core values?

War and peace. Which would help save the world?

And yet, if they were so similar, why couldn't Evander see that she was an active participant in her life? She wasn't sitting around letting it go by, as he seemed to believe.

She vowed not to think about him any longer and finished folding the basket of laundry in her room. Pushing back the curtain, she glanced at the street below. There was a car parked along the curb, the window rolled down. An elbow rested on the sill and she wondered when the reporter would give up. He'd banged on the door, requesting an interview, but Evander had chased him away with threats that had sent chills down her spine. She allowed the curtain to fall back into place.

She needed a way to show Evander she was taking action. Just because she wasn't controlling every little thing and left space for spontaneity didn't mean she was letting her life run her.

Picking up her phone, Daphne dialed Mistral's office. She was going to arrange that meeting she'd told her sisters about. No more pussyfooting. No more waiting for Mistral. Summer was almost over and she needed a decision from him.

"Mistral, please," she said, when the secretary picked up.

"I'm sorry, he's not taking calls right now."

"Now or ever?" Daphne asked with suspicion.

"I do believe his lawyer has advised him not to speak with you." The secretary's voice had a chill that could rival a kiss from a snowman.

"Right. And that's your business how, exactly?" Daphne asked sweetly.

"I will not put your call through."

*Peace, light, and goodwill. No murder via ballpoint pen.*

"You will let him know I called, because that is your job." Daphne hit the red button to end the call, wishing she'd been able to slam the phone down. Maybe next time she could slam it against something and then tell the woman to—no, peace, light, happiness. *Inhale, one, two, three. Exhale, one, two, three.*

Oh, to heck with it.

Daphne picked up the phone and dialed Mistral's cell.

"Yeah?" His voice was curt and dismissive.

For a moment Daphne forgot why she was calling. *Take charge of her life, be active and not a passive participant. Prove to Evander he was wrong. Make him proud of her.*

"Have you had a chance to think about my proposal?" she asked.

"My lawyers advised me not speak with you any longer due to what happened on the road the other day."

"You heard about that, huh? Thanks for your concern."

"Yeah," he said drily, "it was a little embarrassing, being hauled down to the police station for questioning."

"Did you send him after me?"

"Give me some credit."

"Did you?"

"Who do you think I am? Some monster? What if Kim had been with you?"

"I'm fine. Thanks for asking."

"Sorry. I'm sorry. Things are crazy around here right now and it's getting to me."

Daphne bit her tongue so she wouldn't say something snarky. "Does Aaron still work for Rubicore?"

She spied Evander in the hall outside her bedroom. He paused as he went by, his head stuck in his phone as usual. She was starting to dislike his phone. And it felt as though he was using it as a barrier between them, when all she wanted was to find out more about him. To sit. To talk.

And maybe get another one of those kisses like when she'd been hopped up on nerves and adrenaline after he'd brought them into the safety of his home. He'd met her with a passion and need that had cranked her up even further. But then he'd pulled away. Several times. She wasn't sure what would have happened if Tigger hadn't come up the stairs.

She wanted more of Evander, but she knew it was the kind of more that would lead to trouble. They might seem to have some core beliefs in common, but they were still so incredibly different. But the way he handled Tigger and made her eyes dance caused Daphne's heart to warm and swell as though she had a circulatory problem. The worst part was that she desperately wanted Evander to care for her, as well.

"He's a bit of a mess," Mistral said carefully into her ear, and for a moment she thought he was talking about Evander and not Aaron. "He's not dealing well with the roadblocks and I've suggested counseling. I've let him go, but my father has decided to keep him on as his own assistant. It doesn't matter what I do, Dad always undermines me." He let out a sigh as though the weight of the world was pressing on him. "I fired Ricardo, too. I have a new assistant."

"Is he armed?"

"Probably. I'm sorry. I know how you feel about guns."

"Why do you need a bodyguard?"

"I was advised to make sure I had an assistant who was armed, for crossing picket lines up in Muskoka."

"What picket lines?"

"The ones everyone assumes you'll erect against me." He gave a sheepish laugh. "I've had time to think, Daphne. I let my dad blow you up as this big evil force who hated me, but seeing you..." His voice was soft and almost wistful, and Daphne wondered if he was remembering those hot summer nights they'd spent together hiding out at Trixie Hollow, when nobody else was around. "I understand where you're coming from."

She could practically visualize Mistral running a hand through his hair as he let out a jagged breath.

"Thank you. Thank you for saying that." She sagged onto her bed. Mistral was still the good man she'd known him to be. They could still get control of this situation. But they had to work together, and he was going to have to learn how to be a whole lot stronger.

Daphne glanced into the empty hallway, wishing Evander could have heard Mistral, but he'd wandered into his own room on the other side of the wall. She half pictured him pressing his ear against it to hear her side of the conversation. Although it was more likely he had her room or phone bugged.

"This project is my baby," Mistral continued. "It was also Aaron's first real chance to prove himself and get a massive promotion. He didn't take the threat well."

"That's why I'm calling, Mistral. I want to remove the threat by working together."

"You think we can work together without killing each other?" He added quickly, "That's just an expression, by the way."

"I think in a lot of ways we're coming from the same place." She thought of her recent conversation with Evander. The two of them, even though vastly different, had similar core values driving them to take action in differing ways. Mistral hadn't changed so much that they were no longer coming from the same place. They just had different reasons for doing what they were doing.

"You always saw the world differently," he said, "and with a hope that none of us others could ever wish for."

Daphne gave an uneasy laugh. "I'm not sure if that is a compliment or not."

"It is."

Silence stretched out between them.

"So?" she asked. "What do you say? Shall I drive down so we can discuss this plan?"

"You are the most persistent woman I've ever met. And I've met plenty." She could hear papers rustling in the background, then a sigh. "Fine. You win. How can I say no to someone who's always been open and friendly, even when I've been a complete ass and my colleagues have broken into her home and tried to run her off the road? Man, I really need to start listening to my lawyers, don't I?" He gave an uneasy chuckle.

Lesson number one: It was always harder to say no to someone who was smiling, friendly, and expected the best from you.

Evander might not understand her go-with-the-flow, happy attitude, but it was kicking his let's-fight-it-out plan right now.

"How's tomorrow?" she asked. "Any openings?"

"I'm in Toronto."

"Well, in case you haven't heard, the highway does run both ways. How about eleven o'clock?"

"Fine," he said with resignation.

She hung up the phone and began planning.

# Chapter Eleven

*"What do you mean*, you want to go to Toronto and talk to Mistral?" Evander wanted to give Daphne a good, hard shake, but was struggling to squeeze drops into the cat's folded-back ears. Yesterday, he'd been certain she'd understood what he was saying about being an active participant in her life. He knew he'd agreed to help her with peace talks, but this? Several members of the press were waiting out on the street for their chance to go in for the kill, and she was busy whipping up a meeting that would be in the papers all around the planet—without consulting him first, he might add.

"Email your proposal," he said.

How was he supposed to protect her? How was he supposed to keep her safe when she kept shutting him out? He'd thought they understood each other at long last. He'd opened up and yet she was still the same old Daphne, charging on. Nothing had changed.

Rudolph clawed his way loose when Evander unconsciously tightened his grip on the feline. Evander held in a hiss of pain, not wanting to be distracted from the bomb Daphne was imploding at his feet.

"I don't *want* to go, I *am* going," she said, tipping up her chin with determination. "There's a difference."

Brick wandered into the room in a magenta bathrobe. "Oh?

Toronto? Are we all going? I could use better slippers than the ones I packed. I was in such a state." He smiled expectantly at the fighting couple, and Evander scowled, pointing to the door.

"I'll take that as a no." Kyle backed out of the kitchen, hands raised in surrender.

"Did it ever occur to you to run this meeting by me first?" Evander boomed. "That there might be things I need to put in place to ensure your safety? I thought we were a team. A team trying to keep you safe. Meeting with Mistral. Is. Not. Safe."

He should have bugged her cell phone. He should have captured their conversation so he could hear Mistral's side of it. She was too trusting.

"Evander, you're being really..." Daphne wouldn't meet his eyes as she backed away.

"Threatening?"

"Yeah."

He took one massive step, eating the space between them. She bumped against the table, sending Tigger's half-empty glass of milk sloshing. He rested his hands over Daphne's ears and pushed his lips against hers, determined to show he wasn't a threat, and that he only wanted what was best for her. He gave her a hard kiss, then stepped back.

"When I said be active in your life," he said softly, "I didn't mean go running into the open mouth of the roaring lion."

Her cheeks were bright red as she said, "I resent the way you paint me with the stupidity stick."

She placed her tiny hands on her hips and glared at him, her attention focused solely on his lips. He almost laughed, she looked so indignant. But there was a fire in her eyes that he didn't dare mess with. If he didn't handle this right, she would take off without him. And that would be a disaster for sure.

"And," she added, "you need to learn to kiss better." She turned on her heel, trying to beat a hasty escape into the sitting room, where Florence and Tigger were knitting once again.

Evander hooked her around the waist, spinning her into his arms. With one hand on the back of her head, the other wrapped around her slender form, he pulled her warmth against him. With a deliberate slowness, he gently brushed her lips with his. The caress was sweet and he licked her lower lip before giving her a long, slow kiss. Heat sizzled between them and it was all he could do to pull back, to be a gentleman, to not lift her T-shirt dress and lay her flat out on the breakfast table.

He let her go and put his hands on his hips as she had only moments ago, enjoying the way she looked dazed, her chest expanding, but not quite fully able to inhale properly.

"For the record, I *can* kiss. And I understand that you are used to making your own decisions without having to consult with anyone. But in order to do my job and keep you safe—no matter what sweet things that ex of yours whispers in your ear—I need you to consult with me. I can't do my job if you're making plans without talking to me."

"Okay."

Okay? That was it?

Had his kiss blown her difficult side out of commission? If so, he'd have to remember that trick.

"What time do you have to be there?" he asked grudgingly.

Today was going to be endless. After that kiss and her softly giving in, he was going to be thinking with the wrong head all day long.

Daphne checked the slender watch on her wrist. "About three and a half hours."

"And you're just telling me now?" The anger was back. "It's almost a three-hour drive."

"I know. But I thought—"

"You did this so…" No, he wasn't going to argue with her. He was also not going to lock her in a room for her own safety. As appealing as that was.

Tigger came bounding into the kitchen, all lace and flounces in her party dress.

"Is she coming with us?" he snapped, tipping his head toward the small girl. Daphne was never going to think about safety first, was she?

"I'm right here," Tigger said. She gave him a dark look.

"Sorry, kiddo."

"Well, if I can't go, then she can't go," Kyle said, joining them in the kitchen. He pointed to Tigger. "So, I say we stay here and have a TV party with Florence, while the poopy adults fight their way to the city and back. What do you say, Tigger? Does your mother approve of nail polish? I think Granny needs her nails freshened and I bet she's got some colors that would look splendid on those tapered fingers of yours."

"Is it okay if she stays here?" Daphne asked, looking from Brick to Evander. "I was going to take her to hang out with Melanie, since she's still off work, but I'd feel better leaving her here with all the security stuff."

Evander ran a hand down his face, taking in his brother's magenta robe. Would the kid be safe here? It wouldn't be as safe if he was gone, but she sure as heck wasn't coming with them.

"You had time to line up a babysitter, but still didn't think to tell me you were going to Toronto?" he asked, an edge to his voice.

"You were eavesdropping! How did you *not* know?"

"I was not!"

"I think this is our cue to go raid Granny's nail polish," Kyle whispered to Tigger, and they hustled out of the room.

"You're always around, looking over my shoulder," Daphne

said. "You're like, like…" Her hands were fluttering and her cheeks were flushed. They needed to go to bed. Together. That would settle this.

No.

No, he couldn't think that way. He needed to remain focused. Not think about what she'd feel like with her legs wrapped around his hips.

"I only heard you ask if Aaron still works for Mistral," Evander admitted, his jaw clenched.

"He doesn't. And neither does Ricardo."

Evander suddenly felt lighter, with tension draining away as though someone had pulled the plug. "That's promising."

"I thought so."

He checked the time and gave a hefty sigh as he poured coffee into his travel mug. "We'll take my truck even though there's no backseat for Tigger." Why hadn't he bought a bigger truck last winter? Had he really believed he was that alone in the world that he'd never need to give several people a ride—or small people for that matter? "She'll be okay riding up front again. The airbag turns off. Plus, the tires on your van suck and the bumper's still smashed."

Instead of arguing like he expected, Daphne gave him a sunny smile.

Damn women.

EVANDER HAD A VERY FAST, very cold shower while trying to get his frustration with Daphne out of his mind. That and how wonderfully right her body had felt pressed against his as he'd kissed her in the kitchen. Again.

He really needed to stop doing that.

It was becoming harder to get the way she felt out of his mind, as well as those sneaky fantasies that were starting to take over. Fantasies of what they could do together. Alone.

*Focus. Keep her safe.*

*No matter the cost.*

He groaned and buttoned his cotton dress shirt. He jerked the cuffs, inspecting his ironing job. Perfect. At least one area of his life was staying controlled and in line with what he needed. Even if it was only his ironing.

Tigger bounded by his bedroom door. She stopped and doubled back. Grinning, she said, "I'm not going to Aunt Mellie Melon's anymore because we're having a nail polish party instead!"

"You call your aunt that to her face?" He slipped his phone in his back pocket and his wallet in the other. He needed to get Daphne's van worked on. There was a shop a few blocks from here that might be able to get it fixed today while they were out.

The girl giggled. "She likes it."

"You're joking?"

Tigger shook her head. "I like Max. He's Tristen's dog. He has a really big tongue."

"I didn't know that about Tristen. Interesting." Evander grabbed his truck keys and slipped by the girl. They headed down the wood staircase, where sunshine streamed through the window, hitting the landing and blinding him for a half second.

"Max has a big tongue, not Tristen." The girl giggled, her bare feet tapping out a chirpy beat as she trundled down the steps behind him.

"Oh." He pretended to be chagrined. "It's a good thing I didn't say anything to Tristen about his big tongue. That would have been embarrassing."

"You're silly."

"I don't think I've ever been called that before."

They found Daphne in the sitting room talking quietly with his mother. The women paused, looking up as he entered the room.

"Saying good things about me, I hope," Evander said with a grin.

"Always," Florence replied. She got up from her armchair, looking better than she had in days. Having a houseful of distraction was good for at least one of them. "Look at Daphne, Evander. Isn't she a delight? How could a man ever say no to her?"

"You'd be surprised," Daphne replied out of the side of her mouth.

"Could you say no to this lovely face, Evander?" Florence waved a hand over Daphne as though showcasing the woman.

Evander placed a kiss on top of his mother's head, hoping she didn't know the full truth of that. The longer he spent with Daphne, the harder it was for him to be a solid, stubborn wall of "no."

Daphne lightly touched his arm and goose bumps rose along his skin like flames spreading through dry grass.

"Ready?" She pressed her fingers to the base of her throat. A sure sign she was worrying.

"You okay? We don't have to go. Your van is heading into the shop, but we could use picking it up as an excuse to stay."

"That's a horrible excuse," Daphne said, with a laugh that didn't have her usual house-shaking Richter scale level of energy.

"Tigger will be okay here," he said. "Brick is tougher than he looks and there's no way he'll let anyone near her. He's just as protective as I am, even though he likes to wear odd colors." Evander gave her a wink. "I taught him how to defend himself. He's good. And the house is well secured."

His mother nodded. "I haven't nicknamed the place Fort Knox for nothing."

"Would you feel more secure knowing where Tigger was, and being able to check up on her location?" he asked. Not waiting for more than a flicker of agreement from Daphne, he turned his head and called, "Tigger! Come show your mom your new trinket."

The girl bounded out from between the couch and curtains. Little eavesdropper. She danced over to her mother, showing off the lacy ponytail clip he'd given her as soon as he'd heard she'd be separated from him for the day.

"Evander gave it to me. Isn't it pretty?"

Daphne sent him a surprised look.

"Mom and I made it. It connects." He waved his phone, trying to keep the girl in the dark that her hair clip had a tracking chip in it that connected to his phone so he could keep track of her. Loose lips had sunk more ships than torpedoes, and he didn't want the girl giving away the one thing that might keep her safe if things went south.

Daphne frowned thoughtfully as she studied her daughter and Evander rushed through goodbyes, hoping Daphne wouldn't ask about radio signals and brain tumors.

Wishing he had an attached garage or a secret escape tunnel from the house, he locked the front door behind them and headed to the truck. He gave a reporter who looked as though he was about to step onto the property the finger, and opened the door for Daphne, helping her into the truck.

With one last glance at the house, he pulled away down the tree-lined, sun-dappled street. In his rearview mirror, he saw three cars fall in behind him.

Reporters.

If he'd had any time to prepare, he'd have had Tyrone come over to create a diversion. Instead, Evander began going through a few basic maneuvers, such as timing traffic lights in order to run them and lose his followers, and using traffic to create buffers between him and those trying to follow him.

"You're going the wrong way," Daphne said.

"Oh, I'm sorry. I didn't realize you wanted to tip off the reporters that we're going to Toronto? And here I thought it would be smarter to have them think we were heading in the direction of Port Carling."

"Sorry," Daphne muttered. "Do your thing."

By the time they were near the next highway exit, he'd lost the reporters. He circled around Bracebridge, heading out to the highway he really wanted, and crossing his fingers that none of the reporters picked up their trail again.

"I hope this is worth it, Daphne."

"Me, too."


DAPHNE NEEDED A DISTRACTION. Lots of them, and the familiar divided highway wasn't providing any. Having Evander ticked off at her for not telling him about Toronto was draining. His unhappy energy was filling the truck and she discovered she didn't like him being upset with her. Not at all.

"I'm sorry I didn't tell you about Toronto," she said. "I thought you were listening, and sometimes it feels as though you know what's going on more than I do and I just…" The excuses sounded lame. She'd screwed up. Plain and simple.

"You need to tell me things."

"I promise I will from now on. I'm sorry."

He gave a sharp nod and she could tell he was already moving past it, but didn't want her to think that it was that easy to be forgiven for something of this magnitude.

"And I don't think of your house as a bunker, either."

His lips flickered, almost as though he was amused.

The truth was, she felt safer and more at home with Evander than she would have expected. Living with the de la Fosses was good and the idea of returning to their quiet little house in Port Carling held surprisingly little appeal. But how much longer could Florence take the rambunctious Tigger? How much longer until having her daughter following Evander everywhere wore on him?

There were still a lot of kilometers to go and too much time to think. Daphne had a general idea of what she wanted to say to Mistral, but she needed a distraction so she didn't turn into a nervous mess who wondered how on earth she'd ever fallen for a man like her ex.

"Have you traveled a lot?" she asked Evander, hoping he was feeling chatty.

"Yes."

"What was your favorite place?"

"In what way?"

"Um, people?"

"Canada."

"Does that count?"

He smiled at her, his eyes teasing. "Of course it does."

"How so?"

"Look at how much land we have, how diverse we are. I was stationed out in a small farming town in Alberta for a while. The people were very down-to-earth. You could tell they'd been through tough times and they depended on each other. Nobody was an outsider or a stranger. They still pulled over to help if someone had an accident or their car broke down. They looked you in the eye and called you on your bullshit. I liked it."

Daphne smiled at the idea of Evander in the middle of a bunch of tell-it-like-it-is farmers. "It sounds nice." Real. Honest. Very different from the online world she'd come to avoid. It seemed as though her friends and acquaintances presented only their edited, polished, super-mom side, leaving her feeling crappy about her own life and failures. She knew their lives had ups and downs, just like hers, but it still got to her, seeing only the shiny moments.

It was either that or drama created around small things that they'd blown out of proportion. And if there was one thing that bugged Daphne, it was when people competed to see who was having the worst life or the crappiest day.

"Think a town like that would have room for a hippie like me?" she joked.

"It's like Northern Ontario in some ways," Evander continued, ignoring her question. "Although there's maybe more laughing and booze up north."

"There always is. Got to stay warm, right?" This conversation wasn't distracting her. Not nearly enough. Especially the way he was smiling now. It looked good on him, and all she could think about was how those lips had felt against hers this morning in the kitchen. "Why did you keep pushing me away? Upstairs. When I first arrived."

Well, that wasn't supposed to come out.

Evander's eyebrows lifted and his chest expanded as though holding in a breath. Finally, giving her a quick glance, he said, "I've been hired to protect you. If I get involved it will compromise my ability to stay focused and retain a clear mind. I have to be square, not distracted. And you are definitely a distraction."

She liked the idea of being able to distract a man like Evander. He was impenetrable in so many ways, but being able to dig into that armor and get underneath was more than flattering. It was empowering in a way she hadn't expected.

"And I know, too, with this stuff going on, emotions can get out of whack." His voice was lower now, his head tipped to check his blind spot as he changed lanes. "I'd hate to let things get to a point where you'd regret it later."

"Right. Because I obviously don't know my way around birth control." She'd been down this road before with the one man she'd seen since Mistral, back when Tigger was two. Just because Daphne had a child out of wedlock did not mean she didn't understand what sex led to if one wasn't careful.

"Sorry?" Evander looked uncomfortable, maybe even as if he was contemplating jumping out of the moving vehicle.

"Baby out of wedlock."

"Oh."

It seemed as though he didn't believe she was a man trap. That was good. However, that begged the question of what he did believe she was.

"I don't recommend condoms," she added. "They aren't particularly reliable."

He smiled at her tone.

"So your sisters all fell in love recently?" he probed, his curiosity palpable.

"Yeah." She gave a wistful sigh. "All three in the past six weeks."

How had destiny brought all three of them boyfriends in such a short period of time? Especially when they didn't believe in the legend? And what about her? Was destiny going to pass her over? She had only a week before the tax deadline. What if they lost the island? Would she remain single forever? Had Mistral been her one Nymph Island love match?

"Are you hoping Mistral will ask you back?" Evander's question popped out as though he'd been reading her mind, and she could tell he wanted to take it back.

"I would like him to take an interest in Tigger, that's all," she said honestly.

"He's only met her this summer?"

Everyone assumed she'd walked away, head held high, and never looked back. But in reality she'd tried seeing him in Toronto once when Tigger was six months old. She'd been tired, broke, and desperate for child support. His father had turned her away, not recognizing her or Tigger as anything more than a bother on their front step.

"I send him photos of her. Letters. Drawings."

"Did he reply?"

"Not until this summer."

She turned to Evander, whose expression had turned dark. "Do you think it's a game? His sudden interest? My sisters think... Do you think he really wants to be her father? Truly?" Her heart squeezed, waiting for his reply.

She felt as though she knew Mistral and the position he was trapped in, unable to lead his own life. But at the same time, she wasn't sure if her own hopes and wishes were clouding her vision of what was really happening. She wanted to be positive and expect the best, but she knew she had to be realistic, too.

She thought of Mistral trying to play with Tigger at the picnic before Tristen had punched him. Had that all been an act? Because Evander was taking more of an interest in Tigger than Mistral was. Sure, the bodyguard was stuck with her, but he was still being the man she wished Mistral would be, and that wasn't part of the job description.

"It could be a ploy," Evander admitted. "He's a shrewd businessman."

It just seemed so out of character for the young man she had fallen for all those years ago. She wasn't sure who he was now, but it still didn't fit. People didn't change that much in such a short period of time, did they?

"He's successful, isn't he?" Evander added.

"You know, just because he has money doesn't make him special."

"You can say that again." There was a glimmer of a smile playing at Evander's lips.

"He used to be a decent man. He had potential to change the world. Still does."

"I'm sure."

"You have a secret," she said lightly. There was something in the turn of the conversation that was tickling his funny bone. He was keeping something under his hat. Something beyond him thinking Mistral wasn't special because of his money and success. If she didn't know any better she'd think Evander had money or some sort of hidden success.

"We all have secrets."

"Are you carrying a gun today?"

He gave her a look of disbelief. "That's not a secret."

She let out a sigh. "Well, don't bring them into the meeting. In fact, you can stay outside."

"I don't think—"

"Yeah, yeah, yeah." She held up a hand. "I meant outside the room with his latest trigger-happy buddy. You guys can see who has the fastest draw in central Canada while we get down to brass tacks."

He gave her a grudging nod and took a sip of the massive coffee he'd picked up in Barrie when they'd stopped for gas. If she drank that much she'd be peeing all day. That and be as hyper as Tigger on sugar. She supposed on the coffee-cup-to-body-size equivalent scale his extra large was like her drinking her small. Big coffee for a big guy.

"Mistral is following in his father's footsteps because he doesn't know any better," she said, wanting to talk it out with someone who might understand, or at least be an impartial, analytical party. "He doesn't know how to free himself. He thinks being like his father will win him love and pride. But it never will. His dad will never be able to provide what Mistral needs. Everyone deserves love, especially from their parents. It can be so heartbreaking to not have it, and its absence changes a person." She pressed her palm against Evander's warm forearm, thinking about her daughter and the lack of a father figure. It had to be affecting her, just as it had affected Daphne not having a father during her teen years. "Don't you think so?"

He met her gaze, his eyes warm and safe. "I do."

"Mistral needs a lot of love."

"Is that why you're giving him the benefit of the doubt? Why you're trying to talk sense into him?"

"If you don't believe in the good of every person, what's there to believe in?"

"You haven't been to war." His grip tightened on the wheel and Daphne wondered what all he'd seen with those dark eyes of his. The way they shuttered over emotions, keeping his true self hidden away.

As an experiment, she lightly kissed her fingertips, knowing he saw it in his peripheral vision, then gently placed them against his temple, stretching to do so.

He flinched, jerked the wheel, then straightened the truck again. When he glanced at her, surprise was the dominant emotion on his face. Ha! He couldn't shutter everything away.

"Why'd you do that?" he asked softly. The vehicle had slowed, he'd been so taken off guard, and he picked up speed again.

She smiled. She could get to him. Love fixed everything. Maybe even Evander.

EVANDER WAITED OUTSIDE the skyscraper's meeting room. He didn't like the idea of Daphne in there alone with Mistral, even though he was just outside the door. Mistral was a man caught between two worlds, and based on what Evander had seen in his life, that made a man unpredictable. It didn't help that Daphne thought she could fix the guy.

Opening his tracking app, Evander checked on Tigger. Still at home. While he trusted his brother to watch out for the girl, he knew that if Mistral and others knew Daphne was here, they could try to do something behind their backs. Not likely, but knowing Tigger was exposed, despite security measures, left Evander anxious to head back to Bracebridge.

He texted his brother. *Anything unusual?*

His brother texted back, *Yeah, this kid's energy levels.*

*Did you give her sugar? Daphne says it makes the kid wacky.*

*Oh. Oops.*

Evander shook his head and pocketed his phone, then erred on the side of caution and pulled it out to text, *Don't go outside. Stay in the house. Keep the alarm on.*

Feeling better, he studied Mistral's new bodyguard. He seemed familiar and Evander placed him as an acquaintance from his army days. Again, if Daphne had given him more time he could have found out who the new guy was and done a background check.

Smiling, the new man extended his hand for a shake. "Evander, right?"

"Yeah. Sorry, I can place you in the army or navy—no, army—but not your name."

"Leif McClain." They shook hands. The man looked him in the eye, his grip not too firm, but authoritative enough that Evander took a liking to him. "Good to be forgotten, since I never made it out of boot camp. You had to throw me over that stupid wall every single time."

"Ah. Sorry. I threw a lot of people over if it makes you feel better."

"I wasn't cut out for the army, as I still hadn't hit my growth spurt." He patted his biceps. "How'd you do?"

"Navy. JTF 2."

The man's eyebrows rose in appreciation. "Medals?"

"A few."

Mistral was trying to surround himself with honest, levelheaded men, judging by the personable bodyguard. However, Leif really needed to shut up so Evander could keep an ear out for trouble beyond the closed door.

He had a vision of Mistral trying to badger Daphne, and he turned to the door to check in on her. If he'd had more time to prepare, he could have bugged Daphne so he could listen to their conversation via an earpiece. The quiet mumble of voices on the other side grew louder, but as his hand touched the doorknob, Mistral's man lightly tapped his arm and shook his head.

Evander ignored him and opened the door. It was his job to keep Daphne safe, not listen to the lackey hired by the man voted most likely to hurt her.

Quickly taking in the situation, Evander caught Daphne's gaze. She seemed distraught and he was to her side in a moment. "Everything okay?" He kept his eyes on her, knowing Mistral would try to smooth things over.

"No." Daphne glared across the desk at her ex. "But I suppose that is nothing new." She rose with grace and Evander couldn't help but be pleased to think that the trip to the city was coming to completion. There were too many unknown variables when they were treading on enemy ground.

"I have agreed to cooperate. I've proved I'm trustworthy." The way she spit out the word *trustworthy* he figured the man had questioned her loyalty. "You can't blame me because your corporation didn't follow laws. I purposefully stayed out of the Rubicore fight, something you can't seem to comprehend." Her voice was hard, stubborn.

"You led a protest against us closing our own summer camp."

"It wasn't yours to close. It's a charitable organization on land you bought out from under it with the promise that you'd take care of it on Baby Horseshoe Island. Closing it so you can build your resort isn't taking care of it. That camp is important for teenagers, and both you and I know it."

"I'm not the only one who makes decisions around here, Daphne." Mistral's face was flushed and Evander wondered how many decisions the man actually got to make in his own company.

She leaned forward, her voice softening. "Be the hero I know you are and open Camp Adaker somewhere new. Tristen Bell has agreed to cover the cost. You'd look like a saint for looking out for those troubled kids. Think of the publicity and goodwill it would generate around your business."

She paused and Evander felt himself holding his breath so he wouldn't miss Mistral's reply. He noted that the new bodyguard was doing the same.

"I'm on your side," Daphne cooed.

Oh, this man was going down. Who could resist her when she got like that? Not a man who was swinging for Team Heterosexual, that was for sure.

"There's a way to follow the rules with this development and come out on top. Be the good guy, be the hero. As well as make a tidy profit and prove yourself to the corporate world. Everyone could be emulating *you*, Mistral."

Damn, she knew this man's weaknesses and was playing to

them like a major league pitcher. Evander should have told her to be active in her life sooner. Then again, he wouldn't have had the chance to hang out with that firefly kiddo of hers. The girl seriously brightened his days in ways he hadn't expected. Daphne, too, if he was honest with himself.

She collected her purse, saying casually, "Think about it, Mistral. You know me. I wouldn't do anything to hurt you. I have your best interests at heart and I know if we cooperate everyone could get what they want. Everyone."

Daphne turned to the door, and Evander fell into step behind her, shaking himself out of the moment in order to keep one eye on the men. In the doorway, Daphne paused, turning back, and he stepped out of the way so she could see Mistral. "You know it doesn't have to be this way," she said to him. "We could be on the same side again."

"Were we ever really on the same side, Daphne?"

Evander could see there was no love lost between them, yet the hope in Daphne's eyes nearly crushed him. Her desire to have Tigger's father in their lives was almost unbearable to witness, and the worst part was that Evander knew Mistral didn't have the strength of character to be good for either of the Summers.

Daphne was a smart, competent, and confident person, yet she was falling for the same mistakes women made over and over again. She was believing in the wrong man instead of cutting loose, knowing she deserved someone better.

"There was a time when you wanted to make a difference on this earth," she said. "Money wasn't everything and you wanted to be different from your father, but look at you. You couldn't be more like him if you tried." Daphne had moved back to the desk, facing off against her ex-boyfriend, her fingertips resting lightly on the smooth varnish. "Has he accepted you yet? Is he proud? Have you finally received his love?"

Evander watched, intrigued. The man who had been so removed, emotionless and determined shrank in his fine leather chair. She had him by the ball sack and all she had to do was twist and he'd be a crumpled heap on the floor, wailing for his mama.

Evander had definitely underestimated Daphne.

She turned, pausing again in the doorway. "You're a crappy father, Mistral, just like your dad was. I thought you'd want to be different from him in that regard, but I suppose I was wrong."

With that parting shot, she brushed by Evander, the contact making the hairs on his arm stand up. He grinned at the stunned-looking Mistral, then followed Daphne back down on the elevator and out into the street. She may have just picked a fight or she may have put the man in his place. But either way, Daphne's stock had definitely gone up.

"I think I fell in love back there," he said, helping her into his truck.

"Oh, Evander. You did not." She gave him a dry look.

"No, really. Sexiest thing I've ever seen." He held up his hand as though taking a vow.

She blushed. "That wasn't my best side playing him like that."

Maybe not, but it was still dead sexy and revealed just how powerful she could be when she got out of her own way.

# Chapter Twelve

*"Can we go to the island?"* Tigger asked, tugging on her mother's arm. They'd barely made it in the door and the kid was all over her as if they'd been separated for weeks rather than hours.

"What island?" Evander asked. The idea of going somewhere again was exhausting. He wasn't a wimp, but he could use a low-key evening after strutting about in the lion's den with Daphne poking at the snarling beast. He'd had way too much time on the way back to imagine all the ways Mistral could react to her little showdown today. Everything from the good to the bad to the very ugly.

"The cottage," Daphne clarified, brushing a mess of curls out of her face. She looked worn-out, and her usual hurried, brisk movements were methodical as she pulled off her sandals. He steadied her with a hand on her elbow, knowing she needed more than he was offering.

"So? Can we go?" Tigger bounced alongside her mother, and Kyle raised his eyebrows hopefully to Evander. Daphne looked at him as well, deferring the decision. She was going to defer to him on going to the family cottage, but not on going to see the man who could possibly be in charge of having someone attack her with a Hummer? Because while everyone kept pointing to Aaron Bloomwood, the fact of the matter was the man had been working for Mistral, whether he'd ordered the attacks or not. And although Evander hadn't pegged the wishy-washy, weak Mistral as a mastermind, he knew better than to underestimate someone who was scared and easily influenced by others.

"How's Mom?" Evander asked his brother, putting off answering the girl.

"Fine. So? Can we go?" Brick asked. "I've heard all about this magnificent island."

"Why don't you and Tigger go see what you can rustle up for supper, and Daphne and I'll talk about it."

Evander felt fatherly, shocked at how comfortable it was. Then again, Tigger seemed to have a knack for weaving her way into people's hearts, making them feel as though she was theirs.

"That kid is something, isn't she?" He took Daphne's light sweater and hung it on a hook at the door. "So? What's the island about?"

"It's where our cottage is. We go for supper picnics there fairly often."

"You like picnics, don't you?"

"Who doesn't?"

He could think of a few people. Namely those who felt exposed dining out in the middle of nowhere when they had lives to protect.

"You want to go to the island?" he asked, unsure whether Daphne wanted him to be the bad guy and say no to Tigger, or if she was leaving the final call to him due to safety concerns.

She shrugged, a spark of something in her eyes.

She wanted to go.

Of course.

Evander thought back to the short visit he'd had to Nymph Island when he'd been helping Daphne's sister Hailey and her movie star boyfriend, Finian, escape the paparazzi last month.

The island had been dark and remote, with crappy cell service. The building had been run-down and nowhere near secure. And if memory served, it was right across the water from Rubicore's island.

"I don't think your cottage is a safe place to go right now," he said, aware he was crossing his arms.

Daphne placed her hands on her hips, and he could tell by the set of her jaw and the way she was chewing her bottom lip that she was fighting the urge to argue with him. Her life had changed a lot since he'd come into it, and he was beginning to resent the way she held it against him, as if it was his own doing.

"It's a place where I can think," she said.

"They tried to run you off the road, and you practically launched grenades at Mistral today." Evander's temper started to rise. People like Daphne were their own worst enemies. They took control, but over the wrong things. "Do you trust me or not?"

"Trust has nothing to do with this."

"You're not trusting my advice nor my authority."

"Authority?" Her head took a dangerous tilt, and if he had been a smarter man he would have shut up and run. But there was a reason why he was a hired gun and not working in a skyscraper like Mistral. He never shut up. He never ran. It made him good at what he did.

He took a step closer, knowing he was encroaching in her personal space and that she found his size threatening. He would never hurt her, but his number one job was to keep her safe, not become her best friend or give her warm fuzzies.

"Authority?" she repeated.

"Yeah, you have a problem with that?"

"Oh, you are just too much."

Knowing it was a mistake, he bent his head down so his lips

were flush with hers. She tasted like raspberry lip gloss and something comforting. Her eyes drifted shut and when he moved away, breaking the kiss, he had a moment to revel in her unguarded, sweet and innocently beautiful self.

She was the epitome of everything the war had taken from him, and he stepped back, feeling as though he had been hit hard in the chest by a shock wave. She was life and he was falling for her. Hard.

"Are you okay?" Her voice was soft, her touch on his arm more firm.

He was a man. He could get through this. It was just a kiss.

But he needed distance. A distraction. Something to keep him preoccupied.

He opened his mouth and said, "Let's go to the island."

DAPHNE STOOD IN THE front entry of Florence's home and blinked furiously, scrambling to get her bearings. That was some kiss. Again.

He kept doing that.

But this time it was him who looked completely off-kilter afterward.

Head tucked down, Evander strode down the hall with his slight, distinctive limp, disappearing into the kitchen, where Brick and Tigger where hooting with laughter as they worked up dinner plans.

He'd kissed her. Then said they were going to the island.

Which was odd, seeing as she knew he didn't want to take her there for fear that without his million doodads he couldn't keep them safe.

While in Toronto she's seen a lighter side of Evander. One that smiled, and it looked good on him. Unfortunately, he'd seen and liked a side of herself that was awful.

Again, she'd failed in trying to take action. She'd been pushy and mean to Mistral in an attempt to coerce him into working with her and her sisters. She'd said unkind, hurtful things. She'd been the type of woman she hated. And Evander had loved it.

She needed to go to Nymph Island and think. But Evander had made it clear he was willing to die in order to keep her and Tigger safe. That wasn't something she could take lightly, and she feared going to the island would put him in a dangerous position.

In the sitting room she ran the island plan by Florence, half hoping she'd say no. The woman caught Daphne's hands in her own, giving her a steady gaze that reminded her so much of Evander. "Are you okay, dear?"

"Fine. Where did Tigger take off to?"

"She's in the kitchen with Kyle. There's so much life and happiness in that child. You're doing a wonderful job."

Daphne jolted, not expecting the compliment. It felt as though she spent her days trying to keep up with her daughter more than actually guiding and shaping her into someone or something specific. There was very little to take credit for other than a bit of passed-down genetics.

She sat heavily beside Florence, thinking. What kind of parents did Tigger have in her life? A father who destroyed the environment for money and essentially wanted nothing to do with her, and a mother who was cruel to him in hopes of getting him to do things her way.

Maybe letting go of Nymph Island would be for the best. Rubicore and their developments were the future, not old cottages that were lucky to be still standing. Daphne was exhausting herself, trying to make people care about preserving Canada's heritage and environment.

Tigger bounded into the room and Daphne held in a sigh. She didn't have the energy to deal with the girl. Just listening to her natter away at Florence made her want to cry from exhaustion. Being a single mother was all she'd ever known, but the past several days of having support had been eye-opening in regards to how tiring it really was. Especially while trying to keep from getting killed.

She'd always envied how her friends were able to slip off to book club or dance lessons or simply go for a walk on their own. She knew she was lucky that her sisters would step in and take her daughter here and there, so Daphne could get a small reprieve for a few hours. Sometimes all she needed was thirty minutes to herself. Thirty minutes of uninterrupted thoughts, even though the small break often left her feeling guilty. She knew needing that time didn't make her less of a good mother, but it still made her feel that way.

Evander stood over her and she looked up, feeling impossibly small.

"Let's go."

"Are you sure?"

"Yes."

"Really?" Hope bubbled up within her.

"Really."

"We should pack a supper," she said, too exhausted to move.

"Already done. Coming, Mom?"

"I'd love to."

Evander packed everyone into Daphne's repaired van and took the keys. "Mind if I drive? You look beat."

Tears threatened to brim in Daphne's eyes and she nodded, climbing into the back. She didn't know where he'd had her van fixed, how much it cost or even how he'd arranged to get it back to the house. Right now she was just happy not have to do anything but go along for the ride.

Evander nudged her awake in the marina parking lot. Everyone else was already heading down to the dock, and they needed her and the boat key.

"You okay?"

"You were wrong," Daphne said. "I take action in my life. I do things. I organize protests and influence people about the environment." Man, that was an exhausting endeavor. What would it be like when she worked for Environment Canada? More of the same, only every day and not on her terms? It sounded like a sure path to burnout. "I don't let others do everything for me, Evander. I let you fix my van, and I listen when you boss me around about safety stuff now, but that's different. I'm always trying to do what's best for my daughter, as well as ensure we have enough. It's not an easy balance. Today, when I tried to be the person you wanted, I was a bitch, and I didn't like it."

He sat in the captain's chair in the van's middle row, angled back so he could look at her.

"Okay."

"Okay?" she asked.

He seemed thoughtful for a moment. "Maybe I was wrong. I got a charge out of seeing you kick Mistral in the proverbial nads today, but you're right. It's not you." He rubbed the side of his face where the scars were, and she wondered what he was thinking. "That wasn't the peace talk you had in mind."

"So now what?" She shivered, worried she'd made things worse with her trip today instead of better.

"We restrategize."

"Yeah?"

"Yeah." He held out his hand to help her out of her seat, but didn't pull her up yet. "I need to learn how to get out of the way and trust you and your slow-and-steady instincts. You need to do this your way and I need to stop interfering and simply be there to help keep you safe." He swallowed hard, showing her it had been difficult for him to tell her he'd been wrong. She leaned forward, awkwardly hugging him in the cramped space.

"Thank you, Evander. You're a real man, you know that?"

His eyes clouded briefly, then without a word, he nodded, drawing her out of the van and down to where everyone was waiting for them.

At the cottage, Tristen's boat was tied up at the dock, and Daphne sighed, knowing that on top of everything, she didn't have the energy to deal with Melanie tonight.

Her sister and Tristen came down the shaded path hand in hand, and Daphne worried they might be interrupting something.

"I'm surprised you let them out of Fort Knox," Tristen said to Evander, shaking his hand. Although he said it with a grin to show he was kidding, Daphne could see tension return to her big bodyguard. It had slowly begun to creep up on him the closer they got to the island, and now it was back in full force.

"We have a picnic," Kyle said, holding up the basket. "We brought way too much food and I'm sure there's enough for everyone."

"Sixth sense," said Florence, tapping her temple with a finger. "I knew there'd be more people."

"We won't be staying long," Melanie said, and Daphne knew it was a lie even before Tristan shot her sister a look. They'd always been good about sharing the cottage, and any of the sisters were welcome at any time, even if the others were using the place. But now that they were all hooking up, Daphne wondered if she would be the odd woman out in a place that had always felt like home.

"Oh, do stay. I'd love to get to know Daphne's family better," Florence said, as introductions were made.

"Love your dress," Kyle said, eyeing Melanie's 1950s-style frock. "I can see the Summer women have a thing for femininity."

Daphne looked down at her T-shirt dress, then over at her daughter, who was in her usual flounces.

"I'm special," Tigger said.

"You sure are," Florence said, giving her a pat.

Daphne frowned at Tigger. She'd been saying the odd, uncharacteristic thing lately. About not causing a fuss, about being special, and something about cycles or circles.

"I suppose we should go up?" Daphne asked, waving the picnic basket toward the path.

They all made their way up to the cottage, Florence taking the ancient lift so she wouldn't have to deal with the steep hill. On the veranda, Daphne began unloading the picnic on the outdoor dining table as Tristan and Melanie brought more chairs. Evander helped his mother out of the lift and joined Daphne.

"Where's Tigger?" he asked.

"Probably making a fairy house."

"Where?"

"Out there somewhere," she said, waving vaguely toward the underbrush behind the cottage.

Evander tensed, the large muscles in his shoulders bunching up. He squeezed the bridge of his nose and said, "You know you're killing me here."

She gently touched his shoulder, wishing she could massage the tension out of him. "Expect the best."

"How am I supposed to do that when I've seen nothing but the worst?"

"Evander, what a thing to say," his mother scolded.

Daphne kept her attention on setting the table, carefully lining up the utensils beside the plates so she wouldn't cry. How could a man see the horrors she was certain Evander had and still keep on living? How had he not been crushed by the knowledge that the world was a dark and nasty place?

"It's okay," she said softly to Florence. "I'm sure he has. I'll call Tigger back in a minute."

"Did you hear I got heritage status for Nymph Island and Trixie Hollow?" said Melanie, her voice a bit too chipper. "They processed it so fast!"

"That's amazing," Daphne said.

"Going forward we should get more tax breaks due to it being a heritage site. As well, any fix ups we do here may be eligible for grants."

"That would be great."

"Tristen said he knows a guy who can redo our roof in the spring." Melanie whispered, checking to make sure the rest of the group was still around the veranda corner, inspecting the rotting steps. "He said he'd pay for it."

Daphne continued setting the table, feeling even more out of place on the island. All her sister's rich boyfriends were going to spruce up the place, squeezing her, the single mother, out even further. Finian had already fixed the chimney, and now Tristen had plans, as well.

That was assuming the cottage would still be theirs next year.

She sighed and listened to Melanie continue talking about the cottage. "I still haven't figured out how Ada, our great-grandmother, came to own the cottage, though. Christophe—the curator at the Port Carling museum—you met him last year at the antiques show? Anyway, he's trying to find a connection with the cottage's name. You know, combine the names Ada and Stewart Baker to get Adaker?"

Daphne nodded, having heard something about this from Hailey the other day.

"So, I think if I could find out more about that and their relationship, then I could really get the public interested in some sort of heritage claim for Heritage Row. I still feel I'm still missing something major. Like it's right there and I just can't see it."

Daphne made a noncommittal sound as her sister paused to look out over the trees and water to the island across the way, where a few old cottages from the past era still remained.

Silence stretched between them. There was only one more thing for the two of them to discuss. Daphne met her sister's eye and they both looked away.

"How did it go with Mistral?" Melanie asked quietly.

She shrugged. "Time will tell."

"We don't have a lot of that."

Daphne rearranged a few last things on the table. "I think we're about ready to eat. I'll go call Tigger."

Everyone sat, with the exception of Evander, who waited for Daphne to come back with Tigger. When he saw them step onto the veranda, his shoulders relaxed. He helped them into their chairs, then took a seat beside Daphne.

"Have you ever considered yoga?" she asked, as he kept his gaze moving. Always checking for security breaches.

His mother unsuccessfully held back a chortle.

"JTF 2 men do not do downward dog." Evander gave Daphne a look that could have melted steel. She began laughing. It started low in her belly and worked its way up until it was exploding out of her in a way that shook the table. Tigger started in beside her, and soon everyone except Evander was laughing.

The look on his face was priceless, and before long she was

wheezing from the effort of laughing so hard. She wiped the tears from her eyes, and said, "Oh, honey. You know we love you."

Evander's expression twisted.

She leaned over and pulled his large shoulders toward her in a half hug. "Has nobody ever told you they love you?" She knew she was probably playing with fire—well, more like a flamethrower filled with jet fuel—but she couldn't resist poking at his serious side.

"No," he said, his voice not wavering one iota.

"Aw." She gave him an extra squeeze before releasing him.

"Now that's simply not true," said his mother. She folded her napkin carefully beside her plate and gave her son The Eye.

Daphne felt someone move behind her, and turned to see her daughter bouncing up beside Evander. Stretching, the girl reached up and wrapped her arms around his thick neck. She gave him a light kiss on the cheek and said, "I love you, Evander."

Melanie gave a happy sigh and Daphne watched the man's reaction. He was struggling with something, but she couldn't identify what it was. All she knew was that he needed more hugs and kisses as well as love in his life.

As soon as the last fork rested on an empty plate to signal the meal was finished, Evander stood to clear the table. Daphne worried she'd pushed things too far with her joking. He wasn't a regular guy, and he'd been through things she couldn't possibly imagine, and had the scars as proof.

She caught up with him in the kitchen, where he was shoving paper napkins into the small garbage can under the sink. His shoulders were bunched, his movements quick and jerky.

Carefully, Daphne came up behind him and slid her hands around his waist, joining them at his belly button. He jumped, his body rigid. She rested her head against his back, listening to his heart race under the skin, through his rib cage and a pile of muscle.

"I'm sorry if I teased you too much. I hope you didn't think I was making light of what you've done."

Evander didn't move, resembling an animal caught in the sights of a hunter. Not moving, not willing to be seen.

Finally, he said, "It's okay. Most people are afraid to tease me."

"Aw. But you're not scary."

"Yes, I am."

She laughed against his broad back, feeling as though she was hugging a bear, and his body gradually softened under her. He braced himself against the counter with his hands, not slipping from her embrace.

"Daphne, if you knew the things I've done."

"I have a child out of wedlock. I get not being perfect."

"It's not that." He turned, breaking her tight grasp as though it was nothing more than a thin thread binding him. "This is different."

"I don't care. I know who you are now. Here. In this moment."

She wasn't sure what she was saying, but it felt as though she was fighting for him. For them. For a chance that he would let himself live again.

That was the problem. He wasn't allowing himself to live and that's all she wanted—him. Alive. With her. Living and laughing their way through life. Together.

IT WAS A GOOD THING she'd got Evander off Nymph Island when she did. Four generations in the Summer family line had fallen in love there, and she was *not* falling for Evander. But things had gotten sketchy a few hours ago.

Tossing herself onto her side, Daphne pulled the thin blanket up under her chin and stared at the sliver of moonlight peeking through the gap between the wall and the curtain of Florence's guest room. How long until this was all resolved and she could go home?

Today hadn't been as productive as she'd hoped, with Mistral becoming defensive rather than open as he'd been over the phone. She'd gone in strong, thinking he was in line with her suggestions, but he'd pulled back.

Maybe she needed to be more like Maya and show up with a whole plan. A business plan.

Kicking her legs off the bed, Daphne sat up and grabbed her phone off the tall, antique nightstand.

"Hey, hope I'm not calling too late," she said to Maya.

"It's okay, Connor and I were just… Never mind."

Didn't destiny get it? Daphne was the one who needed someone, not her strong sisters. If anyone needed a man to lean on sometimes, it was her.

No, positive thinking only. She would find someone. Eventually.

Evander.

She laughed at herself. There was no way. She was tired and stressed and he was a steady, comforting presence, that was all. They were too dissimilar. She wanted someone in her life right now only because she was feeling vulnerable and lonely. It was just getting to her. The hopes. The stress.

The amazing way Evander was with Tigger. Another reason she shouldn't feel lonely: she had her daughter. But Daphne wanted a relationship with a man. She wanted family. Love. More kids. Stability. A father for Tigger.

Someone to take over when she was too exhausted to see straight.

"Hey, you okay?" Maya asked, breaking into her thoughts.

"I'm just…" She trailed off with a sigh, unsure what to say.
"Yeah."

Her sister got it. Maybe not all of it, but she got it enough that Daphne felt a bit less lonely.

"Can I come over?" Maya asked. "I feel like I haven't seen you in forever."

It was late, but she didn't think that Florence or Evander would mind her having company.

"Sure." Daphne made certain her sister had the address, then clicked off the phone.

Pausing outside Evander's door, she considered knocking, but his light was off. The man needed his rest. He'd be okay with her sister coming over if Daphne was careful about the alarm. Besides, if she saw him sleeping in nothing but his boxers, she wasn't sure she'd be able to hold back. There was a side to him she wanted to learn more about. An intimate side. She had a feeling being Evander's woman would be a very sacred, safe place, and the temptation to try and see if she could fit into that role was all too strong.

A half hour later, her sister and their old friend Polly Pollard were at the front door, and Daphne hoped she remembered the right sequence for turning off the security system so it wouldn't go off and wake the sleeping household.

"I bumped into Polly at the gas station," Maya said as she stepped into the house. "Will Evander have a fit if she comes in, too?"

"Nah, but fair warning…he might try to microchip you, Polly." She winked at the woman to show she was kidding.

Their old friend looked sad and tired, but gave a small smile. She'd married for money rather than love, and it looked as though it was starting to take a toll. Daphne remembered her as a vibrant woman, but lately whenever she saw her she seemed worn down by the world.

"Things are pretty rough?" Polly asked Daphne.

"Kind of, but I'm in good hands here. How are your fundraisers going? Oh, and thanks for getting our mom to go for a mammogram during your breast cancer awareness campaign." If Daphne could rouse people for environmental reasons, Polly could rouse people for a cause. And they were both looking exhausted. Go figure.

"They're going well, thank you for asking." Polly held her hands loosely intertwined in front of her. She was polite and slightly distant. Not at all the girl they'd grown up with.

"Are you okay?" Daphne asked.

"Hey, can we make some margaritas or something?" Maya asked.

Daphne ignored her sister and watched Polly. The woman's eyes brimmed with tears and Daphne pulled her into her arms, squeezing her tight.

"I filed for divorce." Polly sniffed.

"I'm so sorry to hear that."

"I'm not," she said, straightening up. She adjusted the hem of her trim white shorts, pulling herself together. "It was time. No love lost and all that."

"What happened?" Maya asked bluntly.

Daphne flashed her a look. Sometimes her sister got so wrapped up in what she wanted and where she was going in life that she forgot other people might be feeling tender about things.

"I married for money, and not for love," Polly said. "I got tired of it. That about sums it up."

"Oh," Maya said, apparently satisfied with the answer. "Speaking of money, I think I may have managed to convince Connor that I should get some sort of finder's fee for the dental device, as well as an advance on the project we're working on—better than asking him for a loan for the cottage taxes, right? So, it looks like I may be able to foot my portion of the bill. How are you doing?"

"Less than a week left to pay it off," Daphne said gloomily. She led the women into the sitting room where Florence knitted during the day. Daphne was going to be the one who lost the cottage for them all. And not just for them, but for future generations. For Tigger.

The women took seats and Daphne wondered if it would be okay to raid the de la Fosses' liquor cabinet. She'd contributed with groceries, but just barely, due to Evander persistence that they were guests—something his mother agreed with. Getting up, Daphne went into the adjoining kitchen and began digging around. She found a bottle of spiced rum and a few cans of cola in the back of the fridge. Carrying them back into the sitting room, she set the girls up with drinks, figuring that tomorrow she could replace what they consumed.

"Do you think we should take the offer?" Maya asked. She turned to Polly and explained, "The cottage is going to be sold in a tax sale in less than a week if we don't come up with several years' worth of back taxes. We've all decided we'll pay our own equal share, which is a lot. But we've had an offer to purchase."

"Trixie Hollow?" Polly said, a note of loss lowering her voice. "What a shame. Is there anything I can do?"

Polly, when she and Hailey had been close, had spent tons of time at the cottage and likely had good memories of the place, as well. It seemed as though everyone who went there did.

"I don't think so, but thanks," Daphne said, topping up the woman's glass.

"You're that far away from making the payment?" Maya asked.

"Depends if I sell more paintings. It's been doing okay, but I'm still short."

"This sucks."

"Tell me about it."

"What about Simone?" Polly asked. She adjusted her string of pearls and watched the sisters as though unsure whether she was overstepping her bounds.

"You think she'd like to buy a painting?" The honorary Summer sister and boutique owner was expanding into making her own dresses to sell, and it was unlikely that she had money laying around to buy a painting. Not that Daphne charged a lot, but still. She knew money was tight for their friend, too.

"I meant have a show in her boutique, like she did for Hailey last month. That was a success, right?" Polly said.

"Hot diggety," Daphne said. "Why didn't I think of that?"

"That's what I do. Solve problems." Polly tipped back her glass, emptying it.

"How's Melanie doing? Does she have her portion?" Daphne asked, hoping she wouldn't be the only sister who couldn't come up with the money on her own.

"She's been selling her antiques—again," Maya said. "Did you hear what Tristen did?"

Both women nodded. The fact that Tristen had gone out and accidentally bought all the antiques Melanie had put up for sale, and then given them to her as a gift, had become a bit of a legend.

"Add in that tax break she got through the reassessment and I think she's pretty much covered."

"I'm going to be the one who loses it, aren't I?" Daphne moaned.

"Well, as Mom says, it's up to destiny," Maya said with a cackle as she finished her drink.

"I need a sugar daddy," Daphne decided with a laugh.

"Somehow, I can't see you with one of those," Maya said.

"You're currently living with the billionaire," Polly stated.

"Obviously the grapevine has things incredibly inaccurate, as usual," Daphne said, taking a sip of the spiced rum.

"This is Evander de la Fosse's house, right?" Polly said, her glass languidly hanging in her hand as she gazed around the old home, taking in the high ceilings and crown molding.

"It's his mother's. I doubt he's a billionaire in disguise."

"Quite the contrary." Polly leaned forward, elbows on knees, voice dropping to secret-revealing tones. "He used to protect princes. He'd take high-risk jobs protecting royalty over in the Middle East when everything went haywire. He even got himself blown up."

If anyone knew about billionaires, it was Polly, but she was reaching a bit with this one.

"Getting yourself blown up for being a macho man doesn't make you a billionaire," Daphne said.

"If you do it enough times, it does."

"What do you mean?" Daphne's heart thundered at the thought of Evander allowing himself to get blown up over and over again as a way to accumulate wealth.

"You get paid fairly well to protect a prince whose life is in danger. If you get blown up, you not only get a bonus added to that danger pay, but some sort of insurance gives you extra money, as well. It's ridiculous, really. But only the elite can get a job like that. Shake out his couch and see if you can find an extra grand or two. Or, you know. Use your feminine wiles."

"I am not going to sleep with Evander in order to save the cottage."

Polly and Maya focused on something behind Daphne.

"He's in the doorway, isn't he?"

They both nodded silently, eyes round.

"You're drinking my rum and have uninvited guests that you didn't run past me," Evander said, his voice low and unimpressed.

"Sorry, I'll buy you a new bottle. And you know Maya." Daphne stood, turning to Polly, wishing Evander wasn't looking so unwelcoming. "This is Polly Pollard. She's an old friend. I didn't want to wake you and I reset the alarm."

"Nice to meet you," Evander said, stepping into the room to shake her hand before returning to his spot in the doorway.

"You as well," Polly said. "I apologize for drinking your rum." She lifted her glass, looking demure, harmless, and a little bit on the prowl.

Evander said nothing, just stared at Daphne. She felt as though she didn't know this man all of a sudden. "Are you really a billionaire?" she asked, cringing as the words came out of her mouth. It didn't make a difference if he was, and now he'd think it did.

He turned on his heel. "Make sure you reset the alarm when you go to bed."

Daphne eased back onto the sofa and faced the two women. Polly appeared thoughtful, while Maya looked as though she was trying to hold in the giggles.

"Good on you," Maya said. "Just like the rest of us. Shacked up with billionaires, but not asking for a dime. What on earth is wrong with us?" She let out a snort of laughter. "We should be like Great-Grandma Ada and milk it." She laughed again. "There's some awesome irony in here somewhere, isn't there?"

"I guess we're too independent for our own good," Daphne said with a sigh.

"Are you talking about the Ada who started Camp Adaker?" Polly asked.

"The one and only."

"She really did know how to work an angle." Polly lifted her glass in a toast. "Cheers to that."

Maya and Daphne frowned at her.

"Well, I mean she got that cottage given to her when she was pregnant with your grandmother."

"What?" Maya perched on the edge of her armchair. "What? Say that again?"

"It was a baby-keep-quiet gift. He was married. Stewart Baker—the father."

"How do you know that?" Maya leaned forward.

"I work on the camp board."

"And?"

Polly was dishing out fresh info and acting as though it was common knowledge. How did she know more about their family than they did, when Melanie had been digging for weeks?

"Ada and Stewart started the camp."

"Okay. Melanie's suspected that. The camp name part," Maya said.

"It's an epic love story." Polly cozied into her spot, looking dreamy. "Ada and Stewart used to camp out on Nymph Island when they were working on the summer camp. The island became their lover's nook."

"Destiny causes people to fall in love when they're on the island," Maya said, eyes focused on something in the distance.

"Yeah, but how do you know the cottage was a keep-quiet gift?" Daphne asked.

Polly shrugged. "There are old letters at the camp. It's all written between the lines."

"Letters?" Daphne pressed.

"Holy crap. You have to tell Melanie." Maya smacked the table with the flat of her hands. "That's so crazy that they're still around and we had no clue."

Daphne pinched her lower lip between her fingers, thinking. She turned to Maya. "Could you help me create a business plan for an ecotourism retreat?"

"A business plan?"

"Ecotourism is a fun idea," Polly said. "My brother, Josh, the firefighter?" She waited for them to nod in recognition. "He just went on one of those trips. It was expensive, but he said it was incredible."

"I think Mistral could turn Baby Horseshoe Island into a nature retreat instead of the resort he has planned," Daphne said. "He could obey environmental laws and guidelines, as well as have his development. He would have to scale back some of the things he's planning to do, but it could be an ecofriendly retreat. A blending of tourism, development, and environmental awareness. But I need to be able to show him the bottom line."

"It's kind of late to make changes to his plans, isn't it?" Maya asked.

A feeling of defeat washed over Daphne. For some reason she wanted to show Evander that she could do this, more than she wanted Mistral to make changes to his plans—as beneficial as that would be.

She emptied her glass. "I have to try."

# Chapter Thirteen

*Evander barely recognized* Daphne as she sat in the meeting room wearing Maya's borrowed pantsuit. Her hair was swept up into what Tigger had informed him was a French twist. Even though the outfit was a bit big, she looked professional and businesslike. Not at all like the woman he had come to know and feel comfortable with. When people began acting unlike themselves, it was time to worry. That was when the unexpected happened.

He figured after their chat in the van the night before last that she would go back to Miss Take-It-As-It-Comes, instead of trying to be the hard-nosed bitch. But here he was, on his toes again. At least before calling this morning's meeting she'd given him enough of a heads-up that he'd been able to phone Austin Smith, the paparazzi, to create a diversion so they could leave the house in peace. The man, true to his word, had created a buzz that had all the lurking reporters sprinting away from the house, cameras waving so he, Daphne, and Tigger could sneak off to Port Carling to meet with Mistral.

Again.

Evander took up his post at the door of the library's basement meeting room as Daphne greeted Mistral by handing him a stapled bundle of papers.

Maya sat beside Daphne, her lips white from the effort of keeping them pinned shut and not sharing all her business know-how. Outside the room, Tyrone was caring for Tigger, as Kyle had stayed behind to take their mother to her radiation appointment.

Mistral's new hired gun, Leif, leaned back in his chair.

Daphne began outlining the business plan she'd been working on with Maya since the night of the cottage picnic. A plan for an eco-retreat on Baby Horseshoe Island, rather than the monstrosity Mistral had planned.

Evander figured it was a case of being at least a year too late, but admired Daphne's determination, as most people would have given up, then always wondered if they could have made a difference.

Mistral shifted, looking uncomfortable. "I appreciate you going through the bother to put something together, but we're so far into the development that changing plans now could really set us back. Plus, the cost alone…"

Evander had to give it to him, the man at least looked apologetic.

"I understand that," Daphne said softly as she pushed a sheet of paper across the table toward him. "That is why Maya and I came up with this."

Mistral held a finger over the graph, his attention on Daphne. "What is this?"

"Money." She slid a bullet-point list toward him. "And this is how to change direction without losing any. Basically, you're simplifying what you already have planned. So it will actually cut your construction costs. You can make these changes, do it under budget and still open on the scheduled date a year and a half from now. You'll be offering fewer services to your clients, which will lessen your overhead. As well, you'll be offering things you don't have to build or maintain, such as birds and other wildlife, and the peace and quiet of nature. In essence, build less, charge the same."

Mistral leaned back, leaving the graphs on the table.

"Ecotourism isn't a cheap vacation," Maya blurted out. Hands clasped, she glanced at Daphne, then added, "We know you already have plans for the island, but the problem is that at the rate you're running into compliance issues, you're never going to get it built."

Mistral opened his mouth to argue, his face red. Evander took a step closer to the table, arms loose at his side, ready to act.

Maya continued, "I know you've got several agencies hot on your tail, so let's be honest. Things haven't been going easy for you. You're losing money waiting for permits and plans to get pushed through, and the issue with the municipality not following permit protocols is not cool. Nobody's going to back down on that fight." She leveled the man with a steely look and Daphne shifted uncomfortably. Evander didn't blame her. Maya was pretty darn direct. Painfully so.

"You can either carry on with your original plan and hope you don't go belly-up before you get through the delays, or you can give Daphne's idea a serious look. It has incredible merits and I believe she is ahead of the game in terms of trends in tourism."

Maya leaned back. "I honestly don't see how you could fail with this. In fact, Connor MacKenzie took a look at the plans last night, and if you don't do this, he will. You're lucky Daphne's given you first right of refusal."

Mistral's head tilted to the side. They had him.

The Summers had been underestimated again.

Maya stood, and a panicked look flashed across Daphne's face. Evander awaited his cue from her.

"I still don't see how changing my plan is going to allow me to come out financially ahead," Mistral stated. He tried to emulate

Maya's earlier posture by leaning back in his chair, as though he was the one in control. It was obvious the man wanted to learn more.

"Here on page six," Daphne said, pushing papers toward him.

"Read at your leisure," Maya said. "Daphne and I have another meeting to get to." She checked her watch. "If you want to work with us you'd better let us know soon, because we're pulling this off the table in four days."

"Four days?" Mistral began flipping pages and Leif scooted closer to the table to help him find whatever he might be looking for. "I'll have to ask my dad."

Pansy. The man didn't even run his own company? No wonder things were so screwed up.

"Don't forget that we own the rights to this resort plan," Maya said. "Don't try opening it elsewhere."

"I also made a list of the endangered species in the area," Daphne said. "It's something that could—"

Both Maya and Evander reached for her. They had Mistral where they wanted him. It was time to shut up.

"Everything you need to know is in the package," Maya said, pushing Daphne out the door. They left Mistral and Leif hunched over the papers.

Maya shut the door, and said, "I think that went well." She gave them a bright smile that reminded Evander of Daphne.

"Do you think he's interested?" Daphne asked, her hands twisted into a tangle.

"We'll hear from him soon enough," Maya said.

Daphne turned back to the door and Evander cringed, catching her hand. She didn't know when to let well enough alone, did she?

"What did you forget?" he asked.

"I just wanted to ask if he wants to see Tigger, since he's out here today."

Evander shook his head. "One thing at a time. Don't distract him." With a gentle hand on her shoulder, he moved her away from the door, wishing they had the kind of relationship where he could give her a hug.

Maya was watching, her lips pulled into a frown.

Maya would make a good soldier, with her determined, straight-forward approach, but Daphne had too much hope and too much heart. She'd make a lousy soldier, and for that reason it made Evander like her all the more.

Against his better judgment, he pulled her close, wrapping his arms loosely around her. She leaned in, resting her head against his chest. She trembled, making him think of a sapling in need of protection from the storm.

"I'll go round up Tigger." Maya hustled off, and Evander wished she'd come back. He was doing a sister's job right now. He should be rounding up the kid and she should be doing the mumbo-jumbo, loosey-goosey, huggy thing her sister needed. Not him.

He smoothed Daphne's hair, reveling in its straightness when bullied into a twist.

No, definitely not him.

He allowed himself to snuggle her closer.

Mistral and Leif left the room, Mistral not even looking their way, and Evander had to struggle not to go after the man. The way he'd dismissed Daphne during the meeting had bothered him. Daphne was right here, wanting Mistral in her incredible life, and the man couldn't even give a crap. He was taking everything for granted. His freedom. His life. Other people. Even ideas. What was the point of Evander getting blown up and going to war if goofs like Mistral could sit around in offices and ignore great ideas?

This was a democracy. There was freedom to try new things. To live a real and full life. But what was the point of it all if you were going to live by tight rules and never try stepping out of the box? If you were never going to even bother to try and stretch a little?

Evander hadn't gone to war so men like Mistral could ignore their awesome kids. The man didn't have an inkling of what he was missing. If Mistral could see what Evander saw, he'd be a changed man. But Evander didn't have the power to open the man's eyes. Mistral had to make the choice to open them and to see everything he had.

Sometimes, Evander had discovered, you had to go across the world and get shot at in order to understand just how precious one small child growing up in Canada could be.

He shook his head. Mistral didn't even know what section of the dictionary to find the word *lucky* let alone where to see it in his own life.

"Mistral doesn't realize what he is missing," Evander said, hugging Daphne tighter as Tigger came bounding over, her face lit up like sunshine. "He has absolutely no idea."


DAPHNE HAD BEEN MOPING around his mother's house all day and Evander had finally figured out a decent way to distract her. Yesterday's meeting with Mistral had torn a piece out of her, and he could only imagine how she must feel—rejected at every turn.

He peeked into the sitting room, where his mother was patiently teaching Tigger to knit, her usually smooth ball of yarn a mess of tangles at their feet. Kyle was trying to sort it out without getting attacked by Rudolph, laughing whenever the cat pounced. Radiation had gone okay, but Evander could see how tired Florence was.

He climbed the stairs to the bedrooms and found Daphne sitting cross-legged on her bed, her head in her hands, elbows on knees. She was wearing uncharacteristic jeans and a T-shirt, her feet bare.

Gripping the door frame above his head, Evander leaned his torso into the room. "Bored?"

He definitely was.

There hadn't been a hint of danger in almost a week. And the past few days of checking his monitors and security measures for breaches had become a tedious, mindless habit that was making him wonder if he was missing things because there was never anything to see.

Were the Summers finally safe? Oddly enough, Daphne hadn't asked to go back to her house other than to pick up a few things.

She turned to him, her eyes sad. "Just feeling sorry for myself."

"Isn't there a yoga meditation thing for that where you shove your butt in the air while sticking out your tongue?"

"Probably."

It occurred to Evander that he didn't know how to proceed from here. An eight-mile run usually helped him out of any funks, but he didn't think sending Daphne out was a wise idea. Not yet. Who knew if Aaron Bloomwood was still on the warpath, especially if he was indeed working for Mistral's father, who obviously ran Mistral. And if Mistral actually brought Daphne's new development idea to his father's attention, Evander could pretty much guarantee Aaron would do something stupid in order to preserve all he'd been trying to accomplish in making a name for himself within Rubicore and the planned development.

"So?" Evander said, not quite self-centered enough to walk away from the woman and her blues.

"So?" she replied.

"What's got you down?"

She let out a long sigh. "What doesn't?"

He let go of the door casing and sat down beside her on the bed, making the mattress dip so low she had to shift away from him in order to not fall against him. She smelled like sunshine.

"List the blues. It'll be like skeet shooting. You fire, I'll blast them."

He got a flicker of a smile. "For one, I'm stuck living in G.I. Joe's headquarters."

"Ouch." Of all the crappy things she had to choose from, and she picked that first? He'd actually believed they were doing pretty good at the cohabitation thing.

"I'm sorry. That came out wrong. I mean, the food is much better here than in the army, from what I've heard." She gave him a half smile that made him want to kiss her lips.

He shifted farther away.

She began listing more blues-causing grievances. "My ex wants nothing to do with our daughter. My sisters are in a battle with him. His partner tried to run me off the road and break into my home. His bodyguard would have shot me or something if you hadn't intervened." She shuddered and Evander eased closer in case she needed him. "My life has become an action movie. I don't even have the money to help with the cottage. My sisters are all going to be able to raise enough to not only save the place, but their billionaire boyfriends are going to fix it up. Meanwhile, I'm over here, about to lose the island for our family after a hundred years of ownership. All because poor Daphne the single mom is an irresponsible hippie with her head in the clouds, and doesn't understand money. What I understand about money is that there is never enough. No matter how much I budget or skimp or save or buy used."

"Are you looking for an ear? Or do you want me to argue those points and shoot them down?" Evander angled himself so he was facing her more fully. "First of all, I think you're doing a bang-up job of keeping those ducks in a row. Especially that bouncing one you've got going on. But Daphne, you can't control what others do and how they run their own lives. You can only change your own. But by doing so, sometimes we can change someone else's."

"I guess." She paused, running her hands through her hair. "I just wanted to prove that I could take control over my life and that I could make changes. And I can't." She met his eyes. "You were right."

Hearing her say that wasn't as rewarding as he'd thought it would be.

"You're in a tough spot right now and there aren't a lot of directions for you to maneuver. Don't judge yourself based on the ability to take charge over the past week and a half. You've tried a heck of a lot harder than most people would in your situation."

"Are you blowing sunshine?"

"You should know me better than that by now."

"Are you really a billionaire?"

The shock must've shown on his face, judging by her reaction. "Yeah," he said simply. "Pretty much."

Only a few dollars short and a lifetime too late to really enjoy it.

"I would never have figured. You carry it well."

"Was that a compliment?"

"You get so few that you don't recognize them?" She gave him a goofy smile and he could see that she was well on her way to a cheerful mood again. Back to the Daphne he had come to love.

"And," she said, holding up a finger in warning, "complaining about money is not me asking you to save me. I know you heard me, Maya, and Polly talking."

"You'd make a horrible gold digger, Daphne."

She sighed, shoulders drooping. "I know."

"Come." He stood and held out his hand. "I want to show you something hard."

She rolled her eyes with a groan. "I have no interest in touching your gun."

"Don't make this dirty."

She blushed in a way that made him grin inside as he led her out of the house.

DAPHNE SHOULD HAVE KNOWN.

Evander wanted to teach her kung fu. Or karate. Or jiu-jitsu. Some sort of martial art that was not created for aligning one's chi, but rather for killing someone with one's bare hands. The man was never going to understand her, was he?

Digging her bare toes into the soft grass of the sloping backyard, she put her hands on her hips and cocked her head to the side.

"Don't give me that look," Evander said.

"Which one?" She tipped her head to the other side. "The one where I am staring at you as though you are a crazy fool who knows nothing about me even after living elbow to elbow for six days? That one? Or maybe the one where you try to make me into a killer so I can be like you, the big army hero."

He took her down.

She didn't even see it coming. One moment she was giving him sass and the next moment she was flat on her back in the grass, the heavy weight of his body pushing into hers. She kind of liked it.

Even though the move was taught to him for reasons she was opposed to.

"I never said I was a hero." His breath was warm on her forehead. She could stay here awhile. He hadn't even hurt her, laying her out flat.

"Do that again. That was really cool."

"No."

She stuck out her tongue and he pulled her to standing. He maneuvered her hands so they were in front of her face, elbows pointed down. "We'll start with a few blocks."

"I want to take more action in my life, but not in a kung fu action movie way, Evander."

Then again, if she got a chance to hit Evander she probably wouldn't refuse. Yeah, yeah, she was a peace-loving person who believed in words before violence, but she figured she owed him one for the way he'd cramped her style and messed with her chi's alignment. And she hated to admit it, but this was kind of perking her up for some weird reason.

"Take out your frustrations on me," he said, beckoning her with his raised hands. He had them positioned as if he was going to chop through something.

She snorted. "I'm not going to hit you." He'd just block every hit she tried to make, which would lead to immense amounts of frustration.

She contemplated his face, the strength of his bones. She'd probably break her hand if she managed to land a hit. "Can you teach me how to wipe that grin off your face?" she asked.

"Which one?" he teased. "This one where I look at you as though you don't know me after living elbow to elbow for six days?" He gave her a wicked grin that stirred something fizzy deep in her belly. "You liked that one?"

She lunged at him and he caught her, spinning her around,

pushing her up against the trunk of a nearby birch. His breath was tantalizing on her bare neck and she leaned her head to the side, needing to feel his lips graze the tender skin.

Instead he stepped back, releasing her.

"I was having a very nice feel-sorry-for-myself session up there, you know."

"Beating something will fix you up."

Daphne rolled her eyes. Typical man.

Evander made dodging moves as though they were in a boxing ring, and she tried to hold her interest. The sunflowers along the back window were starting to open. Fall was coming. She was going to have to put Tigger into school soon. Would she have enough money to cover the requested back-to-school supplies? She hadn't registered Tigger in the local elementary, unsure why she'd dragged her feet. It was only kindergarten. She hadn't sent her daughter to optional junior kindergarten, figuring too much school would be hard on a bouncy girl like Tigger, even though it would have been cheaper than day care.

Evander's open hand whizzed by Daphne's ear as he faked a jab. Without thinking, she blocked him.

"Good, good!" he said encouragingly.

He threw another jab and she blocked that as well. She had that job interview with Environment Canada tomorrow morning. She'd never thought a nine-to-five position would hold appeal, but with her daughter starting school maybe it was a good answer. Financial stability. Benefits. Retirement package. She'd hadn't saved a nickel for retirement yet. She blocked another jab and yawned. She'd also need flexibility in her schedule. Would they be able to offer that?

But could she make a difference working for the government? She needed that sense of fulfillment in a job if she was going to be there full-time.

"Let's mix things up a bit," Evander said, backing off. Good. He was getting annoying.

Would Environment Canada allow her to take a grassroots approach? She supposed she could always quit if it didn't work out.

Evander did some sort of crazy move, dropping low on the lawn, one leg whipping out to knock her feet out from under her. She landed hard on her butt.

He paled and was over her in an instant. "Are you okay?"

She blinked up at him. This close, she saw the flecks of gold in his eyes that she'd forgotten about. He had nice eyes.

"Daphne?"

His concern was so genuine, her throat closed up. She rolled onto her left hip and stood, giving herself distance. Dusting herself off, she said, "I'm fine. I just wasn't expecting it."

"I'm sorry. You were just blocking everything and I…"

"I was what?"

"You were blocking me like you'd done this before. I figured it was time to step things up. What kind of training do you have?"

"Training?"

"Martial arts. Karate or something?"

"Tai chi. Yoga."

"Huh." He leaned back on his heels. "Maybe I should try yoga, after all. You're good."

The compliment was unexpected and Daphne felt herself blush.

"You went to this sort of Zen place," Evander was saying.

"I was thinking. Are we done? I'm going to get a sunburn. I didn't put on lotion."

Evander repositioned himself, taking on his typical shoulders-back, all-business body language. "I need to teach you self-defense."

"Why?"

"It's something I can do for you."

"Aren't you already doing enough?"

"What's that supposed to mean?"

"Fine." She threw up her hands. "Teach me how to kill someone. Put a dark hue on my aura."

"There's a positive energy associated with using your body to defend yourself. This is going to give you strength and power."

"Okay. Show me." She tipped up her chin, fighting to be positive. She always worked so hard to show the world a happy side, and it seemed as though Evander simply walked up and it all just drifted away as though it had never been there, revealing all her hurt and anger. The hurt and rejection she kept hidden inside. He always released it, and she hated feeling that way. It was out of control and it wasn't happiness. Those emotions were so dark and strong they could take over her life, destroy her. Her feet ate the ground between herself and Evander as she threw all her hurt and anger into her hands, thrusting them against his broad chest. He stumbled backward, his eyes wide.

To her surprise, he shoved back. She caught herself before she fell, and whirled on him, fists clenched and swinging. If he'd been a second slower, she would have hit him a good one right on the cheekbone. Instead, he blocked her and dropped into a ready position, legs bent in a crouch, arms out and ready to block her jab. She imitated his position, glad she was in jeans for once.

He wiggled his fingers at her as though to say, "Give it to me. Give me your best shot."

She knew she couldn't take him. She had nothing in her arsenal that could get through to a man as trained and as ready and aware as he was in this moment. The lawn stretched out behind him, birds chirped in the sky, a light breeze kissed her skin, and in front of her was a man as large as a grizzly bear, ready to take her down as soon as she moved.

She dropped her arms in defeat. This was her life right now. She couldn't move without being taken down. She could throw goodwill and ideas out there and they'd be swatted right back out of the sky again, as though someone was standing over her, swinging a giant flyswatter.

Tumbling into the grass, she held in a choking sob. Evander was wrapped around her in an instant, pulling her onto his lap. He held her so tight it was both confining and comforting. Soothing and painful.

It was perfect.

The sobs spilled out of her and his lips burned trails across her forehead, laying kiss after kiss as though paving a highway of sympathy across her skin.

She tipped her head up so the kisses would land lower on her face. The heat of his skin touching hers left tingles along her cheekbone, over the bridge of her nose, before curving around to her lips.

Their kisses turned greedy and hard, bruising skin as they tried to give away the pain in their souls. Her palms ran up his sides, untucking his perfectly ironed shirt. His skin was hot under her fingers, and she tracked over small ridges of scars as though they were a sandy lake bottom under her touch.

His hand ran up over her T-shirt, cupping her breast, and she sighed. It had been so long since anyone had touched her. Consumed her. Loved her.

Their kisses turned frantic as she straddled him, plucking at the buttons down his front. All thought left her mind for long glorious seconds. Her body tingled with anticipation and everywhere it touched Evander's she felt as though she was caving in to him. She wanted to be his, to be seen, to be felt.

Evander whispered something, his voice raw. She smiled against his mouth, pushing his shirt off his shoulders. It was caught on something. Her fingers stumbled across something hard. His gun.

She scrambled out of his lap, suddenly aware of what she was doing and with whom. He was her bodyguard. He was being paid to protect her. He was a wonderful man, but he'd made it clear that being together would cloud his judgment. She needed him clear-minded for her, for Tigger.

Chest heaving, she fell to the grass, staring at the handsome man who locked his eyes on hers, his gaze echoing what she wanted. What she needed. Echoing the lust. He felt it, too. The connection. It fizzed and sparked between them like wet Pop Rocks candy. Evander was like nothing she'd ever experienced. Not even Mistral.

He was the man she wanted, despite everything. Daphne Summer wanted Evander de la Fosse with everything she had.

# Chapter Fourteen

*Daphne walked slowly* and carefully down the old wood steps the led into the basement. She'd peeled herself off of Evander's smoking hot body on the lawn six hours ago and had spent the last six agonizing hours wanting him. Avoiding him. Six hours of trying to be good. And now she'd had enough.

She hadn't been in the basement before. It wasn't exactly off-limits, but hadn't been part of the welcome tour of the house.

She paused, doubting herself. Would getting involved with Evander put everyone at risk? Would it affect him? Maybe he'd changed his mind about getting involved with a client since nothing dangerous or scary had happened for almost an entire week.

Music and light flooded her way as she continued to creep down the old staircase, a hand trailing along the wall on either side. From her vantage point, the basement looked as though it had been finished. She paused at the bottom, then crossed the laminate floor, stopping in the doorway where the music was pumping from. The room was brightly lit, with mirrors along one wall. Foam exercise mats interlocked across the floor. The stereo played "Demons" by Imagine Dragons loudly enough that Evander, who was in a corner, didn't hear her clear her throat.

He was shirtless, with mounds of muscles rippling. Sweat

slicked his skin, making it shine under the lights. He was tanned, strong, healthy, and utterly irresistible.

The room was filled with exercise equipment, weight machines, and barbells so massive it seemed impossible that anyone should be able to lift them, let alone one man. Evander was pumping iron, doing biceps curls with weights that looked large enough to weigh down a member of the Mafia sent to go swim with the fishes. Watching Evander, Daphne wondered how he managed to not rip through shirts. He was compact and powerful.

His intense focus on his movements made her breath catch. She stood in the doorway, uncertain whether to proceed. The song changed to something dark with a lot of electric guitars, and Evander switched exercises without apparent thought. Setting down the barbells, he stepped to a machine and began doing weighted squats. The machine's round weights were larger than the tires on her minivan, and she wondered if Evander ever worried about being crushed.

When she figured his legs must be burning, he reached for a rope and began skipping. His arms crisscrossed in front of him over and over, picking up speed. She'd thought that Tigger was a good skipper, but Evander was light on his feet in a way that belied his size. The man was dangerous.

She stepped back, preparing to sneak away, feeling as though her intrusion had led to her seeing a side of Evander she wasn't quite prepared for. Her movement caught his eye and his intense focus was gone in a flash. He dropped the rope and came to her, a hint of primal aggression just below the surface despite his concerned look. She stepped back, a hand at her shirt collar.

"What's wrong?" he demanded.

"Nothing. Supper's ready."

He stared at her for a moment, and she knew he'd seen

through the lie. All week, his mother and brother had planned meals around his routine, and today was no different. He always said to go along without him if he wasn't ready in time. Daphne had intruded upon his space, crossed the line.

Evander watched her with those dark, brooding, probing eyes of his and she felt exposed. Around him, nothing ever stayed hidden.

"You're a crappy liar," he said, though his expression was kind, amused.

She moved her mouth, but no words could come out. He was so *masculine*. Large. His shoulders so broad, his waist so tapered, hips so narrow. He was so *man*. It made her hungry. And not for supper.

Slowly, as though it was just dawning on Evander that his body was holding her under its spell, he gave a hint of a knowing smile.

So few emotions ever made it to Evander's surface that Daphne felt similar to a blind woman seeking hints under her fingertips to find out what was going on with the man.

She wished it was her body making *him* speechless, throwing him off, making him be the one wanting more than he could have.

Without thinking, she reached out, placing her hands on either side of his sweaty face, bringing his lips down to hers. For all his strength, there wasn't a hint of resistance, and he made the move as easily and fluidly as though it was his idea.

Daphne slid her tongue inside his mouth, the warm sweetness overpowering her. There was something about Evander that felt right. Safe. Hers.

She pushed her body against his and his arms slowly came around her, cupping her in a way that felt as though a piece of what had always been missing was coming home at last. It felt as though this was the only place she was ever supposed to be.

Sighing against his mouth, she broke the kiss. Keeping her eyes closed, she savored the moment, tucking it away for later, when he would surely slip out of her life. The thundering of the music's bass echoed in her chest cavity, jumbling her irregular heartbeat in a way that felt like discord. Welcoming discord.

"What do you want, Daphne?"

"You."

"You know I can't do real life," he whispered, his voice anguished. "Relationships. Family. I can't be the man you need. The man you deserve."

"Try going with the flow to see what happens. You might surprise yourself." She teased a finger down his chest, loving the way it slid in one long glide, making her think of other things. More carnal things.

"You are the kind of woman men wait for," he said, removing her finger from where it had paused between his hot skin and the elastic of his workout shorts.

She sighed. That sounded really good, but it wasn't what she was looking for. She sagged against his body, wondering why he wouldn't just do what they obviously both wanted.

"Don't you want me?" she asked, hating the vulnerability in her voice.

"Want has nothing to do with this."

"Is it because I'm a mom?"

"Not in the way that you think."

"Why do men always have a problem with dating or screwing a mother?"

She could tell her language had caught him off guard. He ran his fingers through his hair, then gently rested a heavy hand on top of her head.

"Because mothers are special, Daphne. Sacred. You treat them with the honor and respect that they deserve. You only take them to your bed if you feel you can do their lives justice."

Great. Now she was going to bawl.

"Fine." She made her voice harsh, turning on her heel before stomping up every single step to the main level. She hoped he realized that respect and honor were not what she was looking for with him. She needed someone to hold her tight and tell her it would be okay. She needed someone strong enough to make her forget her problems and responsibilities for a few moments. Not one more man rejecting her.

Being together for a moment in time didn't have to be complicated. Because when it came to love, it was the simplest thing in the world, and she wasn't even asking for that.

EVANDER PARKED HIS TRUCK outside the government office for Daphne's job interview. He came around and let her out, holding his umbrella over her head. He should have brought two, but his mind was elsewhere. Pushing Daphne away when she was offering herself, no strings attached, last night had been one of the hardest things he'd ever had to do. Ever since, she'd been giving him the cold shoulder, which told him that, somehow, whether Daphne realized it or not, there would have been strings attached to a night of lovemaking. And those strings most likely would have been feelings. Deep, honest, true feelings.

"Happy birthday!" Tigger squealed to her mother before Evander closed the door.

"Good luck," he said to Daphne as she hustled into the building, ignoring the rain and leaving him standing under the umbrella.

Not for the first time, he wished he had something more to offer her. A woman such as Daphne deserved more than a one-night stand. Deserved a whole lot more than he could ever give her.

"We have to go bake her a cake while she's at her interview," Tigger announced when he climbed into the truck.

"We don't have time. Sorry, kiddo," Evander replied, watching through the large windows as Daphne was checked in by the building's security. It was refreshing to see someone intent on his job. "Hang on two secs. Stay here, doors locked."

He splashed across the sidewalk to the building, noting that the weather was similar to his mood. Bleak. His mother had scolded him when he'd pulled the dishes out of the dishwasher and slammed them the cupboards that morning. *Too loud. Take it easy. Don't forget to smile.*

Canadian summers were short and once again he'd been lulled into taking their beauty for granted. He dashed through the drizzle to the security guard, slipping him fifty bucks. "Keep an eye on that woman. She doesn't leave the building with anyone but me."

"And who are you? Her stalker?" the man asked, eyes narrowing with suspicion.

"Her bodyguard," he said simply. He handed him his business card. "Check with the police if you don't believe me."

He returned to the truck, Tigger picking up the cake thread of conversation as he settled back into the cab's dry warmth. "We could buy a cake. The bakery will put swirly writing on it."

"Yeah, okay." Evander glanced at the building, hesitant to drive away. He should be inside, waiting outside the interview room. His mother was at home, having a good day, Brick holding a meeting on the phone with some guys back at the office. The press hadn't followed Evander's truck today. Were things safe? Could he risk leaving to buy a cake?

Would he ever actually feel Daphne was safe?

Yeah, when she was permanently ensconced at his side.

So probably never.

"We need to have a party, too." Tigger was bouncing in place beside him as he pulled away from the building. "A *surprise* party. Mom's always wanted one."

"We don't have time to plan something like that."

"Hand me your phone." Tigger held out her palm. "I can call everyone and tell them to meet us at the house after Mom's interview."

The kid actually made it sound as though it was that simple. Buy a cake, invite people over. It was a party.

"What about decorations?" he asked.

The girl thought for approximately one nanosecond before saying, "There's a dollar store near the bakery."

"You have a solution for everything, don't you?"

"Yep."

If only his life was as easy as this kid made hers out to be. But maybe that was the beauty of childhood—things were simplified, black-and-white. No mazes full of shades of gray to get lost in.

"Tell you what, if you can convince my mother to hold a party at our house after the interview, then we will have a party."

Celebrating Daphne's birthday would be an easy way to show her that there were no hard feelings and that he still liked her. In fact, he liked her quite a lot. Too much.

But Daphne was a woman who could use someone caring for her, showing her she was loved. And while he couldn't show her in the way she wanted, he could show her in other ways, and his family could help.

"Can I have your phone?" Tigger asked.

"Even better," Evander said, as he hit the button on his steering wheel to connect his phone to the car's Bluetooth and speaker system. He said to the truck, "Call home."

Tigger, hands clasped in her lap, leaned forward. The sound of dialing and a phone ringing worked its way through the truck speakers.

His mother answered the phone and Evander said, "Hi, Mom, I have someone here who would like to ask you something." He raised his eyebrows at Tigger as he turned down the street to the bakery

"Granny Flo, can we have a birthday party at your house for my mom after her interview? Evander said we could buy her a cake and there is a dollar store where we can get decorations like balloons and streamers. She really wants a surprise party, so is it okay if we invite people over?" The girl paused to take a breath and Evander let out a chuckle.

"Today? In an hour?" asked his mother in surprise. He really hoped his mom was up for a party.

"Yes, please."

"You have such lovely manners, Tigger. Yes, of course you may have a party for your mother. That is a splendid idea. What do I need to do to help you out?"

Tigger looked at Evander thoughtfully, then froze, hands out as though someone was whispering something important in her ear. "No. We have to have the party at the cottage."

"It's raining, dear," Florence said.

"I know. But Mom and my aunts are about to lose it. Shh. They don't want me to know, so pretend you don't know the secret. Trixie Hollow is a special place. The party has to be there."

"Well, I suppose that's settled, then," his mother said, much to his surprise. "We're all waterproof, right, Evander?"

"We are," he admitted reluctantly. "Are you sure you'll be okay, Mom?" Having a few people over for cake was one thing, but trekking through the rain to an island was something else.

"Would you like me to make some punch?" Florence asked.

"Yes, please."

"You know what? I bet I have some balloons and streamers in the basement. I'll send Brick down to look. We'll try and decorate the cottage before you get there."

"Thank you," Tigger said crisply, ever the in-charge kiddo. Evander reached over and ruffled her hair. So little and yet so sure of herself. She had a good mom.

"How much time do we have?" Florence asked.

Tigger and Evander looked at each other.

"About an hour?" he said. "Plus travel time to get to the cottage. We'll send Hailey or someone over to pick you up."

"Thanks, Evander."

"Thank *you*, Mom." He ended the call and parked the truck in front of the bakery. "We're going to have to be very efficient, Tigger."

"That means getting things done really fast, right?"

"Yup."

They bought a cake, and while they waited for the baker to add swirly writing that said Happy Birthday, Daphne, the girl used his phone to call Daphne's sisters and mother, as well as a few family friends. By the time the cake was ready, Evander figured Tigger had invited approximately a dozen people. This girl got the idea of efficiency, that was for sure. When it was safe for Daphne and Tigger to move back into their own home he was certainly going to miss them and they ray of sunshine they brought to every challenge in their lives.

It felt right having them around, and he only wished he could offer them something to make them stay.


EVANDER RELAXED AS DAPHNE climbed into his truck, smiling. The warmth that had been there a few days ago had returned, and he hadn't realized how much it had bothered him having her upset and feeling rejected.

"How did it go?" he asked, pulling out onto the rainy street.

"The job sounds really interesting." She paused, biting her lower lip, her long lashes emphasizing the sparkle in her eyes. "Really good, actually."

Tigger was staring straight out the windshield, barely moving, barely blinking. The cake and snacks were hidden in what was likely becoming a soggy cardboard box in the truck's box, and he would have to drive carefully to ensure it didn't slide around. He nudged the girl who was sitting between him and Daphne and rolled his shoulders, trying to hint that she should loosen up so she didn't give away the surprise.

"When will you hear back?" he asked Daphne.

"I have it, if I want it." She stopped worrying her lip with her teeth and gave him a grin so huge he felt as though a shock wave from an explosion had hit him in the chest. He was left momentarily breathless and focused on keeping the truck in its lane. Across the heated cab he could catch waves of Daphne's gentle scent, could practically feel her touch, wild and electric, despite the space between them.

He needed to get his head on straight. Having her this close for this many days was starting to get to him.

"Are you going to take the job?" he asked.

"I think so. I told them I needed to think about it for a day. They offered me a signing bonus, though." The grin was back.

"Environment Canada? Wow, they must really love you."

"Yeah." He thought he saw a flash of sadness, but if he had it was long gone already. She looked like an entirely different person than she had only yesterday afternoon, when she'd collapsed in a fit of self-pity. The woman had some serious resiliency and was bouncing back already.

She probably wouldn't need him in her life much longer.

An ache started within him, spreading slowly like an acid burn. Deep and vicious.

"So?" Daphne asked Tigger. "What did you do while you were waiting for me?"

The girl's eyes grew round.

"We went to the grocery store and grabbed a few snacks. Tigger wanted to have a birthday picnic on the island. Is that okay? It's kind of rainy, though."

He glanced at Tigger, who was acting as though he'd just revealed the entire surprise.

"You actually left your post to get snacks?" Daphne laughed, bracing her hands on her thighs, the truck rocking with the familiar happy sound. "What on earth could ever pull you away from—" She stopped short, and he covered for her so Tigger wouldn't know the full reason they were staying with him.

"We needed snacks," he said simply. "Plus, I talked to the security guard." He felt the familiar worry creep up inside him. He *had* left her unprotected. A rookie mistake. This lull could very well be the quiet before the storm, and not the quiet before everything went back to normal and she no longer needed his services.

Unable to help himself, he asked, "Nothing suspicious happened while we were away?"

"Whew," she said. "I was wondering what had happened to the real Evander. And whatever you said to that security guard must have worked. He really didn't want me to leave, until I pointed out that you were waiting for me."

"It's my job," Evander said grumpily.

"I thought your job was saving the whales?" Tigger gave him a confused pout.

"I was teasing your mom. When you find a man who cares

about you, Tigger, he's going to want to make sure you stay safe all the time. It's what men do." Evander focused on the road that led down to the marina where the Summers kept their boat, cursing himself for making it sound as though he cared about Daphne. Which he did. Damn.

He wasn't supposed to get involved, and caring about her in the way he did was definitely involved. He was going to have to pull himself off the case, but who would take his place? Even with his objectivity compromised he still did a better job than most.

As he parked his truck he began to worry that something in the marina would give away the surprise. Familiar vehicles parked along the road. Stragglers trying to get to the island ahead of them. It was a workday, so how many people would be available to drop what they were doing and go to an impromptu party?

What if nobody came?

He glanced around for any reporters. Not even Austin today. Maybe they didn't like the rain.

He parked in the empty spot reserved for the Summers. "Hang on, I have an umbrella. Let me come around." He grabbed the damp umbrella out of the door's cubbyhole and, shaking it out, hurried around the truck. The marina was suspiciously quiet and Evander decided that surprise parties were not a good idea for a retired JTF 2 man. Everything in place seemed suspicious. He should see hints, shouldn't he? Extra vehicles? Boats scooting out of the harbor before being noticed by the birthday girl?

Holding the umbrella above the passenger side door, he helped Daphne and Tigger slide out of the truck.

Handing Daphne the umbrella, he grabbed the wet box from the back of the truck, letting the rain drip off him as he followed them to the old aluminum boat. Instead of stomping through puddles, Tigger walked somberly beside her mother.

"You're awfully quiet. Are you feeling all right?" Daphne paused on the dock to press a palm to her daughter's forehead, nearly catching Evander in the eye with the umbrella's points as he climbed into the boat. "You feel fine."

"Tigger," Evander asked, "can you help us launch the boat, please?"

The girl sprang to life, and before long they were all standing in the vessel's small overhang enclosure, trying to stay dry despite the wind and rain.

As they pulled between Daphne's island and Baby Horseshoe all was quiet. Other than a few extra boats parked across the way at the neighbor's, Nymph Island looked and sounded vacant, causing Evander a moment of doubt. From down here everything looked normal. No balloons. No streamers. No security guards trying to hide. His heart began picking up its pace and he worried that something had gone wrong, and most of all, that nobody had come for Daphne.

DAPHNE WALKED UP TO the cottage, the damp path silent under her feet. Fat raindrops fell off the leaves above, striking Evander's umbrella as she held it over her and Tigger. Her daughter was acting strange, which was unusual, as hanging out with Evander usually made her extra sparkly.

Daphne glanced back at Evander. His head was bowed, drops of rain sparkling in his hair as he cradled the soggy cardboard box of snacks. She felt a tug of fondness for the man, as well as something she couldn't quite identify. It was almost a possessive feeling. One of wanting to make him happy, to lift his sorrows and love him until he smiled.

She was going to miss him when they moved back to their own house. Who in her life would let her take the umbrella and carry the snacks through the rain to a dilapidated old cottage? Who else would take care of all the little things so she could worry about being a mother?

Daphne swiped at her damp eyes. She really needed to stop thinking about Evander or it was going to be even harder leaving him when this was all over. As it was, it would be difficult enough.

She thought back to her job interview. She was definitely going to accept Environment Canada's offer if it got her closer to a life like this, with fewer worries. It was ironic that the stability she'd mocked for years was what she now craved via a steady job. It was her own version of Evander. A constant, steady, reliable something to lean on that would take care of the details—which in her case would be the money side of things.

Taking this job would be a milestone in her life. One where she grew up and planned a bit more, so she didn't end up in a corner where she couldn't even pay the taxes on the cottage. It was time to join the rat race.

All she had left to figure out was Mistral.

No. It was her birthday. No thinking about a man who hadn't done a thing she'd wanted in the past six years. He was a waste of dreams and energy. It was time to let that hope go and move forward so she could find something better. Someone more deserving. Tigger was worth it and so was she.

Evander gripped her elbow, steering her around the broken step, third from the top.

She stopped halfway onto the veranda. The main room's glass door was open, leaving the cottage unsecured by the flimsy screen door that was closed over it. She turned to Evander, nearly knocking him with the umbrella. "The door's open."

Behind her, she heard the screen open and she turned to face the threat. She stepped back in surprise, arms flying out, crashing into the box in Evander's arms.

People flooded out of the cottage, shouting, "Surprise!"

Behind her, she could feel Evander fumbling with the box against her back. Something tumbled past her on its way to the floor. Cool, moist splatters hit the backs of her bare legs and she turned to see Evander looking as crushed as the birthday cake lying on the veranda floor.

Without thinking, she reached up and cupped his stubbly cheek. He leaned into her touch as though about to collapse from disappointment.

"It's okay," she said softly, "I'm sure we can salvage some of it." She glanced down at the ruined cake and began laughing. "We won't even have to cut it, we can just scoop it out onto plates." Her laughter took hold and she had to clutch her sides to support herself. Leave it to her to smash her own cake.

Hailey bent to fuss over the mess, and Maya, with an arm around Daphne, began laughing as well. Tigger dipped her finger into the creamy icing, licking it clean before aiming her finger at a broken sugar rose covered in splatters of pink icing. Melanie stopped her with a gentle hand. "No double dipping."

The sisters saved as much of the cake as they could while Daphne greeted a veranda crowded with people she loved. Her environmental protest buddies. Her sisters' boyfriends. Her mother and her friends. Even new friends such as Evander, Kyle, and Florence.

She turned to Evander. "Did you plan this?"

"The kid did." He tipped his head toward Tigger, who was licking the icing off a bag of chips that had been in with the cake.

"Oh, boy. When the sugar hits—look out."

"Don't worry about Tigger. I'll take care of her. You enjoy your party."

Daphne watched Evander for a moment, surprised at the affection in his body language. Had it always been there? Had she just been so determined to make him into her enemy that she hadn't noticed this sweet man inside the warrior? Or was it something new?

"Thank you, Evander."

He gave a small shrug as if to say it was nothing.

"For everything." She held his gaze for a long moment, to ensure he knew she meant more than just the party. More than just the offer to take care of a sugar-buzzed child.

He gave a bashful half smile before turning away.

Her love was changing the man. Or maybe he was changing her.

"Happy birthday, Daphne," said someone to her left.

"Mrs. Star!" Daphne gave the woman a cheek kiss and a hug. She hadn't seen her mother's old friend in ages. "How have you been?"

"Like a snowflake in a sudden storm. Great!" She leaned closer to confide, "I've been winning several bets against my sister Elsie in Blueberry Springs lately. She owes me twenty bucks now. Although I may have to go to that little mountain town and collect it from her. You know how she is."

"I heard about your bet over Hailey and Finian."

Agnes Kowski, another friend of her mother's, joined them, pushing her walker up close to Daphne's toes. "I can't believe you ruined the cake."

While her mother never complained about the food at the nursing home, Mrs. Kowski, her neighbor, certainly made up for it by complaining double.

"Now, now," Catherine said, from her position in a nearby wicker chair. "At least it isn't red icing, and the girls managed to save most of it. I'll make sure you get a slice."

"The cake they serve at the home is a disgrace," declared Agnes.

Daphne took a seat beside her mother as Hailey handed her a piece of smashed cake, ensuring that Mrs. Kowski got a slice, as well.

"We opted not to sing Happy Birthday. Is that okay?" Hailey asked Daphne.

"I tried to convince her you wouldn't mind blowing out candles on a broken cake," Finian said.

Daphne assured them it was fine. Having a room full of people she loved meant so much more than a perfect cake.

"I told you so," Hailey said to her boyfriend as they went to serve more cake.

Shawn McNeil, an environmentalist friend, handed Daphne a small wrapped gift.

"Oh, Shawn. You didn't have to get me anything."

He looked bashful. "I've had it for a while. I heard your birthday was coming."

Evander stood off to the side, watching, not eating.

"Do you want cake?" Daphne offered her piece to him, but he shook his head and smiled, his eyes doing their typical flick around the area for potential dangers. The veranda's perimeter was dotted with men she figured were the security agents the boyfriends had shadowing her sisters.

What a complete mess she'd made of things. Hopefully, next year would be better. Hopefully, she'd grow up with her new job and quit messing things up for others.

Daphne set the cake down and carefully unwrapped the gift. She held up three six-inch-wide slabs of wood, slices from a tree showing the growth rings. She glanced up at Shawn. "These are wonderful, thank you."

The man ran a hand through his longish hair. "They're heat

pads. Like big coasters." He took them from her grasp and laid them out on the coffee table in front of her. With gangly, awkward moves he snatched plates of cake from bystanders, setting them on top of the short stumps. He stood back. "See? But you put hot stuff on them."

Daphne smiled. The gifts were so Shawn, who was training as an arborist. "They're wonderful, thank you."

He gave a smile and his body relaxed. "Yeah? You like them?"

She nodded.

Connor, who had been standing nearby, eating cake, said to Shawn, "Knock any trees down lately?" His voice with was without humor, and Daphne could tell that he still wasn't over last month's incident that had endangered Tigger. Shawn had been taking down some trees, as well as testing some of the bigger ones for rot, and despite his precautions, one of them had fallen too close to Tigger. If it hadn't been for Connor, there would have been a funeral. Daphne's gut clenched at the thought of what could have happened, and her fingers gripped her plate. Forcing herself to relax, she looked up to see Evander watching her.

"What happened?" he asked, coming to her side.

"No, nothing."

"What did he do?" Evander's neck was strung tight, veins popping as he fought for control. Fists bunched, he whirled to face Shawn. "What did you do?"

Shawn backed up so quickly he tripped over the coffee table and went sprawling, sending cake and tea crashing to the floor.

"Oh, dear," Florence said, surveying the mess. "Evander, honey, please go get a dustpan."

Daphne jumped up, not liking the way he was pulling Shawn to his feet. "What did you do to Daphne and Tigger?" Evander demanded.

Connor stepped in. "No harm, no foul. Tigger interfered with some safeties."

"Connor saved her from a falling tree," Maya said, giving her fiancé's arm a squeeze, her engagement ring sparkling in the late afternoon sun streaming through the rain clouds.

"Mom! A rainbow!" Tigger came bouncing over, her eyes lit up, pink icing smeared around her mouth like clown makeup. "Come see! Come see! Come see!" She hauled on Daphne's hand until she had no choice but to follow.

She glanced over her shoulder to where Evander was still burning holes into Shawn with his eyes. Then, with a short nod, Evander glanced around the gathered group to ensure all was okay, before heading to the kitchen.

Dutifully, Daphne admired the rainbow until Tigger was satisfied. As she chatted with friends, she watched Evander host. He ensured his mother had all she needed, while he moved in and out of the kitchen with fresh pots of tea, juice boxes, and dirty dishes. All he needed was a frilly apron. Daphne smiled, loving to see the domestic side of the big burly man. He was constantly surprising her in ways that made her smile.

"Someone has a crush," Simone said, sidling up beside Daphne as the group drifted away to talk to Melanie.

"On who?" Daphne asked her old friend.

"Your bodyguard. It's very Whitney Houston of you."

Daphne let out a bark of laughter, and Evander glanced her way, his shoulders loosening when he realized all was okay.

"You're blushing," Simone teased. "Please tell me you've brought that hunk of man to the island several times in the past week and a half."

"Not on your life. I am not letting destiny get her hands on that one."

"Why not?"

"Because we're total opposites." *Liar.* At first, she'd believed it, but the more she got to know him, the more she discovered that they were more alike than different.

Simone gave her a smile that suggested she didn't believe her for one second. "I'm going to go find me a hunk and get you to bring us here to see if the island's magic works on honorary Summer sisters."

Daphne laughed.

"There's nothing to lose. Oh, speaking of nothing to lose, when did you want to have a show of your paintings in my boutique?" She rubbed her hands eagerly. "I can't wait to premiere Daphne Summer."

"Can you hold a show tomorrow so I can make a few grand by Friday?"

"Tax deadline?"

"Yeah."

"Unfortunately I'm just finishing up a show, but in September I could."

Daphne sighed. Once she started her new job she probably wouldn't have time for painting. Not while balancing being a mother, too.

Why did it seem as though any time one good thing came into her life, she had to let go of something else?

Tigger bounded over, trailing a string of balloons, and dropped to the floor, grabbing Simone tight around the ankles before shoving her shoulder behind the woman's knees, toppling her.

Daphne reached out for Simone, who caught herself against the veranda railing.

"Tigger! What on earth was that?" Daphne scolded. "Enough sweets. You know what sugar does to you."

"Evander taught me that!" Tigger chirped loudly.

A few feet away, Evander smiled with pride.

"What's he going to do next? Teach you how to fire a gun?" Daphne muttered.

"He says I'm too young and you have to say yes first. Can I? I'm not that small anymore. I get to go to kindergarten next month."

Across the veranda, Evander bent over to allow Mrs. Kowski to whisper in his ear while she pointed at Tristen.

"No guns. Are you okay, Simone?" Daphne asked.

"Oh, yeah. Fine. Good one, kiddo."

"Don't do that again," Daphne told her daughter.

"But now Rigby doesn't pick on me at the babysitter's anymore," Tigger said, looking pleased with herself.

"I imagine if you used that move on him he found out pretty darn quick who he was dealing with," Simone said. "But a nonviolent takedown? Love it. That'll serve you well in life, little ninja."

"Rigby didn't even see it coming," Tigger said, bouncing in place.

Evander was laughing with Mrs. Kowski now, and Daphne frowned. She didn't realize the woman knew how to laugh. He was turning everything in Daphne's life upside down, and right now, she wasn't sure how that made her feel.

"You keep telling me to solve everything with love, light, and forgiveness," Tigger said. "And sometimes understanding. But Evander taught me how to get even." She smacked her small fist into her waiting palm and narrowed her eyes before cruising the room for more goodies.

Daphne shut her eyes, unsure whether to be mad at Evander or relieved that he'd helped her daughter in what had hopefully been a not-too-violent takedown. Drawing a deep breath, Daphne reeled herself in. It wasn't as though he'd taught her how to give the boy a knock-out punch. It could have been worse, and if she was honest with herself, there'd been times where she'd lain awake at night, worried that her sweet daughter would be taken advantage of or forced to do something she didn't want to. She didn't believe in violence, but she did believe in self-defense.

Therefore, upside down was good. Evander was good.

"Tristen Bell," Melanie said in a strong, loud voice.

The party grew quiet and Tristen, licking his lips uncertainly, pushed his way out of the cluster of people he was talking to, his teenaged daughter, Dot, looking concerned.

"Yes, Melanie?"

Melanie, eyes teary, dropped on one knee. Daphne's heart constricted as the women around her let out happy sighs.

"Will you marry me, Tristen?"

The man was across the veranda in a heartbeat, pulling Daphne's sister to her feet in order to kiss her thoroughly.

"That must be a yes," Simone whispered to Daphne, smoothing her form-fitting dress. "I tell ya, you've got to get me in on this cottage action."

Daphne snorted, feeling oddly alone despite the crowd gathered in her honor. Forcing a smile, she joined the cluster congratulating the couple.

With the hubbub still going on, she went to stand in a corner with a cup of tea from Evander, and watched Tigger's antics. First her daughter hit up her grandmother for more sugar—but Catherine knew better. Then she moved on to her next mark, like a druggie in need of a fix. Daphne caught Evander eyeing the girl from the edge of the crowd. He had a slice of cake and was eating while he watched, not missing a thing. His wistful smile grew as Tigger worked the crowd, and Daphne found herself wondering what Evander was wishing for.

Then his back straightened and the window she'd been peeking through shuttered closed, blocking off the real man behind the bodyguard persona. His attention flickered over his checkpoints with practice precision and she wondered if he ever truly relaxed. If he'd ever marry. If he'd ever know love like her sisters Melanie and Maya did with their fiancés, and Hailey with her boyfriend.

It was sad to think that a man who had begun to mean so much to her couldn't enjoy the small things most took for granted.

## Chapter Fifteen

*Daphne, exhausted and* happy, ushered guests into the rowboats Connor and Tristen were using to shuttle guests across the strait to the Fredericksons' dock, where most of them had moored their boats to avoid ruining the surprise. The word was that Evander and Tigger had pulled together this surprise party with less than an hour's notice.

When the majority of the partyers had been seen off, she went up to the cottage, where Evander was trying to get Tigger to eat a slice of cheese in hopes that it would absorb some of the sugar running like cocaine through her veins. He looked exhausted and Daphne couldn't help but feel pleased that he was the one dealing with the sugar rush that he'd all but pooh-poohed the other day.

Out on the veranda, Maya prepped the lift to take Florence down to the dock where Kyle was already waiting for her, then it would take their mother.

"It was such a pleasure meeting you," Florence said, taking Catherine's hand in her own to give it a squeeze as they said goodbye. "Your daughter is such a fine artist. I hope she continues painting."

"Thank you," Catherine said.

Maya helped Florence into the lift, before heading down the path to help Kyle in case the lift's old latching mechanism needed the special Summer touch—a tap with a hammer or large stone—in order to open.

"He sure is good with Tigger," Catherine said to Daphne, as the little girl's laughter rolled out of the kitchen.

Daphne tucked her sweater tighter around herself. "He is."

"He's become like a father figure for her. Will you stay in touch with him?"

"I hope so." The truth was, with Evander around everything was easier in her life. She should be melting down, but instead she was growing and changing. And laughing.

"Are you still hoping Mistral will step up as a dad?" her mother asked.

At her ex's name, a flash of anger rocketed through Daphne. Mistral wasn't strong enough to be the father figure Tigger needed. He didn't have the strength of morals or the ability to do what was right in the face of differing opinions. She'd kidded herself for years, but now with Evander in her life she could see just how wrong a fit Mistral was.

She'd expected too much from him and had thought his words would make up for his lack of action.

How was it that this broken billionaire in disguise, an ex-military bodyguard, could be the man that she wanted and needed?

*Wanted and needed?* Had she lost her mind? It was this island, wreaking havoc on her heart. She didn't love Evander. She couldn't.

She gave her head a shake and asked her mother, "How did you manage to raise all four of us after dad died?"

"Like you, I rolled with the punches, one day at a time." Her mom gave her a secret smile. "And sometimes I secretly fantasized about the day when the house would be empty and nobody would have any pressing demands on me. But don't tell your sisters. They wouldn't understand."

Daphne smiled. She'd had a few of those days herself. At the same time, she would pull those wishes back so fast. She didn't want to wish away her days with her daughter, who was already growing so fast, but it was still hard. There was always more she could do to be a better mother, a better person. She could be a better cook. Keep a cleaner house. Be more focused and diligent at work. Listen more attentively when her daughter told her stories about her day. The list could go on and on.

Catherine rubbed Daphne's arm. "You're doing a fine job."

"Thanks." The sound of Evander's laughter boomed across the veranda and Daphne paused. Laughter. Evander. That may have been the first time she'd ever heard him laugh. A real, true laugh. And she'd missed it.

"He's really good with her, isn't he?" Catherine said, smiling.

"Surprisingly, yes."

"Why surprising?"

"Because he carries a gun and he's all…manly."

Her mother laughed. "That is the most ridiculous reason I've ever heard for a man not being good with kids."

"I know. He just surprises me, is all."

"You know, you used to laugh all the time and today you were laughing more again. If living with this man helps you with that, go with it."

The laughing had felt good. Really good. And she knew a big part of finding that joy again had to do with Evander.

"Are you suggesting I should shack up with him?" Daphne asked.

"It's obvious the two of you care for each other."

"As friends, Mom."

She was turning into such a liar when it came to Evander. She cared for him as more than a friend, but that didn't make it easier to accept or any less scary.

What if she got involved with him and he got hurt? What would that do to her? To Tigger?

"Make sure you take those blinders off before it's too late."

"I know, but it's scary. It's not just me in a relationship. Tigger is, too."

Catherine laid a warm hand over hers. "I completely understand."

"Did you ever date after Dad?" Daphne asked, not remembering her ever going out on dates as a widow.

"No. Sometimes the one you get on the first try is The One and nobody else can compare. But in your case, I think destiny brought you even better seconds, if you know what I mean." Her mom gave her a wink as Maya came up the steps to help her into the lift.

"Your taxi awaits," Maya said, bowing as she gestured to the now vacant device. "Good thing I didn't let Connor talk me into letting him ride this thing during his stay last month or he'd have broken it and where would we be today?"

"Probably riding a new lift, knowing him," their mother laughed. "He so likes to help out, doesn't he? Oh, and remind me to thank him for fixing the screen door. I keep forgetting to mention it."

"Okay," Maya replied.

Evander joined them on the veranda.

"It was lovely meeting you, Evander," said Catherine. "And thank you so much for all you're doing for my girls." She reached out and gave him a weak hug, her stroke-affected side hanging limp. He gave her a gentle, tender hug in return, and Daphne's eyes filled with tears.

"It's truly my pleasure, Mrs. Summer," he said, his voice a quiet rumble.

The affectionate note in his voice made Daphne itch. Her mother had to be wrong. She herself had to be wrong. She and Evander couldn't care for each other in that way. It was too scary. Too big. Too real. It was all just adrenaline and the way he was so kind that made her think she wanted him sometimes. He was a sexy man, that was all. Not her type. He didn't want to be with her. They would never make it.

"You okay?" Evander asked, lightly touching her elbow. Electricity shot up her arm and she flinched.

"Fine." She pushed past him, helping settle her mother in the lift, even though Maya was already there. She needed to get away from Evander, from everything running through her mind like wildfire.

She wanted Evander so bad it scared the daylights out of her.

"Mistral is not the man you need in your life," Catherine whispered, her expression serious. "Open your eyes to what you've got before you let it go."

Daphne squeezed them shut.

"I agree," Maya murmured.

Daphne closed the lift's gate, allowing Maya to take over. She needed to climb to the top of the island, sit on a rock and think. But when she turned back to the veranda she saw that Evander had Tigger riding high on his shoulders. Her daughter was laughing down at him, patting the top of his head as he beamed up at her. They looked just like the family she'd always dreamed of having.

But they were the family she could never have, because Evander had made it clear he was not cut out for real life. And having kids and a family was as real life as you got.

He rolled Tigger off his shoulders and the girl came bounding over to her. She wasn't going to get that thinking space, was she?

"Mom, brains and beauty won't buy you everything. You should marry for money."

"What?" Daphne looked at Evander, who shrugged.

"I am a sweet and quiet girl and I promise to not cause a stir."

"A stir about what?" Who had her daughter been talking to today?

"Mistral—Dad—said if I want to stop the circle I have to step out of it."

"What circle?" Angry heat spread through Daphne.

"He said I can be someone special."

Evander's face was red, his fists clenched, jaw tight. He looked as though he was holding back a deluge of anger, just as she was.

Daphne dropped to her knees. "Mistral's not your father."

Tigger's face scrunched in confusion.

"I mean, he is. But he—a dad shouldn't…" She looked to Evander for help.

He scooped up the girl. "I happen to think you're already somebody special." He leaned over to give Daphne a peck on her cheek. "And I think your mom has the power to change the world. Do you understand how amazing that is, Tigger? Because secretly, I hope you cause a really big stir every day for the rest of your entire life." He gave the girl a kiss on the cheek, then lowered her carefully to the ground.

And in that small action, Daphne lost her grip and fell in love with the man she had sincerely hoped to resist.

DAPHNE WAS STORMING DOWN the rickety old stairs of the veranda and Evander worried she would fall through the third step from the top, which was rotting through. He quickly scooped Tigger up onto his shoulders and followed Daphne down to the dock. A bee had definitely zipped into her bonnet with Tigger's talk of being special, and he worried she was going to leave the island without them.

Maya, Florence, Kyle, and Catherine were on the dock and looked startled at the trio's abrupt arrival.

"Is everything okay?" Catherine asked.

Voices drifted across the water and Daphne stormed to the end of the dock. Untying the rowboat that was bobbing there, she climbed in. If she was rowing, she wasn't planning to go far. Which meant she was going across to the other island. To enemy territory.

Evander passed Tigger to Maya and, ignoring Catherine's questions, climbed into the wobbly boat at the last second, nearly falling into the water as Daphne started pulling the boat with surprising speed and strength across the calm strait. The rain had let up, but the air was cool and damp, and moving through it felt like moving through a rain cloud.

"Dare I ask where we're going?" Evander said.

Daphne didn't reply, but climbed out on the opposite shore, yanking the bow upon land even before he jump out of the boat. She was out of breath from the brisk row, and was panting as he followed her through the trees.

"Daphne, are you okay?"

"I'm going to settle this once and for all."

He had a feeling things were about to get crazy. He patted his side, ensuring his concealed handgun was still with him, then flexed his calf to check on his knife.

She was moving fast and he had to jog lightly to keep up.

She bounded up to an old cottage, where he could hear deep voices discussing something. Daphne flung open the door, heading inside. Evander followed, quickly taking in the room. It was an open concept cottage like Trixie Hollow, with a main room that had several doors leading off it. A fireplace covered half the opposite wall; screened doors and windows were at their backs. Were the doors ahead dead-end bedrooms? How many viable exits were there?

The men in the room were recovering from the shock of having uninvited guests barge in. Evander quickly identified Mistral, a gray-haired man who was Mistral's father, Aaron Bloomwood, and the third, less active Rubicore owner, Jim Hanna. The new bodyguard, Leif, had drawn his weapon, as did Evander.

As the screen door slammed shut behind him, a man who rivaled Evander's size came out of one of the side rooms. He looked dark and mean. Mario La Toya, Aaron's right-hand man according to Tyrone's background checks. Interesting that he was finally showing up. Yet, no trigger-happy Ricardo. That alone was good, but that still didn't make this a friendly place to be—and especially with Daphne all fired up.

The room had a few tables he could turn up as protection. A few glasses half full of liquid. Flinging them would make a man flinch, buying Evander what could possibly be a lifesaving split second or two.

Daphne strode straight to Mistral, stopping a few feet from him. "It's done. You had your chance, and you blew it. Do not ever talk to our daughter again. Do not talk to me. And the offer to work together on the development has been withdrawn."

Mistral paled and his father smirked. Mistral's father. That would make him Tigger's grandfather. Evander hated him already.

"What did I do?" Mistral asked softly. He angled himself as though trying to shut out his father.

"Telling Tigger she could be special if she stepped out of the circle I'm in. You're already trying to divide us. I know you don't approve of how I live my life, but putting our daughter between us is a game ender. You will not get custody. Ever. You will drop your claim right now and never speak to either of us ever again."

Mistral glanced at his father, then whispered to Daphne, trying to draw her away from the men. Evander heard him say, "I told her she should step out of *my* circle. I want her to be able to break the cycle my family is in, where money and prestige are more important than love." He turned to his father, raising his voice. "The way the Johnson family lives is not healthy, and I want my daughter to have more than I did as a child. That's part of why I haven't stepped up, Daphne. She deserves more."

"You got that right," Evander said. He shut his mouth and stepped back, wishing he'd kept quiet. This wasn't his fight, but with Tigger involved, it felt as if it should be. The girl was like an RPG missile, her sole purpose to break through men's armored shields, as she'd done with him.

Mistral's father rolled his eyes. "Not this again. You had everything you could possibly want as a child, Mistral."

"I never had the one thing I truly wanted. I wanted and needed a father to be there for me."

"I was out earning a living."

"You never approved of me."

"And how have you shown me that you're worth approval?"

Evander wasn't a sappy, touchy-feely, let's-hug-it-out sort of guy, but the sudden urge to punch Mistral's father made his knuckles itch. He figured it was a good time to put his gun away, so he didn't shoot the man in the foot accidentally-on-purpose.

"And hiding a grandchild from me?" Mistral's father continued. "I had to learn about Kimberly from the press rather than my own son. You're lucky I didn't disown you."

Evander wasn't sure whether he should punch Mistral's father now or comfort Daphne, who looked as though someone had yanked a rug out from under her.

"I can't believe you lied to your own son," she whispered. She gave the man a look that could kill. Almost automatically, Evander covered his nuts. Daphne turned to address her ex. "Mistral, I guess your father never told you that he shooed me and Tigger off when we came to see you once. He knew exactly who we were."

Mistral paled, and Evander wasn't sure if the man figured he was busted in some old lies or whether he hadn't realized just how deeply his dad had been meddling with his life.

"Your father was afraid I'd convince you to give up the life he'd laid out for you," Daphne said.

Mistral ran his hands through his hair, shoulders hunched. Evander shook his head, wishing he could give the man enough strength to break free. If only for Daphne and Tigger's sake.

"She's a slutty liar!" Mistral's father shouted, pointing a finger at Daphne.

Evander broke the man's nose.

He hadn't even felt himself move. He was suddenly in front of him, his fist stinging, with the man bent over, blood gushing. Leif pulled Evander's arms back in a weak lock that he could break by sneezing.

"You son of a—" Mistral's father shouted as his men bustled around, trying to take control again.

"You don't talk to the mother of my child that way," Mistral said, stepping between his father and Daphne.

"Mistral," she said softly.

"No," he replied. "It's time I stood up to him. It's time I broke free and lived the life I want." He moved closer to Daphne and Evander broke Leif's grip, getting between the two, one hand resting lightly on his holstered gun in warning. He didn't like the way Mistral was changing his tune. Sure, it was probably good that he was standing up to his father after years of submission, but it wasn't enough.

"And what life do you want to live?" Daphne asked.

Evander got the feeling they were touching on a discussion they'd had years before.

"Anyone want to buy an island?" Mistral called, letting out a pained laugh.

"Don't you dare," commanded his father. "I bought you this island so you could finally break free of this woman and show her she no longer has a hold on you. You go through with this development plan. Show her who's boss. Show her who and what really runs this world."

"I don't know what runs this world, Dad, but I know it isn't you." Mistral positioned himself at Daphne's side. "I can't believe I've let you be in charge of my life for so long. I can't believe I didn't walk away when you hired Aaron after I fired him. I don't even know why he isn't in jail. And you want to know the truth, Dad? Your development plans are unoriginal crap. Who needs another exclusive resort that ruins the environment? Nobody. And certainly not me. This is my island and I'm asking you and everyone associated with you to leave. Effective immediately."

Mistral's father, a handkerchief held to his bleeding nose, gaped at him. Then his face turned as red as the blood still flowing from his nose as he realized he'd finally lost his son.

"So?" asked Evander. "Is that offer to buy the island still up for grabs?"

DAPHNE WAS ALREADY shoving the rowboat into the water by the time Evander caught up with her.

"You don't have to buy this island," she said, clambering into the boat. "I don't need another rich man trying to alter my life or trying to save me."

"You don't need anyone to save you, period."

She looked at him in surprise.

"I've never met anyone as strong as you are," he said.

She gave a snort, then stiffened. Evander turned to see what was bothering her. It was Mistral, looking half scared and half triumphant. He came to a stop on the shore, several feet away.

"I understand that you don't want me to have anything to do with Tigger, but I really like the way you're raising her," Mistral said. "She's an amazing person and is going to be a lot like you."

"Yeah, well, that's too bad for her, because it means you will never love her," Daphne said, standing tall in the wobbling boat. Evander steadied its bow, partly so she wouldn't have an embarrassing incident where the boat tipped her into the lake, and partly so she wouldn't leave without him.

"I did love you," Mistral said. "I still do—"

Evander thought he heard someone growl, but it didn't seem to be Daphne.

"I hope to find a way to be the father figure that Tigger so greatly needs," Mistral said.

"If she needs a father figure, I'll be that man," Evander said. "That's a right you have to earn by putting in the time and love, and you have a long way to go. Just because she shares half your genetic code does not make you a father."

"He's right," Daphne agreed. "Being a father is a right that has to be earned."

"You start at square one," Evander continued. "You have to start by earning Daphne's trust. Then Tigger's. You pay attention to that girl when Daphne goes out of her way to set up a meeting." He let go of the boat, stepping forward to poke the man's chest, furious at how he had overlooked his own child.

"You're right," Mistral said, and Evander tried to grant him the love and understanding Daphne was so good at, rather than hit him for being such a pushover. He knew that sometimes people got wounded bad enough it caused them to give up. For Mistral it had likely been one drawn-out emotional blow as a child as he'd sought love and approval. The man had taken a crippling hit and Evander recognized the hollowed-out result. The bravado might still be there, but there was little left but shell.

Mistral might get his spirit back one day, but it would be a long, difficult journey, and he was kidding himself if he thought he could get there with a few smooth words to his ex-girlfriend.

"Get some damn balls and grow up," Evander said. He turned to the boat, pushing it off with Daphne still inside. "We're done here."

DAPHNE STUMBLED OUT OF the rowboat, her legs weak from the waning adrenaline rush of the confrontation. She was shaky and less than exuberant.

What box of Pandora's had she opened in the middle of the Johnson family?

Evander steadied her with a hand at her elbow. He'd been a constant strength behind her for the past few days. The man she'd been seeking for years, but had always been looking in the wrong direction. And she couldn't have him.

Maya, standing on the edge of the dock, already had the mothers, Kyle, and Tigger loaded into Connor's boat, along with their bodyguard. Maya shared a look with Connor. "We have Tigger for the night," she said. "Connor has lots of security."

"I think everything is over," Daphne said, considering the possible effects of her trip to Baby Horseshoe.

Her sister tipped her head. "What do you mean?"

"Mistral told his father and his development plans to get off his island. I told Mistral he wasn't welcome in our life." She glanced at Tigger, her heart breaking as the girl frowned, obviously trying to connect the pieces and figure out the implications. "I know Mistral's words are often different than his actions, but I think this time…"

A warm hand caressed her shoulder and she leaned into it, knowing it was Evander looking out for her.

"Is it okay if Tigger goes?" she asked him. Daphne needed time to think. Time to sort everything out.

"Who've you got?" Evander asked Connor.

"Tyrone's on. The other guy's sick and Tyrone said something about you having his head if he sent in a newbie."

"Good. You'll all be fine, but don't let your guard down. Just in case." Evander nodded and the boat pulled out, leaving them alone at the cottage.

Daphne waved them out of sight, then collapsed into one of the Muskoka chairs. She picked at its flaking white paint. When she looked up, there was something in Evander's eyes that made her gut tug tight. A low hum of need and desire was sparking in his eyes, a feeling that was echoed in her veins.

She stood, her dress and sweater feeling like a barrier between them. She gently hooked her fingers in his, resting her head against his chest. "Thank you."

"You keep thanking me, but for what?"

"Everything. I couldn't have done any of this without you and your strength, and knowing that you were here… I always thought I was independent and could do things on my own, but you helped me do more. To stand up for myself and to have the courage to say to myself and to Mistral that he wasn't the right fit for us, no matter how much I wanted it for Tigger."

With his free hand, Evander thumbed away the wetness on her cheeks.

His voice was low and unsteady when he said, "I need to thank you, too."

Daphne smiled with uncertainty, quirking her head. What could he possibly need to thank her for? An ulcer caused by her inability to listen to him?

He scooped both of her hands into his, and in the cool damp air, his body heat felt welcoming and familiar. Like something she never wanted to leave.

"You showed me that real life is still possible."

"Of course it is," she said softly.

"You gave me hope that I may still be capable of participating in it. That maybe I could be more than an ex-warrior."

Her heart broke as she pulled her hands from his grip, cupping his face while trying to see inside him. How could a man like him ever make it through the things he'd been through? He had such a kind and caring soul that going to war should have torn him apart. She stroked the scars along the side of his face, ran a thumb along his eyebrow and another faint scar.

He rested his forehead against hers and she smiled. This was who they were, leaning against each other in ways the other didn't understand or even realize. While she had thought that he was saving her, she had possibly been saving him. Fixing his broken spirit.

"So? Ready for the real test to see if you're fixed?" she asked with a playful smile.

"I don't know," he said, with such seriousness she had to laugh.

"Is the glass half empty or half full?"

"You tell me." He angled his lips over hers, drawing her in for a sweet kiss. He broke the kiss, watching her with heavy eyes, waiting for her to reply.

"It's always been half-full in my books." She slid her arms up over his shoulders, toying with the short hairs on the nape of his neck. He was so tall and broad it made her feel sexy and small and feminine. Wonderful.

"I'm starting to see it that way, too."

"I knew I'd get to you."

"Who says it was you?"

"Because love conquers all."

"Yeah? And do you love me?" His voice was even, low.

"Yes," she said playfully, realizing it was true, and that it felt good to have it out in the open. To admit to it. To claim it.

He kissed her hard, nothing held back. His large hands, which had been covering her shoulders, slipped to her back, drawing her so close she could feel his anticipation through his cargo pants. Letting out a soft moan, Daphne went up on her tiptoes so their mouths would stop breaking apart because of their height difference. Evander cupped her buttocks, pulling her up his body in a move so slow and sensual that by the time her legs were wrapped around his waist she was ready to shed clothes and get down to business.

"Let's go somewhere more private," he said, and she'd never heard a man suggest anything better in all her life.

# Chapter Sixteen

*Daphne and Evander* lay entwined in her cottage bedroom. Sighing against his bare chest, she smiled.

Destiny had come through for her just under the wire, with a man she'd never have expected but who couldn't have been more perfect. And on her birthday, no less. He'd sneaked in like the trained man he was.

Resting her chin on a fist, she stared into his dark eyes. He tried to hold back a smile as he pushed a heavy hand through her curly hair, giving her tangles the most delicious tugs.

Being with Evander was like nothing she'd ever experienced. He was sweet and tender, yet insistent in all the ways a lover should be. He'd been almost bashful while undressing her in the small bedroom, yet reverent and sensual. He was the same man in the bedroom as outside of it. In control, caring and protective.

"You're beautiful," he said, his voice almost breaking. He swallowed hard and pulled her head against his chest, breathing her in.

He was struggling with something.

"Let go," she said, tipping her head up to meet him eye to eye. "I'll catch you."

"You already have."

"Then let it out."

He took a deep breath, then whispered, eyes shut tight, arms wrapped around her as though afraid she'd disappear with the words he spoke. "I love you, Daphne Summer. I love you so damned much it scares me more than being shot at."

She laughed, her body rocking against his. "Don't worry, I won't leave any holes."

"You'd better not." He pulled her closer so he could kiss her, the bedsheets tangled around them. "I said I would protect you so you can change the world, Daphne. That's a promise I intend to keep. In fact, I plan to talk to Finian, Connor, and Tristen to see if they'd like to go partners in a new venture I have planned."

"What's that?" She couldn't see the other men wanting to be bodyguards, but then Evander had given Mistral that focused look of his when he had an idea and was about to make it happen.

"This woman I know—" Evander said.

"Hey, no mentioning other women in the bedroom!"

He caught her hands as she pretended to fight him. "It's you! It's you!" He laughed, and she'd never heard anything better in all her life.

He settled her and continued, "If the four of us can get the island, then maybe you would be interested in creating a place that is relaxing, teaches people about the environment, preserves our heritage, and maybe creates a new legacy within your family for a little girl who has snuck her way into my life and heart."

"Are you talking about Baby Horseshoe Island?" Daphne sat up, not caring that her chest was exposed. Around him, it didn't matter what she wore, he would always see through it to the real Daphne. The one she hadn't felt strong enough to reveal to the world. To herself, even.

"It's going to take a lot of time." She had to take the job with Environment Canada, and needed to arrange for a signing bonus ASAP. It was Tuesday, and by Friday she had to have enough to pay the taxes on this place or it would be gone forever. Legacy ended.

"It will," he admitted.

"We both have jobs."

"True."

"I never really wanted to work behind a desk, though." She let out a sigh. She really wanted this. Badly. As soon as she had started telling Mistral the small dream all those years ago it had begun to feel real. And the hope was still there. The desire to make it happen.

The timing was off, though. She couldn't have the cottage *and* build this island retreat.

The men didn't even own the land yet.

But it felt so right. She couldn't imagine saying no.

*If the cottage is meant to stay with us, destiny will find a way.* Wasn't that what her mother always said?

Evander took her left hand, his large and warm around hers. "Will you be my partner?"

Although he was talking about the island, Daphne couldn't help but feel as though he was asking for more than that.

And for the second time that day, she followed her heart.

"Yes, Evander. I will be your partner in anything that comes our way, and especially this. That is a promise."

He smiled and swept her up into his arms. "How did I ever become so lucky to have you walk into my life?"

"You were special-ordered by destiny, sweetheart."

Now all she had to do was hope destiny could save the cottage, too.

EVANDER WAS AFRAID. Things were so good with Daphne. Unexpected and entirely frightening. In war he'd had moments of fear, but was never afraid. He knew what his odds were. The other men were there of their own accord, had made their own peace with the fact that they might not come out alive.

But this was different. Daphne had the power to destroy what war had never been able to touch.

And he could break something here more precious than anything he'd ever been responsible for.

But he loved her. With all his might, and the hope and brightness he saw on his horizon was something so exciting it nearly split him apart with the possibilities of what his future could be with Daphne at his side.

The past ten days had changed them both and that crushing weight that had been following him, pressing down hard on his chest, had lifted as though it had never been there.

He looked in the old cottage bathroom mirror and caught himself smiling. No, not smiling, grinning like a mad fool.

He was that man. That man in love who whistled everywhere he went, with a bounce in his step. He let out a chuckle at his turn in fate.

The Summer women said this place was enchanted, and for the first time, he believed. The force of love was something that could never be underestimated and he'd do everything in his power to nurture and protect it.

He lifted his face to the ceiling and whispered, "Thank you. Thank you for Daphne and a chance at living a real life."

# Chapter Seventeen

*Melanie burst onto the* veranda, her fiancé, Tristen, in tow, the last couple to arrive as they said goodbye to the cottage before heading down to the tax office. Snacks and a pitcher of margaritas were set out, but nobody was diving into them.

"Mr. Valos from the municipality got arrested."

The sisters and their men all whirled to gape at Melanie.

"He was taking money under the table."

"No!" exclaimed Maya in disbelief.

"Of course he was," Tristen said, slipping an arm around Melanie's waist.

"Thank goodness. One less jerk to worry about in your life," Evander said, cozying up behind Daphne to give her a kiss on the ear.

"You were worried about him?" she asked.

"Of course. He was part of the Aaron-Mistral mishap."

"And Aaron Bloomwood is up on charges, too," Melanie said.

"Mistral?" Daphne asked, and Evander's grip tightened around her waist.

"Nope." Melanie gave her a smile. "Although I heard through the grapevine that he's officially no longer part of Rubicore."

Connor raised his eyebrows at Evander, who slipped away from Daphne to stand with the other men.

"We have something to tell you all," Evander said.

"We bought Baby Horseshoe Island," Finian announced.

"What about your charity?" Hailey asked, her mouth hanging open. Finian had been supporting piles of charities back in his old neighborhood. How could he afford an island, when he barely fed himself half the time in order to make sure others in need got enough?

"I'm going to fly kids out to the camp to spend time in nature. What better way to make a difference in their lives? Daphne was telling me that time spent in nature reduces blood pressure, anxiety, depression, ADHD, and all sorts of other stuff."

"The camp?" Melanie interrupted, hands clasped in front of her.

"I was talking to Polly Pollard, who's on the camp board," Tristen said, taking Melanie's hands in his, "and she says they would be more than happy to reopen Camp Adaker on the island again."

"I always liked Polly," Maya said, pouring herself a margarita. She took a big sip and, wincing, gripped her forehead. "Ugh. Brain freeze."

The sisters laughed, turning to see who was coming up the steps to join them.

"Simone!" They all got up to hug their friend, who had turned in her usual fashionista look for old cutoff jeans and a dinosaur T-shirt.

"What's with the new look?"

"I was painting a few walls in my boutique." She waved her checkbook in the air and the mood turned somber. "I brought money to save Trixie Hollow."

Daphne checked her watch. "We have three hours until the tax office closes."

She swallowed hard. She knew that she, for one, was short on the amount she needed to save the cottage from the tax sale.

Turning down Environment Canada had felt like a relief, but it also meant she didn't have a signing bonus to bring her to the amount she needed to cover the tax bill.

"Your money is no good here," Hailey said crisply. "We made a deal among us."

Melanie and Daphne shared a look. "Do you have enough?" Melanie whispered.

Daphne gave a minute shake of her head and Evander, at her side again, gave her shoulder a reassuring squeeze. He already knew she was short and wouldn't accept a loan. How could she? She was a single mother starting a new eco-retreat venture with four billionaires. It wouldn't be easy to pay him back.

But it had felt right, choosing Baby Horseshoe Island, even though it meant she might have to say goodbye to the cottage if destiny felt it was time to let the island go.

Trading one for the other.

Because the one thing she'd learned in her life was that you couldn't have it all, and sometimes you had to make sacrifices to keep what was truly important.

Tears streaked down Daphne's cheeks, and with one arm, Evander effortlessly pivoted her into his hold, cradling her.

"Please? Will you let me help?" he asked.

She shook her head. She wanted to nod, but he'd already done so much. Besides, she and her sisters had been clear when they made their pact last month. They had to do this on their own, because if they couldn't do it now, how would they ever be able to keep doing it through all the years ahead? The cottage definitely wasn't getting any younger, and its maintenance costs would go nowhere but up.

"How is my money no good?" Simone was saying. "You've let me use the place like I own it for years, but you won't let me contribute to it? I say we take a vote." Simone slapped her checkbook on the table and took a large gulp of Maya's drink.

"I vote yes," Melanie said, her back straight, her hand in the air. "All in favor?"

"We can't change our minds. We made a deal," Hailey said.

"Is that heritage claim stuff going to get us a tax break, Melanie?" Maya asked.

"We won't hear back for a bit yet. But even if they say yes it won't be an immediate tax break."

Maya took a careful sip of her drink. "So getting a heritage-related tax break this year is out of the question."

"Oh!" Melanie turned to the men. "You own Heritage Row now!" She wildly pointed across the water to where the old cottages stood.

Tristen nodded. "Yes. All of it."

Melanie froze. "Are you going to—"

"Save Heritage Row? Don't be ridiculous. Of course we are. My fiancée would have my head if I didn't." He grinned as she launched herself into his arms.

"Wait…back up a second," Daphne said. "Rubicore really bought the Fredericksons' cottage?"

"I told you they did," Maya said, arms crossed.

"I thought you were speculating."

Maya smiled modestly and shrugged. "I was."

Connor explained, "Rubicore had just taken possession of their cottage, and seeing as we bought every stitch of land from them, it's now ours. We own Heritage Row and Baby Horseshoe Island in its entirety. Even Camp Adaker. The island and everything on it has officially been saved."

The sisters cheered, then slowly grew quiet.

"We're going to lose Nymph Island if we don't accept help from others," Daphne said quietly, turning away from Evander's broad chest and the aftershave she'd come to equate with love and security. "I vote yes to help. Simone is one of us. She's a sister and we said sisters." She whispered, "Sorry, Evander."

He gave her a squeeze in reply.

Hailey blinked twice at Daphne's response, then waited for Maya to vote.

"I don't care one way or the other," Maya stated.

Tigger came bouncing through. "I saw a chippie!" She crooked her finger at Evander, who dutifully lowered his head questioningly. The girl placed a noisy kiss on his cheek and then scuttled down the veranda steps. Evander, looking bashful and pleased, called out a warning about the rotten step.

"I know, Evander-dander!" Tigger called back.

"Help would be nice." Maya elbowed Connor in the ribs. "My boss here just spent all of his money on an island and won't give me the size of advance I surely deserve for finding him wonderful new venture capital clients, so I'm in. I'd like to be able to eat between now and my next paycheck."

"I bought that island for *you*. And it wasn't all my money," Connor said darkly. "Plus, if you'd let me help with the taxes this could all be resolved in five seconds."

"No," Maya said. "Haven't you been listening? We don't want to get behind again. It's do or die. Not beg and borrow."

"So it's settled?" Simone asked Hailey.

Hailey froze for a moment, before stepping forward and embracing their friend in a massive hug. "It's settled," she said. "Pay up."

Laughing and wiping tears from her eyes, Hailey said, her voice shaking, "Okay, let's see if we have enough to save this place."

The men looked solemn as the women counted what they had between them.

"Are you sure we can't help?" Tristen asked quietly.

Melanie held her breath for a long moment, then slowly shook her head.

"We're four dollars short." Maya laughed, sitting back in an old wicker chair, hands on her knees.

The men shared a look and dug into their pockets.

"No," the sisters said at once.

"I'm sure I have change in the ashtray in my car," Maya said.

"In the couch," Daphne said.

"I have four dollars," said a small voice. Daphne turned to see Tigger watching them quietly.

"Do you, Tigger?"

"Yeah. The fairies won't mind if I take their decorations. It's to save their island!" She dashed off and the sisters looked at each other.

Destiny.

You just never knew what she was going to pull out of her hat next.

DAPHNE STOOD BESIDE HER sisters, Simone, and Tigger in front of the municipal tax office.

"Shall we?" Maya asked.

Daphne turned back to where Evander was waiting, leaning against his truck. He smiled and nodded. He was at ease, an entirely different man than he'd been only days ago.

Love conquered the world. Saved the day and changed men.

Everything was going to be okay. Everything was working out.

For the first time, Daphne was really and truly happy. While her earlier happiness had never been an act, her old self felt like a sepia photo compared to where she was now. She was blessed to be a part of something bigger—a true, loving relationship with Evander. They were good for each other. Not just today, but tomorrow, and in the coming months and years. He was a keeper. Evander made her want to try harder. To be a better person and to make a bigger difference and she knew she could with him by her side.

Nate from Environment Canada had texted her on the drive over, asking her if she'd work as a consultant here and there. She'd said yes. She could still help change the world, but still have the freedom to be where she needed to be. For Tigger. For Evander. For herself.

She blew her boyfriend a kiss, waited for him to catch it with a shy smile, then turned to go inside with her sisters, who were holding the door for her.

They had the money. They'd done it with their talents and skills and a lot of good luck. Daphne looked up at the ceiling, silently thanking destiny for not only the island that kept the sisters together, but for the men who had come into their lives that summer.

Love.

Lots of love.

She caught up with Tigger, who hadn't stopped smiling since Daphne had asked if she'd like to move in with Evander and Florence permanently. Tigger would be starting kindergarten after the long weekend, with a whole lot of love in her life thanks to Evander and his mother. Tigger would finally have that father figure in her life, as well as someone to build a tree house for her in the backyard. A man who loved her, doted on her and taught her all the things Daphne was afraid to, such as how to defend herself physically.

And as for Mistral, she agreed with Evander. He had to man up. A lot. She'd give him a chance when he was ready, but she wasn't going to pin her hopes on him as she had for the past six years. She had someone else in mind when it came to dreaming about her and Tigger's future.

The sisters stepped up to the counter along with Simone and Tigger. The five adults put checks in front of the clerk as Tigger carefully laid out her coins, one by one, counting softly under her breath.

"This is for Nymph Island," Daphne said, speaking for all of them.

It was time she stopped acting like the baby in the family, because in many ways she was the most grown-up, the only mother in the group. Well, as far as she knew. Her sisters had each spent a lot of time on the island over the summer and, as Daphne knew, destiny had a way of spreading her love by adding new members to the Summer family.

*Hello Summer Sisters Readers!*

Do you enjoy reading romance?
&

Would you like to be the first to hear about new releases from Jean Oram?
&

Do you love saving money on ebooks?
&

Do you want to get in on exclusive giveaways and FREEBIES?
&

If you answered yes to any of these questions you're going to love my author newsletter.

For fast & easy online sign up go to:
**www.jeanoram.com/FREEBOOK**

## Book Club Discussion Starters

1) Despite the signs, why do you believe Daphne had such high hopes for Mistral as a father figure in Tigger's life?

2) Do you feel is common for opposites, such as Daphne (hippie) and Evander (former military man), to come from a similar place (love) yet see the solutions to issues very differently (peace vs. war)? Do you feel the world's issues are often people coming from a similar place but seeing and acting upon different solutions? Discuss an example from a world war as well as a recent world news story.

3) Which do you believe will save the day? War, peace, or neither? Why?

4) If you were in the Summer's shoes, would your have done the same thing about the cottage, or would you have done something different?

5) Would you have fought the development across the water? Why or why not?

6) Discuss the nymph symbolism of the Summers names & the symbolism/parallels in the heroes and their 'god' names.

**Hailey**—Water nymph. (Presides over sea and seashores. Daughter of marine gods.)
**Maya**—Celesteal nymph. (Partner of Zeus and mother of Hermes. Greek fertility god.)

**Melanie**—Fresh water nymph who presides over subterranean springs. (In the 5th century was a saint who gave her wealth to charity.)

**Daphne**—Woodland and plant nymph. (In mythology while under attack, Daphne called to the river god who then turned her into a laurel tree.)

**Finian**—Handsome/fair. People with this name tend to be dedicated to building their lives on order and service.

**Connor**—Represents wisdom, counsel, and strength. Early king of Ulster.

**Tristen**—Represents tumult/riot/outcry. Was a knight of the Round Table.

**Evander**—Represents manliness/good man. Fought a Trojan hero.

7) Magic (falling in love on the island has happened for four generations) and mythology are woven through the series. What do you think this adds to the books? Do you believe there is magic in falling in love?

8) Who was your favorite character in the Summer Sisters series and why?

9) After reading the last paragraph of Love and Danger, do you think the Summer sisters are pregnant and that destiny will carry on for another generation of Summer women?

10) Did reading the series and the issues of Muskoka leave you 'changed' in any way? Whether more knowledgeable, able to see things from a different point of view, or maybe even just understanding someone in your life a bit better?

## The Summer Sisters Tame the Billionaires

One cottage. Four sisters. And four billionaires who will sweep them off their feet.

*Love and Rumors ~ Love and Dreams*
*Love and Trust ~ Love and Danger*

## The Blueberry Springs Collection

*Book 1: Champagne and Lemon Drops—ALSO AVAILABLE IN AUDIO*
*Book 2: Whiskey and Gumdrops*
*Book 3: Rum and Raindrops*
*Book 4: Eggnog and Candy Canes*
*Book 5: Sweet Treats*
*Book 6: Vodka and Chocolate Drops (Coming Summer 2015)*
*Book 7: Tequila and Candy Drops (Coming Winter 2015)*

# Do you have questions, feedback, or just want to say hi? Connect with me! I love chatting with readers.

**Youtube:** www.youtube.com/user/AuthorJeanOram
**Facebook:** www.facebook.com/JeanOramAuthor
**Twitter:** www.twitter.com/jeanoram
**Website & Lovebug Blog:** www.jeanoram.com
**Email:** jeanorambooks@gmail.com (I personally reply to all emails!)
**Full book list—I'm always adding to it:** www.jeanoram.com

I'd love to hear from you.

Thanks for reading,

*Jean*

Jean Oram grew up in an old schoolhouse on the Canadian prairie, and spent many summers visiting family in her grandmother's 110-year-old cottage in Ontario's Muskoka region. She still loves to swim, walk to the store, and go tubing—just like she did as a kid—and hopes her own kids will love Muskoka just as she did when she was young(er).

You can discover more about Jean and her hobbies—besides writing, reading, hiking, camping, and chasing her two kids and several pets around the house and the great outdoors—on her website: www.jeanoram.com.

Made in the USA
Charleston, SC
15 May 2015